Dwellers in the Mirage

by
Abraham Merritt

Cover Photo by Susi Havens-Bezaire

Contents

BOOK OF KHALK'RU

I. SOUNDS IN THE NIGHT

I raised my head, listening,--not only with my ears but with every square inch of my skin, waiting for recurrence of the sound that had awakened me. There was silence, utter silence. No soughing in the boughs of the spruces clustered around the little camp. No stirring of furtive life in the underbrush. Through the spires of the spruces the stars shone wanly in the short sunset to sunrise twilight of the early Alaskan summer.

A sudden wind bent the spruce tops, carrying again the sound-- the clangour of a beaten anvil.

I slipped out of my blanket, and round the dim embers of the fire toward Jim. His voice halted me.

"All right, Leif. I hear it."

The wind sighed and died, and with it died the humming after-tones of the anvil stroke. Before we could speak, the wind arose. It bore the after-hum of the anvil stroke--faint and far away. And again the wind died, and with it the sound.

"An anvil, Leif!"

"Listen!"

A stronger gust swayed the spruces. It carried a distant chanting; voices of many women and men singing a strange, minor theme. The chant ended on a wailing chord, archaic, dissonant.

There was a long roll of drums, rising in a swift crescendo, ending abruptly. After it a thin and clamorous confusion.

It was smothered by a low, sustained rumbling, like thunder, muted by miles. In it defiance, challenge.

We waited, listening. The spruces were motionless. The wind did not return.

"Queer sort of sounds, Jim." I tried to speak casually. He sat up. A stick flared up in the dying fire. Its light etched his face against the darkness--thin, and brown and hawk-profiled. He did not look at me.

"Every feathered forefather for the last twenty centuries is awake and shouting! Better call me Tsantawu, Leif. Tsi' Tsa'lagi--I am a Cherokee! Right now--all Indian."

He smiled, but still he did not look at me, and I was glad of that.

"It was an anvil," I said. "A hell of a big anvil. And hundreds of people singing...and how could that be in this wilderness...they didn't sound like Indians..."

"The drums weren't Indian." He squatted by the fire, staring into it. "When they turned loose, something played a pizzicato with icicles up and down my back."

"They got me, too--those drums!" I thought my voice was steady, but he looked up at me sharply; and now it was I who averted my eyes and stared at the embers. "They reminded me of something I heard...and thought I saw...in Mongolia. So did the singing. Damn it, Jim, why do you look at me like that?"

I threw a stick on the fire. For the life of me I couldn't help searching the shadows as the stick flamed. Then I met his gaze squarely.

"Pretty bad place, was it, Leif?" he asked, quietly. I said nothing. Jim got up and walked over to the packs. He came back with some water and threw it over the fire. He kicked earth on the hissing coals. If he saw me wince as the shadows rushed in upon us, he did not show it.

"That wind came from the north," he said. "So that's the way the sounds came. Therefore, whatever made the sounds is north of us. That being so--which way do we travel to-morrow?"

"North," I said.

My throat dried as I said it.

Jim laughed. He dropped upon his blanket, and rolled it around him. I propped myself against the bole of one of the spruces, and sat staring toward the north.

"The ancestors are vociferous, Leif. Promising a lodge of sorrow, I gather--if we go north...'Bad Medicine!' say the ancestors... 'Bad Medicine for you, Tsantawu! You go to Usunhi'yi, the Darkening-land, Tsantawu!...Into Tsusgina'i, the ghost country! Beware! Turn from the north, Tsantawu!'"

"Oh, go to sleep, you hag-ridden redskin!"

"All right, I'm just telling you."

Then a little later:

"'And heard ancestral voices prophesying war'--it's worse than war these ancestors of mine are prophesying, Leif."

3

"Damn it, will you shut up!"

A chuckle from the darkness; thereafter silence.

I leaned against the tree trunk. The sounds, or rather the evil memory they had evoked, had shaken me more than I was willing to admit, even to myself. The thing I had carried for two years in the buckskin bag at the end of the chain around my neck had seemed to stir; turn cold. I wondered how much Jim had divined of what I had tried to cover...

Why had he put out the fire? Because he had known I was afraid? To force me to face my fear and conquer it?...Or had it been the Indian instinct to seek cover in darkness?...By his own admission, chant and drum-roll had played on his nerves as they had on mine...

Afraid! Of course it had been fear that had wet the palms of my hands, and had tightened my throat so my heart had beaten in my ears like drums.

Like drums...yes!

But...not like those drums whose beat had been borne to us by the north wind. They had been like the cadence of the feet of men and women, youths and maids and children, running ever more rapidly up the side of a hollow world to dive swiftly into the void...dissolving into the nothingness...fading as they fell...dissolving... eaten up by the nothingness...

Like that accursed drum-roll I had heard in the secret temple of the Gobi oasis two years ago!

Neither then nor now had it been fear alone. Fear it was, in truth, but fear shot through with defiance...defiance of life against its nega-tion...upsurging, roaring, vital rage...frantic revolt of the drowning against the strangling water, rage of the candle-flame against the hov-ering extinguisher...

Was it as hopeless as that? If what I suspected to be true was true, to think so was to be beaten at the beginning!

But there was Jim! How to keep him out of it? In my heart, I had never laughed at those subconscious perceptions, whatever they were. that he called the voices of his ancestors. When he had spoken of Usunhi'yi, the Darkening-land, a chill had crept down my spine. For had not the old Uighur priest spoken of the Shadow-land? And it was as though I had heard the echo of his words.

I looked over to where he lay. He had been more akin to me than my own brothers. I smiled at that, for they had never been akin to me. To all but my soft-voiced, deep-bosomed, Norse mother I had been a stranger in that severely conventional old house where I had been born.

The youngest son, and an unwelcome intruder; a changeling. It had been no fault of mine that I had come into the world a throw-back to my mother's yellow-haired, blue-eyed, strong-thewed Viking forefathers. Not at all a Langdon. The Langdon men were dark and slender, thin-lipped and saturnine, stamped out by the same die for generations. They looked down at me, the changeling, from the family portraits with faintly amused, supercilious hostility. Precisely as my father and my four brothers, true Langdons, each of them, looked at me when I awkwardly disposed of my bulk at their table.

It had brought me unhappiness, but it had made my mother wrap her heart around me. I wondered, as I had wondered many times, how she had come to give herself to that dark, self-centred man my father-- with the blood of the sea-rovers singing in her veins. It was she who had named me Leif--as incongruous a name to tack on a Langdon as was my birth among them.

Jim and I had entered Dartmouth on the same day. I saw him as he was then--the tall, brown lad with his hawk face and inscrutable black eyes. pure blood of the Cherokees, of the clan from which had come the great Sequoiah, a clan which had produced through many centuries wisest councillors, warriors strong in cunning.

On the college roster his name was written James T. Eagles, but on the rolls of the Cherokee Nation it was written Two Eagles and his mother had called him Tsantawu. From the first we had recognized spiritual kinship. By the ancient rites of his people we had become blood-brothers, and he had given me my secret name, known only to the pair of us, Degataga--one who stands so close to another that the two are one.

My one gift, besides my strength, is an aptness at languages. Soon I spoke the Cherokee as though I had been born in the Nation. Those years in college were the happiest I had ever known. It was during the last of them that America entered the World War. Together we had left Dartmouth, gone into training camp, sailed for France on the same transport.

Sitting there, under the slow-growing Alaskan dawn, my mind leaped over the years between...my mother's death on Armistice Day...my return to New York to a frankly hostile home...Jim's recall to his clan...the finishing of my course in mining engineering...my wanderings in Asia...my second return to America and my search for

Jim...this expedition of ours to Alaska, more for comradeship and the wilderness peace than for the gold we were supposed to be seeking--

A long trail since the War--the happiest for me these last two months of it. It had led us from Nome over the quaking tundras, and then to the Koyukuk, and at last to this little camp among the spruces, somewhere between the headwaters of the Koyukuk and the Chandalar in the foothills of the unexplored Endicott Range. A long trail...I had the feeling that it was here the real trail of my life began.

A ray of the rising sun struck through the trees. Jim sat up, looked over at me, and grinned.

"Didn't get much sleep after the concert, did you?"

"What did you do to the ancestors? They didn't seem to keep you awake long."

He said, too carelessly: "Oh, they quieted down." His face and eyes were expressionless. He was veiling his mind from me. The ancestors had not quieted down. He had lain awake while I had thought him sleeping. I made a swift decision. We would go south as we had planned. I would go with him as far as Circle. I would find some pretext to leave him there.

I said: "We're not going north. I've changed my mind."

"Yes. why?"

"I'll tell you after we've had breakfast," I said--I'm not so quick in thinking up lies. "Rustle up a fire, Jim. I'll go down to the stream and get some water."

"Degataga!"

I started. It was only in moments of rare sympathy or in time of peril that he used the secret name.

"Degataga, you go north! You go if I have to march ahead of you to make you follow..." he dropped into the Cherokee..."It is to save your spirit, Degataga. Do we march together--blood-brothers? Or do you creep after me--like a shivering dog at the heels of the hunter?"

The blood pounded in my temples, my hand went out toward him. He stepped back, and laughed.

"That's better, Leif."

The quick rage left me, my hand fell.

"All right, Tsantawu. We go--north. But it wasn't--it wasn't because of myself that I told you I'd changed my mind."

"I know damned well it wasn't!"

He busied himself with the fire. I went after the water. We drank the strong black tea, and ate what was left of the little brown storks they call Alaskan turkeys which we had shot the day before. When we were through I began to talk.

II. RING OF THE KRAKEN

Three years ago, so I began my story, I went into Mongolia with the Fairchild expedition. Part of its work was a mineral survey for certain British interests, part of it ethnographic and archeological research for the British Museum and the University of Pennsylvania.

I never had a chance to prove my value as a mining engineer. At once I became good-will representative, camp entertainer, liaison agent between us and the tribes. My height, my yellow hair, blue eyes and freakish strength, and my facility in picking up languages were of never-ending interest to them. Tartars, Mongols, Buriats, Kirghiz--they would watch while I bent horseshoes, twisted iron bars over my knees and performed what my father used to call contemptuously my circus tricks.

Well, that's exactly what I was to them--a one-man circus. And yet I was more than that--they liked me. Old Fairchild would laugh when I complained that I had no time for technical work. He would tell me that I was worth a dozen mining engineers, that I was the expedition's insurance, and that as long as I could keep up my act they wouldn't be bothered by any trouble makers. And it is a fact that they weren't. It was the only expedition of its kind I ever knew where you could leave your stuff unwatched and return to find it still there. Also we were singularly free from graft and shake-downs.

In no time I had picked up half a dozen of the dialects and could chatter and chaff with the tribesmen in their own tongues. It made a prodigious bit with them. And now and then a Mongol delegation would arrive with a couple of their wrestlers, big fellows with chests like barrels, to pit against me. I learned their tricks, and taught them ours. We had pony lifting contests, and some of my Manchu friends taught me how to fight with the two broadswords--a sword in each hand.

Fairchild had planned on a year, but so smoothly did the days go by that he decided to prolong our stay. My act, he told me in his sardonic fashion, was undoubtedly of perennial vitality; never again would science have such an opportunity in this region--unless I made up my mind to remain and rule. He didn't know how close he came to prophecy.

In the early summer of the following year we shifted our camp about a hundred miles north. This was Uighur country. They are a strange people, the Uighurs. They say of themselves that they are descendants of a great race which ruled the Gobi when it was no desert but an earthly Paradise, with flowing rivers and many lakes and teeming cities. It is a fact that they are apart from all the other tribes, and while those others cheerfully kill them when they can, still they go in fear of them. Or rather, of the sorcery of their priests.

Seldom had Uighurs appeared at the old camp. When they did, they kept at a distance. We had been at the new camp less than a week when a band of twenty rode in. I was sitting in the shade of my tent. They dismounted and came straight to me. They paid no attention to anyone else. They halted a dozen feet from me. Three walked close up and stood, studying me. The eyes of these three were a peculiar grey-blue; those of the one who seemed to be their captain singularly cold. They were bigger, taller men than the others.

I did not know the Uighur. I gave them polite salutations in the Kirghiz. They did not answer, maintaining their close scrutiny. Finally they spoke among themselves, nodding as though they had come to some decision.

The leader then addressed me. As I stood up, I saw that he was not many inches under my own six feet four. I told him, again in the Kirghiz, that I did not know his tongue. He gave an order to his men. They surrounded my tent, standing like guards, spears at rest beside them, their wicked long-swords drawn.

At this my temper began to rise, but before I could protest the leader began to speak to me in the Kirghiz. He assured me, with deference, that their visit was entirely peaceful, only they did not wish their contact with me to be disturbed by any of my companions. He asked if I would show him my hands. I held them out. He and his two comrades bent over the palms, examining them minutely, pointing to a mark or a crossing of lines. This inspection ended, the leader touched his forehead with my right hand.

And then to my complete astonishment, he launched without explanation into what was a highly intelligent lesson in the Uighur tongue. He took the Kirghiz for the comparative language. He did not seem to be surprised at the ease with which I assimilated the tuition; indeed, I had a puzzled idea that he regarded it as something to be expected. I mean that his manner was less that of teaching me a new language, than of recalling to me one I had forgotten. The lesson lasted for a full hour. He then touched his forehead again with my hand, and gave a command to the ring of guards. The whole party walked to their horses and galloped off.

There had been something disquieting about the whole experience. Most disquieting was my own vague feeling that my tutor, if I had read correctly his manner, had been right--that I was not learning a new tongue but one I had forgotten. Certainly I never picked up any language with such rapidity and ease as I did the Uighur.

The rest of my party had been perplexed and apprehensive, naturally. I went immediately to them, and talked the matter over. Our ethnologist was the famous Professor David Barr, of Oxford. Fairchild was inclined to take it as a joke, but Barr was greatly disturbed. He said that the Uighur tradition was that their forefathers had been a fair race, yellow-haired and blue-eyed, big men of great strength. In short, men like myself. A few ancient Uighur wall paintings had been found which had portrayed exactly this type, so there was evidence of the correctness of the tradition. However, if the Uighurs of the present were actually the descendants of this race, the ancient blood must have been mixed and diluted almost to the point of extinction.

I asked what this had to do with me, and he replied that quite conceivably my visitors might regard me as of the pure blood of the ancient race. In fact, he saw no other explanation of their conduct. He was of the opinion that their study of my palms, and their manifest approval of what they had discovered there, clinched the matter.

Old Fairchild asked him, satirically, if he was trying to convert us to palmistry. Barr said, coldly, that he was a scientist. As a scientist, he was aware that certain physical resemblances can be carried on by hereditary factors through many generations. Certain peculiarities in the arrangement of the lines of the palms might persist through centuries. They could reappear in cases of atavism, such as I clearly represented.

By this time, I was getting a bit dizzy. But Barr had a few shots left that made me more so. By now his temper was well up, and he went on to say that the Uighurs might even be entirely correct in what he deduced was their opinion of me. I was a throwback to the ancient Norse. Very well. It was quite certain that the Aesir, the old Norse gods and goddesses--Odin and Thor, Frigga and Freya, Frey and Loki of the Fire and all the others--had once been real people. Without question they had been leaders in some long and perilous migration.

After they had died, they had been deified, as numerous other similar heroes and heroines had been by other tribes and races. Ethnologists were agreed that the original Norse stock had come into North-eastern Europe from Asia, like other Aryans. Their migration might have occurred anywhere from 1000 B.C. to 5000 B.C. And there was no scientific reason why they should not have come from the region now called the Gobi, nor why they should not have been the blond race these present-day Uighurs called their forefathers.

No one, he went on to say, knew exactly when the Gobi had become desert--nor what were the causes that had changed it into desert. Parts of the Gobi and all the Little Gobi might have been fertile as late as two thousand years ago. Whatever it had been, whatever its causes, and whether operating slowly or quickly, the change gave a perfect reason for the migration led by Odin and the other Aesir which had ended in the colonization of the Scandinavian Peninsula. Admittedly I was a throwback to my mother's stock of a thousand years ago. There was no reason why I should not also be a throwback in other recognizable ways to the ancient Uighurs--if they actually were the original Norse.

But the practical consideration was that I was headed for trouble. So was every other member of our party. He urgently advised going back to the old camp where we would be among friendly tribes. In conclusion he pointed out that, since we had come to this site, not a single Mongol, Tartar or any other tribesman with whom I had established such pleasant relations had come near us. He sat down with a glare at Fairchild, observing that this was no palmist's advice but that of a recognized scientist.

Well, Fairchild apologized, of course, but he over-ruled Barr on returning; we could safely wait a few days longer and see what developed. Barr remarked morosely that as a prophet Fairchild was probably a total loss, but it was also probable that we were being closely watched and would not be allowed to retreat, and therefore it did not matter.

That night we heard drums beating far away, drumming between varying intervals of silence almost until dawn, reporting and answering questions of drums still further off.

The next day, at the same hour, along came the same troop. Their leader made straight for me, ignoring, as before, the others in the camp. He saluted me almost with humility. We walked back together to my tent. Again the cordon was thrown round it, and my second lesson abruptly began. It continued for two hours or more. Thereafter,

11

day after day, for three weeks, the same performance was repeated. There was no desultory conversation, no extraneous questioning, no explanations. These men were there for one definite purpose: to teach me their tongue. They stuck to that admirably. Filled with curiosity, eager to reach the end and learn what it all meant, I interposed no obstacles, stuck as rigorously as they to the matter in hand. This, too, they seemed to take as something expected of me. In three weeks I could carry on a conversation in the Uigher as well as I can in English.

Barr's uneasiness kept growing. "They're grooming you for something!" he would say. "I'd give five years of my life to be in your shoes. But I don't like it. I'm afraid for you. I'm damned afraid!"

One night at the end of this third week, the signalling drums beat until dawn. The next day my instructors did not appear, nor the next day, nor the day after. But our men reported that there were Uighurs all around us, picketing the camp. They were in fear, and no work could be got out of them.

On the afternoon of the fourth day we saw a cloud of dust drifting rapidly down upon us from the north. Soon we heard the sound of the Uighur drums. Then out of the dust emerged a troop of horsemen. There were two or three hundred of them, spears glinting, many of them with good rifles. They drew up in a wide semi-circle before the camp. The cold-eyed leader who had been my chief instructor dismounted and came forward leading a magnificent black stallion. A big horse, a strong horse, unlike the rangy horses that carried them; a horse that could bear my weight with ease.

The Uighur dropped on one knee, handing me the stallion's reins, I took them, automatically. The horse looked me over, sniffed at me, and rested its nose on my shoulder. At once the troop raised their spears, shouting some word I could not catch, then dropped from their mounts and stood waiting.

The leader arose. He drew from his tunic a small cube of ancient jade. He sank again upon his knee, handed me the cube. It seemed solid, but as I pressed it flew open. Within, was a ring. It was of heavy gold, thick and wide. Set in it was a yellow, translucent stone about an inch and a half square. And within this stone was the shape of a black octopus.

Its tentacles spread out fan-wise from its body. They had the effect of reaching forward through the yellow stone. I could even see upon their nearer tips the sucking discs. The body was not so clearly defined. It was nebulous, seeming to reach into far distance. The black octopus had not been cut upon the jewel. It was within it.

12

I was aware of a curious mingling of feelings--repulsion and a peculiar sense of familiarity, like the trick of the mind that causes what we call double memory, the sensation of having experienced the same thing before. Without thinking, I slipped the ring over my thumb which it fitted perfectly, and held it up to the sun to catch the light through the stone. Instantly every man of the troop threw himself down upon his belly, prostrating himself before it.

The Uighur captain spoke to me. I had been subconsciously aware that from the moment of handing me the jade he had been watching me closely. I thought that now there was awe in his eyes.

"Your horse is ready--" again he used the unfamiliar word with which the troop had saluted me. "Show me what you wish to take with you, and your men shall carry it."

"Where do we go--and for how long?" I asked.

"To a holy man of your people," he answered. "For how long--he alone can answer."

I felt a momentary irritation at the casualness with which I was being disposed of. Also I wondered why he spoke of his men and his people as mine.

"Why does he not come to me?" I asked.

"He is old," he answered. "He could not make the journey."

I looked at the troop, now standing up beside their horses. If I refused to go, it would undoubtedly mean the wiping out of the camp if my companions attempted, as they would, to resist my taking. Besides, I was on fire with curiosity.

"I must speak to my comrades before I go," I said.

"If it please Dwayanu"--this time I caught the word--"to bid farewell to his dogs, let him." There was a nicker of contempt in his eyes as he looked at old Fairchild and the others.

Definitely I did not like what he had said, nor his manner.

"Await me here," I told him curtly, and walked over to Fairchild. I drew him into his tent, Barr and the others of the expedition at our heels. I told them what was happening. Barr took my hand, and scrutinized the ring. He whistled softly.

"Don't you know what this is?" he asked me. "It's the Kraken--that super-wise, malignant and mythical sea-monster of the old Norsemen. See, its tentacles are not eight but twelve. Never was it pictured with less than ten. It symbolized the principle that is inimical to Life--not Death precisely, more accurately annihilation. The Kraken--and here in Mongolia!"

13

"See here, Chief," I spoke to Fairchild. "There's only one way you can help me--if I need help. And that's to get back quick as you can to the old camp. Get hold of the Mongols and send word to that chief who kept bringing in the big wrestlers--they'll know whom I mean. Persuade or hire him to get as many able fighting men at the camp as you can. I'll be back, but I'll probably come back running. Outside of that, you're all in danger. Not at the moment, maybe, but things may develop which will make these people think it better to wipe you out. I know what I'm talking about, Chief. I ask you to do this for my sake, if not for your own."

"But they watch the camp--" he began to object.

"They won't--after I've gone. Not for a little while at least. Everyone of them will be streaking away with me." I spoke with complete certainty, and Barr nodded acquiescence.

"The King returns to his Kingdom," he said. "All his loyal subjects with him. He's in no danger--while he's with them. But--God, if I could only go with you, Leif! The Kraken! And the ancient legend of the South Seas told of the Great Octopus, dozing on and biding his time till he felt like destroying the world and all its life. And three miles up in the air the Black Octopus is cut into the cliffs of the Andes! Norsemen--and the South Sea Islanders--and the Andeans! And the same symbol--here!"

"Please promise?" I asked Fairchild. "My life may depend on it."

"It's like abandoning you. I don't like it!"

"Chief, this crowd could wipe you out in a minute. Go back, and get the Mongols. The Tartars will help. They hate the Uighurs. I'll come back, don't fear. But I'd bet everything that this whole crowd, and more, will be at my heels. When I come, I want a wall to duck behind."

"We'll go," he said.

I went out of that tent, and over to my own. The odd-eyed Uighur followed me. I took my rifle and an automatic, stuffed a toothbrush and a shaving-kit in my pocket, and turned to go.

"Is there nothing else?" There was surprise in his question.

"If there is, I'll come back for it," I answered.

"Not after you have--remembered," he said, enigmatically.

Side by side we walked to the black stallion. I lifted myself to his back.

The troop wheeled in behind us. Their spears a barrier between me and the camp, we galloped south.

III. RITUAL OF KHALK'RU

The stallion settled down to a steady, swinging lope. He carried my weight easily. About an hour from dusk we were over the edge of the desert. At our right loomed a low range of red sandstone hills. Close ahead was a defile. We rode into it, and picked our way through it. In about half an hour we emerged into a boulder-strewn region, upon what had once been a wide road. The road stretched straight ahead of us to the north-east, toward another and higher range of red sandstone, perhaps five miles away. This we reached just as night began, and here my guide halted, saying that we would encamp until dawn. Some twenty of the troop dismounted; the rest rode on.

Those who remained waited, looking at me, plainly expectant. I wondered what I was supposed to do; then, noticing that the stallion had been sweating, I called for something to rub him down, and for food and water for him. This, apparently, was what had been looked for. The captain himself brought me the cloths, grain and water while the men whispered. After the horse was cooled down, I fed him. I then asked for blankets to put on him, for the nights were cold. When I had finished I found that supper had been prepared. I sat beside a fire with the leader. I was hungry, and, as usual when it was possible, I ate voraciously. I asked few questions, and most of these were answered so evasively, with such obvious reluctance, that I soon asked none. When the supper was over, I was sleepy. I said so. I was given blankets, and walked over to the stallion. I spread my blankets beside him, dropped, and rolled myself up.

The stallion bent his head, nosed me gently, blew a long breath down my neck, and lay down carefully beside me. I shifted so that I could rest my head on his neck. I heard excited whispering among the Uighurs. I went to sleep.

At dawn I was awakened. Breakfast was ready. We set out again on the ancient road. It ran along the hills, skirting the bed of what had long ago been a large river. For some time the eastern hills protected us from the sun. When it began to strike directly down upon us, we rested under the shadow of some immense rocks. By mid-afternoon we were once more on our way. Shortly before sun-down, we crossed the dry river bed over what had once been a massive bridge. We passed into another defile through which the long-gone stream had flowed, and just at dusk reached its end.

Each side of the end of the shallow gorge was commanded by stone forts. They were manned by dozens of the Uighurs. They shouted as we drew near, and again I heard the word "Dwayanu" repeated again and again.

The heavy gates of the right-hand fort swung open. We went through, into a passage under the thick wall. We trotted across a wide enclosure. We passed out of it through similar gates.

I looked upon an oasis hemmed in by the bare mountains. It had once been the site of a fair-sized city, for ruins dotted it everywhere. What had possibly been the sources of the river had dwindled to a brook which sunk into the sands not far from where I stood. At the right of this brook there was vegetation and trees; to the left of it was a desolation. The road passed through the oasis and ran on across this barren. It stopped at, or entered, a huge square-cut opening in the rock wall more than a mile away, an opening that was like a door in that mountain, or like the entrance to some gigantic Egyptian tomb.

We rode straight down into the fertile side. There were hundreds of the ancient stone buildings here, and fair attempts had been made to keep some in repair. Even so, their ancientness struck against my nerves. There were tents among the trees also. And out of the buildings and tents were pouring Uighurs, men, women and children. There must have been a thousand of the warriors alone. Unlike the men at the guardhouses, these watched me in awed silence as I passed.

We halted in front of a time-bitten pile that might have been a palace--five thousand years or twice that ago. Or a temple. A colonnade of squat, square columns ran across its front. Heavier ones stood at its entrance. Here we dismounted. The stallion and my guide's horse were taken by our escort. Bowing low at the threshold, my guide invited me to enter.

I stepped into a wide corridor, lined with spearsmen and lighted by torches of some resinous wood. The Uighur leader walked beside me. The corridor led into a huge room--high-ceilinged, so wide and long that the flambeaux on the walls made its centre seem the darker. At the far end of this place was a low dais, and upon it a stone table, and seated at this table were a number of hooded men.

As I drew nearer, I felt the eyes of these hooded men intent upon me, and saw that they were thirteen--six upon each side and one seated in a larger chair at the table's end. High cressets of metal stood about them in which burned some substance that gave out a steady, clear white light. I came close, and halted. My guide did not speak. Nor did these others.

Suddenly, the light glinted upon the ring on my thumb.

The hooded man at the table's end stood up, gripping its edge with trembling hands that were like withered claws. I heard him whisper--"Dwayanu!"

The hood slipped back from his head. I saw an old, old face in which were eyes almost as blue as my own, and they were filled with stark wonder and avid hope. It touched me, for it was the look of a man long lost to despair who sees a saviour appear.

Now the others arose, slipped back their hoods. They were old men, all of them, but not so old as he who had whispered. Their eyes of cold blue-grey weighed me. The high priest, for that I so guessed him and such he turned out to be, spoke again:

"They told me--but I could not believe! Will you come to me?"

I jumped on the dais and walked to him. He drew his old face close to mine, searching my eyes. He touched my hair. He thrust his hand within my shirt and laid it on my heart. He said:

"Let me see your hands."

I placed them, palms upward, on the table. He gave them the same minute scrutiny as had the Uighur leader. The twelve others clustered round, following his fingers as he pointed to this marking and to that. He lifted from his neck a chain of golden links, drawing from beneath his robe a large, flat square of jade. He opened this. Within it was a yellow stone, larger than that in my ring, but otherwise precisely similar, the black octopus--or the Kraken--writhing from its depths. Beside it was a small phial of jade and a small, lancet-like jade knife. He took my right hand, and brought the wrist over the yellow stone. He looked at me and at the others with eyes in which was agony.

"The last test," he whispered. "The blood!"

He nicked a vein of my wrist with the knife. Blood fell, slow drop by drop upon the stone; I saw then that it was slightly concave. As the blood dripped, it spread like a thin film from bottom to lip. The old priest lifted the phial of jade, unstoppered it, and by what was plainly violent exercise of his will, held it steadily over the yellow stone. One drop of colourless fluid fell and mingled with my blood.

17

The room was now utterly silent, high priest and his ministers seemed not to breathe, staring at the stone. I shot a glance at the Uighur leader, and he was glaring at me, fanatic fires in his eyes.

There was an exclamation from the high priest, echoed by the others. I looked down at the stone. The pinkish film was changing colour. A curious sparkle ran through it; it changed into a film of clear, luminous green.

"Dwayanu!" gasped the high priest, and sank back into his chair, covering his face with shaking hands. The others stared at me and back at the stone and at me again as though they beheld some miracle. I looked at the Uighur leader. He lay flat upon his face at the base of the dais.

The high priest uncovered his face. It seemed to me that he had become incredibly younger, transformed; his eyes were no longer hopeless, agonized; they were filled with eagerness. He arose from his chair, and sat me in it.

"Dwayanu," he said, "what do you remember?"

I shook my head, puzzled; it was an echo of the Uighur's remark at the camp.

"What should I remember?" I asked.

His gaze withdrew from me, sought the faces of the others, questioningly; as though he had spoken to them, they looked at one another, then nodded. He shut the jade case and thrust it into his breast. He took my hand, twisted the bezel of the ring behind my thumb and closed my hand on it.

"Do you remember--" his voice sank to the faintest of whispers-- "Khalk'ru?"

Again the stillness dropped upon the great chamber--this time like a tangible thing. I sat, considering. There was something familiar about that name. I had an irritated feeling that I ought to know it; that if I tried hard enough, I could remember it; that memory of it wasfirst over the border of consciousness. Also I had the feeling that it meant something rather dreadful. Something better forgotten. I felt vague stirrings of repulsion, coupled with sharp resentment.

"No," I answered.

I heard the sound of sharply exhaled breaths. The old priest walked behind me and placed his hands over my eyes.

"Do you remember--this?"

My mind seemed to blur, and then I saw a picture as clearly as though I were looking at it with my open eyes. I was galloping through the oasis straight to the great doorway in the mountain. Only now it was no oasis. It was a city with gardens, and a river ran sparkling through it. The ranges were not barren red sandstone, but green with trees. There were others with me, galloping behind me--men and women like myself, fair and strong. Now I was close to the doorway. There were immense square stone columns flanking it...and now I had dismounted from my horse...a great black stallion...I was entering...

I would not enter! If I entered, I would remember--Khalk'ru! I thrust myself back...and out...I felt hands over my eyes...I reached and tore them away...the old priest's hands. I jumped from the chair, quivering with anger. I faced him. His face was benign, his voice gentle.

"Soon," he said, "you will remember more!"

I did not answer, struggling to control my inexplicable rage. Of course, the old priest had tried to hypnotize me; what I had seen was what he had willed me to see. Not without reason had the priests of the Uighurs gained their reputation as sorcerers. But it was not that which had stirred this wrath that took all my will to keep from turning berserk. No, it had been something about that name of Khalk'ru. Something that lay behind the doorway in the mountain through which I had almost been forced.

"Are you hungry?" The abrupt transition to the practical in the old priest's question brought me back to normal. I laughed outright, and told him that I was, indeed. And getting sleepy. I had feared that such an important personage as I had apparently become would have to dine with the high priest. I was relieved when he gave me in charge of the Uighur captain. The Uighur followed me out like a dog, he kept his eyes upon me like a dog upon its master, and he waited on me like a servant while I ate. I told him I would rather sleep in a tent than in one of the stone houses. His eyes flashed at that, and for the first time he spoke other than in respectful monosyllables.

"Still a warrior!" he grunted approvingly. A tent was set up for me. Before I went to sleep I peered through the flap. The Uighur leader was squatting at the opening, and a double ring of spearsmen stood shoulder to shoulder on guard.

Early next morning, a delegation of the lesser priests called for me. We went into the same building, but to a much smaller room, bare of all furnishings. The high priest and the rest of the lesser priests were awaiting me. I had expected many questions. He asked me none; he had, apparently, no curiosity as to my origin, where I had come from, nor how I had happened to be in Mongolia. It seemed to be enough that they had proved me to be who they had hoped me to be--whoever that was. Furthermore, I had the strongest impression that they were anxious to hasten on to the consummation of a plan that had begun with my lessons. The high priest west straight to the point.

"Dwayanu," he said, "we would recall to your memory a certain ritual. Listen carefully, watch carefully, repeat faithfully each inflection, each gesture."

"To what purpose?" I asked.

"That you shall learn--" he began, then interrupted himself fiercely. "No! I will tell you now! So that this which is desert shall once more become fertile. That the Uighurs shall recover their greatness. That the ancient sacrilege against Khalk'ru, whose fruit was the desert, shall be expiated!"

"What have I, a stranger, to do with all this?" I asked.

"We to whom you have come," he answered, "have not enough of the ancient blood to bring this about. You are no stranger. You are Dwayanu--the Releaser. You are of the pure blood. Because of that, only you--Dwayanu--can lift the doom."

I thought how delighted Barr would be to hear that explanation; how he would crow over Fairchild. I bowed to the old priest, and told him I was ready. He took from my thumb the ring, lifted the chain and its pendent jade from his neck, and told me to strip. While I was doing so, he divested himself of his own robes, and the others followed suit. A priest carried the things away, quickly returning. I looked at the shrunken shapes of the old men standing mother-naked round me, and suddenly lost all desire to laugh. The proceedings were being touched by the sinister. The lesson began.

It was not a ritual; it was an invocation--rather, it was an evocation of a Being, Power, Force, named Khalk'ru. It was exceedingly curious, and so were the gestures that accompanied it. It was clearly couched in the archaic form of the Uighur. There were many words I did not understand. Obviously, it had been passed down from high priest to high priest from remote antiquity. Even an indifferent churchman would have considered it blasphemous to the point of damnation. I was too much interested to think much of that phase of it. I had the same odd sense of familiarity with it that I had felt at the first naming of Khalk'ru. I felt none of the repulsion, however. I felt strongly in earnest. How much this was due to the force of the united wills of the twelve priests who never took their eyes off me, I do not know.

I won't repeat it, except to give the gist of it. Khalk'ru was the Beginning-without-Beginning, as he would be the End-without-End. He was the Lightless Timeless Void. The Destroyer. The Eater-up of

20

Life. The Annihilator. The Dissolver. He was not Death--Death was only a part of him. He was alive, very much so, but his quality of living was the antithesis of Life as we know it. Life was an invader, troubling Khalk'ru's ageless calm. Gods and man, animals and birds and all creatures, vegetation and water and air and fire, sun and stars and moon--all were his to dissolve into Himself, the Living Nothingness, if he so willed. But let them go on a little longer. Why should Khalk'ru care when in the end there would be only--Khalk'ru! Let him withdraw from the barren places so life could enter and cause them to blossom again; let him touch only those who were the enemies of his worshippers, so that his worshippers would be great and powerful, evidence that Khalk'ru was the All in All. It was only for a breath in the span of his eternity. Let Khalk'ru make himself manifest in the form of his symbol and take what was offered him as evidence he had listened and consented.

There was more, much more, but that was the gist of it. A dreadful prayer, but I felt no dread--then.

Three times, and I was letter-perfect. The high priest gave me one more rehearsal and nodded to the priest who had taken away the clothing. He went out and returned with the robes--but not my clothes. Instead, he produced a long white mantle and a pair of sandals. I asked for my own clothes and was told by the old priest that I no longer needed them, that hereafter I would be dressed as befitted me. I agreed that this was desirable, but said I would like to have them so I could look at them once in a while. To this he acquiesced.

They took me to another room. Faded, ragged tapestries hung on its walls. They were threaded with scenes of the hunt and of war. There were oddly shaped stools and chairs of some metal that might have been copper but also might have been gold, a wide and low divan, in one corner spears, a bow and two swords, a shield and a cap-shaped bronze helmet. Everything, except the rugs spread over the stone floor, had the appearance of great antiquity. Here I was washed and carefully shaved and my long hair trimmed--a ceremonial cleansing accompanied by rites of purification which, at times, were somewhat startling.

These ended, I was given a cotton undergarment which sheathed me from toes to neck. After this, a pair of long, loose, girdled trousers that seemed spun of threads of gold reduced by some process to the softness of silk. I noticed with amusement that they had been carefully repaired and patched. I wondered how many centuries the man who had first worn them had been dead. There was a long, blouse-like coat of the same material, and my feet were slipped into cothurms, or high buskins, whose elaborate embroidery was a bit ragged.

The old priest placed the ring on my thumb, and stood back, staring at me raptly. Quite evidently he saw nothing of the ravages of time upon my garments.

I was to him the splendid figure from the past that he thought me.

"So did you appear when our race was great," he said. "And soon, when it has recovered a little of its greatness, we shall bring back those who still dwell in the Shadow-land."

"The Shadow-land?" I asked.

"It is far to the East, over the Great Water," he said. "But we know they dwell there, those of Khalk'ru who fled at the time of the great sacrilege which changed fecund Uighuriand into desert. They will be of the pure blood like yourself, Dwayanu, and you shall find mates among the women. And in time, we of the thinned blood shall pass away, and Uighuriand again be peopled by its ancient race."

He walked abruptly away, the lesser priests following. At the door he turned.

"Wait here," he said, "until the word comes from me."

IV. TENTACLE OF KHALK'RU

I waited for an hour, examining the curious contents of the room, and amusing myself with shadow-fencing with the two swords. I swung round to find the Uighur captain watching me from the door-way, pale eyes glowing.

"By Zarda!" he said. "Whatever you have forgotten, it is not your sword play! A warrior you left us, a warrior you have returned!"

He dropped upon a knee, bent his head: "Pardon, Dwayanu! I have been sent for you. It is time to go."

A heady exaltation began to take me. I dropped the swords, and clapped him on the shoulder. He took it like an accolade. We passed through the corridor of the spearsmen and over the threshold of the great doorway. There was a thunderous shout.

"Dwayanu!"

And then a blaring of trumpets, a mighty roll of drums and the clashing of cymbals.

Drawn up in front of the palace was a hollow square of Uighur horsemen, a full five hundred of them, spears glinting, pennons flying from their shafts. Within the square, in ordered ranks, were as many more. But now I saw that these were both men and women, clothed in garments as ancient as those I wore, and shimmering in the strong sunlight like a vast multicoloured rug of metal threads. Banners and bannerets, torn and tattered and bearing strange symbols, fluttered from them. At the far edge of the square I recognized the old priest, his lesser priests flanking him, mounted and clad in the yellow. Above them streamed a yellow banner, and as the wind whipped it straight, black upon it appeared the shape of the Kraken. Beyond the square of horsemen, hundreds of the Uighurs pressed for a glimpse of me. As I stood there, blinking, another shout mingled with the roll of the Uighur drums.

"The King returns to his people!" Barr had said. Well, it was like that.

A soft nose nudged me. Beside me was the black stallion. I mounted him. The Uighur captain at my heels, we trotted down the open way between the ordered ranks. I looked at them as I went by. All of them, men and women, had the pale blue-grey eyes; each of them was larger than the run of the race. I thought that these were the nobles, the pick of the ancient families, those in whom the ancient blood was strongest. Their tattered banners bore the markings of their clans. There was exultation in the eyes of the men. Before I had reached the priests. I had read terror in the eyes of many of the women.

I reached the old priest. The line of horsemen ahead of us parted. We two rode through the gap, side by side. The lesser priests fell in behind us. The nobles followed them. A long thin line upon each side of the cavalcade, the Uighur horsemen trotted--with the Uighur trumpets blaring, the Uighur kettle-drums and long-drums beating, the Uighur cymbals crashing, in wild triumphal rhythms.

"The King returns--"

I would to heaven that something had sent me then straight upon the Uighur spears!

We trotted through the green of the oasis. We crossed a wide bridge which had spanned the little stream when it had been a mighty river. We set our horses' feet upon the ancient road that led straight to the mountain's doorway a mile or more away. The heady exultation grew within me. I looked back at my company. And suddenly I remembered the repairs and patches on my breeches and my blouse. And my following was touched with the same shabbiness. It made me feel less a king, but it also made me pitiful. I saw them as men and women driven by hungry ghosts in their thinned blood, ghosts of strong ancestors growing weak as the ancient blood weakened, starving at it weakened, but still strong enough to clamour against extinction, still strong enough to command their brains and wills and drive them toward something the ghosts believed would feed their hunger, make them strong again.

Yes, I pitied them. It was nonsense to think I could appease the hunger of their ghosts, but there was one thing I could do for them. I could give them a damned good show! I went over in my mind the ritual the old priest had taught me, rehearsed each gesture.

I looked up to find we were at the threshold of the mountain door. It was wide enough for twenty horsemen to ride through abreast. The squat columns I had seen, under the touch of the old priest's hands, lay shattered beside it. I felt no repulsion, no revolt against entering, as I then had. I was eager to be in and to be done with it.

The spearsmen trotted up, and formed a guard beside the opening. I dismounted, and handed one of them the stallion's rein. The old priest beside me, the lesser ones behind us, we passed over the threshold of the mined doorway, and into the mountain. The passage, or vestibule, was lighted by wall cressets in which burned the clear, white flame. A hundred paces from the entrance, another passage opened, piercing inward at an angle of about fifteen degrees to the wider one. Into this the old priest turned. I glanced back. The nobles had not yet entered; I could see them dismounting at the entrance. We went along this passage in silence for perhaps a thousand feet. It opened into a small square chamber, cut in the red sandstone, at whose side was another door, covered with heavy tapestries. In this chamber was nothing except a number of stone coffers of various sizes ranged along its walls.

The old priest opened one of these. Within it was a wooden box, grey with age. He lifted its lid, and took from it two yellow garments. He slipped one of these garments over my head. It was like a smock, falling to my knees. I glanced down; woven within it, its tentacles encircling me, was the black octopus.

The other he drew over his own head. It, too, bore the octopus, but only on the breast, the tentacles did not embrace him. He bent and took from the coffer a golden staff, across the end of which ran bars. From these fell loops of small golden bells.

From the other coffers the lesser priests had taken drums, queerly shaped oval instruments some three feet long, with sides of sullen red metal. They sat, rolling the drumheads under their thumbs, tightening them here and there while the old priest gently shook his staff of bells, testing their chiming. They were for all the world like an orchestra tuning up. I again felt a desire to laugh;

I did not then know how the commonplace can intensify the terrible.

There were sounds outside the tapestried doorway, rustlings. There were three clangorous strokes like a hammer upon an anvil. Then silence. The twelve priests walked through the doorway with their drums in their arms. The high priest beckoned me to follow him, and we passed through after them.

I looked out upon an immense cavern, cut from the living rock by the hands of men dust now for thousands of years. It told its immemorial antiquity as clearly as though the rocks had tongue. It was more than ancient; it was primeval. It was dimly lighted, so dimly that hardly could I see the Uighur nobles. They were standing, the banners of their clans above them, their faces turned up to me, upon the stone floor, a hundred yards or so away, and ten feet below me. Beyond them and behind them the cavern extended, vanishing in darkness. I saw that in front of them was a curving trough, wide--like the trough between two long waves--and that like a wave it swept upward from the hither side of the trough, curving, its lip crested, as though that wave of sculptured stone were a gigantic comber rushing back upon them. This lip formed the edge of the raised place on which I stood.

The high priest touched my arm. I turned my head to him, and followed his eyes. A hundred feet away from me stood a girl. She was naked. She had not long entered womanhood and quite plainly was soon to be a mother. Her eyes were as blue as those of the old priest, her hair was reddish brown, touched with gold, her skin was palest olive. The blood of the old fair race was strong within her. For all she held herself so bravely, there was terror in her eyes, and the rapid rise and fall of her rounded breasts further revealed that terror.

She stood in a small hollow. Around her waist was a golden ring, and from that ring dropped three golden chains fastened to the rock floor. I recognized their purpose. She could not run, and if she dropped or fell, she could not writhe away, out of the cup. But run, or writhe away from what? Certainly not from me! I looked at her and smiled. Her eyes searched mine. The terror suddenly fled from them. She smiled back at me, trustingly.

God forgive me--I smiled at her and she trusted me! I looked beyond her, from whence had come a glitter of yellow like a flash from a huge topaz. Up from the rock a hundred yards behind the girl jutted an immense fragment of the same yellow translucent stone that formed the jewel in my ring. It was like the fragment of a gigantic shattered pane. Its shape was roughly triangular. Black within it was a tentacle of the Kraken. The tentacle swung down within the yellow stone, broken from the monstrous body when the stone had been broken. It was all of fifty feet long. Its inner side was turned toward me, and plain upon all its length clustered the hideous sucking discs.

Well, it was ugly enough--but nothing to be afraid of, I thought. I smiled again at the chained girl, and met once more her look of utter trust.

The old priest had been watching me closely. We walked forward until we were half-way between the edge and the girl. At the lip squatted the twelve lesser priests, their drums on their laps.

The old priest and I faced the girl and the broken tentacle. He raised his staff of golden bells and shook them. From the darkness of the cavern began a low chanting, a chant upon three minor themes, repeated and repeated, and intermingled.

It was as primeval as the cavern; it was the voice of the cavern itself.

The girl never took her eyes from me.

The chanting ended. I raised my hands and made the curious gestures of salutation I had been taught. I began the ritual to Khalk'ru...

With the first words, the odd feeling of recognition swept over me--with something added. The words, the gestures, were automatic. I did not have to exert any effort of memory; they remembered themselves. I no longer saw the chained girl. All I saw was the black tentacle in the shattered stone.

On swept the ritual and on...was the yellow stone dissolving from around the tentacle...was the tentacle swaying?

Desperately I tried to halt the words, the gesturing. I could not!

Something stronger than myself possessed me, moving my muscles, speaking from my throat. I had a sense of inhuman power. On to the climax of the evil evocation--and how I knew how utterly evil it was--the ritual rushed, while I seemed to stand apart, helpless to check it.

It ended.

And the tentacle quivered...it writhed...it reached outward to the chained girl...

There was a devil's roll of drums, rushing up fast and ever faster to a thunderous crescendo...

The girl was still looking at me...but the trust was gone from her eyes...her face reflected the horror stamped upon my own.

The black tentacle swung up and out!

I had a swift vision of a vast cloudy body from which other cloudy tentacles writhed. A breath that had in it the cold of outer space touched me.

The black tentacle coiled round the girl...

She screamed--inhumanly...she faded...she dissolved...her screaming faded...her screaming became a small shrill agonized piping...a sigh.

I heard the dash of metal from where the girl had stood. The clashing of the golden chains and girdle that had held her, falling empty on the rock.

The girl was gone!

I stood, nightmare horror such as I had never known in worst of nightmares paralysing me--

The child had trusted me...I had smiled at her, and she had trusted me...and I had summoned the Kraken to destroy her!

Searing remorse, white hot rage, broke the chains that held me. I saw the fragment of yellow stone in its place, the black tentacle inert within it. At my feet lay the old priest, flat on his face, his withered body shaking; his withered hands clawing at the rock. Beside their drums lay the lesser priests, and flat upon the floor of the cavern were the nobles--prostrate, abased, blind and deaf in stunned worship of that dread Thing I had summoned.

I ran to the tapestried doorway. I had but one desire--to get out of the temple of Khalk'ru. Out of the lair of the Kraken. To get far and far away from it. To get back...back to the camp-home. I ran through the little room, through the passages and, still running, reached the entrance to the temple. I stood there for an instant, dazzled by the sunlight.

There was a roaring shout from hundreds of throats--then silence. My sight cleared. They lay there, in the dust, prostrate before me--the troops of the Uighur spearsmen.

I looked for the black stallion. He was close beside me. I sprang upon his back, gave him the reins. He shot forward like a black thunderbolt through the prostrate ranks, and down the road to the oasis. We raced through the oasis. I had vague glimpses of running crowds, shouting. None tried to stop me. None could have stayed the rush of that great horse.

And now I was close to the inner gates of the stone fort through which we had passed on the yesterday. They were open. Their guards stood gaping at me. Drums began to beat, peremptorily, from the temple. I looked back. There was a confusion at its entrance, a chaotic milling. The Uighur spearsmen were streaming down the wide road.

The gates began to close. I shot the stallion forward, bowling over the guards, and was inside the fort. I reached the further gates. They were closed. Louder beat the drums, threatening, commanding.

Something of sanity returned to me. I ordered the guards to open. They stood, trembling, staring at me. But they did not obey. I leaped from the stallion and ran to them. I raised my hand. The ring of Khalk'ru glittered. They threw themselves on the ground before me-- but they did not open the gates.

I saw upon the wall goatskins full of water. I snatched one of these and a sack of grain. Upon the floor was a huge slab of stone. I lifted it as though it had been a pebble, and hurled it at the gates where the two halves met. They burst asunder. I threw the skin of water and sack of grain over the high saddle, and rode through the broken gates.

The great horse skimmed through the ravine like a swallow. And now we were over the crumbling bridge and thundering down the ancient road.

We came to the end of the far ravine. I knew it by the fall of rock. I looked back. There was no sign of pursuit. But I could hear the faint throb of the drums.

It was now well past mid-afternoon. We picked our way through the ravine and came out at the edge of the sandstone range. It was cruel to force the stallion, but I could not afford to spare him. By nightfall we had readied semi-arid country. The stallion was reeking with sweat, and tired. Never once had he slackened or turned surly. He had a great heart, that horse. I made up my mind that he should rest, come what might.

I found a sheltered place behind some high boulders. Suddenly I realized that I was still wearing the yellow ceremonial smock. I tore it off with sick loathing. I rubbed the horse down with it. I watered him and gave him some of the grain. I realized, too, that I was ravenously hungry and had eaten nothing since morning. I chewed some of the grain and washed it down with the tepid water. As yet, there were no signs of pursuit, and the drums were silent. I wondered uneasily whether the Uighurs knew of a shorter road and were outflanking me. I threw the smock over the stallion and stretched myself on the ground. I did not intend to sleep. But I did go to sleep.

I awakened abruptly. Dawn was breaking. Looking down upon me were the old priest and the cold-eyed Uighur captain. My hiding place was ringed with spearsmen. The old priest spoke, gently.

"We mean you no harm, Dwayanu. If it is your will to leave us, we cannot stay you. He whose call Khalk'ru has answered has nothing to fear from us. His will is our will."

I did not answer. Looking at him, I saw again--could only see-- that which I had seen in the cavern. He sighed.

"It is your will to leave us! So shall it be!"

The Uighur captain did not speak.

"We have brought your clothing, Dwayanu, thinking that you might wish to go from us as you came," said the old priest.

I stripped and dressed in my old clothes. The old priest took my faded finery. He lifted the octopus robe from the stallion. The captain spoke:

"Why do you leave us, Dwayanu? You have made our peace with Khalk'ru. You have unlocked the gates. Soon the desert will blossom as of old. Why will you not remain and lead us on our march to greatness?"

I shook my head. The old priest sighed again.

"It is his will! So shall it be! But remember, Dwayanu--he whose call Khalk'ru has answered must answer when Khalk'ru calls him. And soon or late--Khalk'ru will call him!"

He touched my hair with his trembling old hands, touched my heart, and turned. A troop of spearsmen wheeled round him. They rode away.

The Uighur captain said:

"We wait to guard Dwayanu on his journey."

I mounted the stallion. We reached the expedition's new camp. It was deserted. We rode on, toward the old camp. Late that afternoon we saw ahead of us a caravan. As we came nearer they halted, made hasty preparations for defence. It was the expedition--still on the march. I waved my hands to them and shouted.

I dropped off the black stallion, and handed the reins to the Uighur.

"Take him," I said. His face lost its sombre sternness, brightened.

"He shall be ready for you when you return to us, Dwayanu. He or his sons," he said. He touched my hand to his forehead, knelt. "So shall we all be, Dwayanu--ready for you, we or our sons. When you return."

He mounted his horse. He faced me with his troop. They raised their spears. There was one crashing shout--

"Dwayanu!"

They raced away.

I walked to where Fairchild and the others awaited me.

As soon as I could arrange it, I was on my way back to America. I wanted only one thing--to put as many miles as possible between myself and Khalk'ru's temple.

I stopped. Involuntarily my hand sought the buckskin bag on my breast.

"But now," I said, "it appears that it is not so easy to escape him. By anvil stroke, by chant and drums--Khalk'ru calls me '"

V. THE MIRAGE

Jim had sat silent, watching me, but now and again I had seen the Indian stoicism drop from his face. He leaned over and put a hand on my shoulder.

"Leif," he said quietly, "how could I have known? For the first time, I saw you afraid--it hurt me. I did not know..."

From Tsantawu, the Cherokee, this was much. "It's all right, Indian. Snap back," I said roughly. He sat for a while not speaking, throwing little twigs on the fire.

"What did you friend Barr say about it?" he asked abruptly.

"He gave me hell," I said. "He gave me hell with the tears streaming down his cheeks. He said that never had anyone betrayed science as I had since Judas kissed Christ. He was keen on mixed metaphors that got under your skin. That went deep under mine, for it was precisely what I was thinking of myself--not as to science but as to the girl. I had given her the kiss of Judas all right. Barr said that I had been handed the finest opportunity man ever had given him. I could have solved the whole mystery of the Gobi and its lost civilization. I had run away like a child from a bugaboo. I was not only atavistic in body, I was atavistic in brain. I was a blond savage cowering before my mumbo-jumbos. He said that if he had been given my chance he would have let himself be crucified to have learned the truth. He would have, too. He was not lying."

"Admirably scientific," said Jim. "But what did he say about what you saw?"

"That is was nothing but hypnotic suggestion by the old priest. I had seen what he had willed me to see--just as before, under his will, I had seen myself riding to the temple. The girl hadn't dissolved. She had probably been standing in the wings laughing at me. But if everything that my ignorant mind had accepted as true had been true then my conduct was even more unforgivable. I should have remained, studied the phenomena and brought back the results for science to examine. What I had told him of the ritual of Khalk'ru was nothing but the second law of thermo-dynamics expressed in terms of anthropo-morphism. Life was an intrusion upon Chaos, using that word to describe the unformed, primal state of the universe. An invasion. An accident. In time all energy would be changed to static heat, impotent to give birth to any life whatsoever. The dead universes would float lifelessly in the illimitable void. The void was eternal, life was not. Therefore the void would absorb it. Suns, worlds, gods, men, an things animate, would return to the void. Go back to Chaos. Back to Noth-ingness. Back to Khalk'ru. Or if my atavistic brain preferred the term--back to the Kraken. He was bitter."

"But the others saw the girl taken, you say. How did he explain that?"

"Oh, easily. That was mass hypnotism--like the Angels of Mons, the ghostly bowmen of Crecy and other collective hallucinations of the War. I had been a catalyzer. My likeness to the traditional ancient race, my completeness as a throwback, my mastery at Khalk'ru's ritual, the faith the Uighurs had in me--all this had been the necessary element in bringing about the collective hallucination of the tentacle. Obviously the priests had long been trying to make work a drug in which an es-sential chemical was lacking. I, for some reason, was the missing chemical--the catalyzer. That was all." Again he sat thinking, breaking the little twigs.

"It's a reasonable explanation. But you weren't convinced?"

"No, I wasn't convinced--I saw the girl's face when the tentacle touched her." He arose, stood staring toward the north.

"Leif," he asked suddenly, "what did you do with the ring?"

I drew out the little buckskin pouch, opened it and handed the ring to him. He examined it closely, returned it to me.

"Why did you keep it, Leif?"

"I don't know." I slipped the ring over my thumb. "I didn't give it back to the old priest; he didn't ask for it. Oh, hell--I'll tell you why I kept it--for the same reason Coleridge's Ancient Mariner had the alba-tross tied round his neck. So I couldn't forget I'm a murderer."

I put the ring back in the buckskin bag, and dropped it down my neck. Faintly from the north came a roll of drums. It did not seem to travel with the wind this time. It seemed to travel underground, and died out deep beneath us.

"Khalk'ru!" I said.

"Well. don't let's keep the old gentleman waiting," said Jim cheerfully.

32

He busied himself with the packs, whistling. Suddenly he turned to me.

"Listen, Leif. Barr's theories sound good to me. I'm not saying that if I'd been in your place I would have accepted them. Maybe you're right. But I'm with Barr--until events, if-when-and-how they occur, prove him wrong."

"Fine!" I said heartily, and entirely without sarcasm.

"May your optimism endure until we get back to New York--if-when-and-how."

We shouldered the packs, and took up our rifles and started northward.

It was not hard going, but it was an almost constant climb. The country sloped upward, sometimes at a breathtaking pitch. The forest, unusually thick and high for the latitude, began to thin. It grew steadily cooler. After we had covered about fifteen miles we entered a region of sparse and stunted trees. Five miles ahead was a thousand-feet-high range of bare rocks. Beyond this range was a jumble of mountains four to five thousand feet higher, treeless, their peaks covered with snow and ice, and cut by numerous ravines which stood out glistening white like miniature glaciers. Between us and the nearer range stretched a plain, all grown over with dwarfed thickets of wild roses, blueberries and squawbemes, and dressed in the brilliant reds and blues and greens of the brief Alaskan summer.

"If we camp at the base of those hills, we'll be out of that wind," said Jim. "It's five o'clock. We ought to make it in an hour."

We set off. Bursts of willow ptarmigans shot up around us from the berry thickets like brown rockets; golden plovers and curlews were whistling on all sides; within rifle shot a small herd of caribou was feeding, and the little brown cranes were stalking everywhere. No one could starve in that country, and after we had set up camp we dined very well.

There were no sounds that night--or if there were we slept too deeply to hear them.

The next morning we debated our trail. The low range stood directly in our path north. It continued, increasing in height, both east and west. It presented no great difficulties from where we were, at least so far as we could see. We determined to climb it, taking it leisurely. It was more difficult than it had appeared; it took us two hours to wind our way to the top.

We tramped across the top toward a line of huge boulders that stretched like a wall before us. We squeezed between two of these, and drew hastily back. We were standing at the edge of a precipice that dropped hundreds of feet sheer to the floor of a singular valley. The jumble of snow-and-ice-mantled mountains clustered around it. At its far end, perhaps twenty miles away, was a pyramidal-shaped peak.

Down its centre, from tip to the floor of the valley, ran a glittering white streak, without question a glacier filling a chasm which split the mountain as evenly as though it had been made by a single sword stroke. The valley was not wide, not more than five miles, I estimated, at its widest point. A long and narrow valley, its far end stoppered by the glacier-cleft giant, its sides the walls of the other mountains, dropping, except here and there where there had been falls of rock, as precipitously into it as the cliff under us.

But it was the floor of the valley itself that riveted our attention. It seemed nothing but a tremendous level field covered with rocky rubble. At the far end, the glacier ran through this rubble for half the length of the valley. There was no trace of vegetation among the littered rocks. There was no hint of green upon the surrounding mountains; only the bare black cliffs with their ice and snow-filled gashes. It was a valley of desolation.

"It's cold here, Leif." Jim shivered.

It was cold--a cold of a curious quality, a still and breathless cold. It seemed to press out upon us from the valley, as though to force us away.

"It's going to be a job getting down there," I said.

"And hard going when we do," said Jim. "Where the hell did all those rocks come from, and what spread them out so flat?"

"Probably dropped by that glacier when it shrunk," I said. "It looks like a terminal moraine. In fact this whole place looks as though it had been scooped out by the ice."

"Hold on to my feet, Leif, I'll take a look." He lay on his belly and wriggled his body over the edge. In a minute or two I heard him call, and pulled him back.

"There's a slide about a quarter of a mile over there to the left," he said. "I couldn't tell whether it goes all the way to the top. We'll go see. Leif, how far down do you think that valley is?"

"Oh, a few hundred feet."

"It's all of a thousand if it's an inch. The cliff goes down and down. I don't understand what makes the bottom seem so much closer here. It's a queer place, this."

We picked up the packs and marched off behind the wall--like rim of boulders. In a little while we came across a big gouge in the top, running far back. Here frost and ice had bitten out the rock along some fault. The shattered debris ran down the middle of the gouge like giant stepping-stones clear to the floor of the valley.

"We'll have to take the packs off to negotiate that," said Jim. "What shall be do--leave them here while we explore, or drop them along with us as we go?"

"Take them with us. There must be an outlet off there at the base of the big mountain."

We began the descent. I was scrambling over one of the rocks about a third of the way when I heard his sharp exclamation.

Gone was the glacier that had thrust its white tongue in among the rubble. Gone was the rubble. Toward its far end, the valley's floor was covered with scores of pyramidal black stones, each marked down its centre with a streak of glistening white. They stood in ranks, spaced regularly, like the dolmens of the Druids. They marched half-down the valley. Here and there between them arose wisps of white steam, like smokes of sacrifices.

Between them and us, lapping at the black cliffs, was a blue and rippling lake! It filled the lower valley from side to side. It rippled over the edges of the shattered rocks still far below us.

Then something about the marshalled ranks of black stones struck me.

"Jim! Those pyramid-shaped rocks. Each and every one of them is a tiny duplicate of the mountain behind them! Even to the white streak!"

As I spoke, the blue lake quivered. It flowed among the black pyramids, half-submerging them, quenching the sacrificial smokes. It covered the pyramids. Again it quivered. It was gone. Where the lake had been was once more the rubble-covered floor of the valley.

There had been an odd touch of legerdemain about the transformations, like the swift work of a master magician. And it had been magic--of a kind. But I had watched nature perform that magic before.

"Hell!" I said. "It's a mirage!"

Jim did not answer. He was staring at the valley with a singular expression.

"What's the matter with you, Tsantawu? Listening to the ancestors again? It's only a mirage."

"Yes?" he said. "But which one? The lake--or the rocks?"

I studied the valley's floor. It looked real enough. The theory of a glacial moraine accounted for its oddly level appearance--that and our height above it. When we reached it we would find that distribution of boulders uncomfortably uneven enough, I would swear.

"Why, the lake of course."

"No," he said, "I think the stones are the mirage."

"Nonsense. There's a layer of warm air down there. The stones radiate the sun's heat. This cold air presses on it. It's one of the conditions that produces mirages, and it has just done it for us. That's all."

"No," he said, "it isn't all."

He leaned against the rock.

"Leif, the ancestors had a few things more to say last night than I told you."

"I know damned well they did."

"They spoke of Ataga'hi. Does that mean anything to you."

"Not a thing."

"It didn't to me--then. It does now. Ataga'hi was an enchanted lake, in the wildest part of the Great Smokies, westward from the headwaters of the Ocana-luftee. It was the medicine lake of the animals and birds. All the Cherokee knew it was there, though few had seen it. If a stray hunter came close, all he saw was a stony flat, without blade of grass, forbidding. But by prayer and fasting and an all-night vigil, he could sharpen his spiritual sight. He would then behold at daybreak a wide shallow sheet of purple water, fed by springs, spouting from the high cliffs around. And in the water all kinds of fish and reptiles, flocks of ducks and geese and other birds flying about, and around the lake the tracks of animals. They came to Ataga'hi to be cured of wounds or sickness. The Great Spirit had placed an island in the middle of the lake. The wounded, the sick animals and birds swam to it. When they had reached it--the waters of Ataga'hi had cured them. They came up on its shores--whole once more. Over Ataga'hi ruled the peace of God. All creatures were friends."

"Listen, Indian, are you trying to tell me this is your medicine lake?"

"I didn't say that at all. I said the name of Ataga'hi kept coming into my mind. It was a place that appeared to be a stony flat, without blade of grass, forbidding. So does this place. But under that illusion was--a lake. We saw a lake. It's a queer coincidence, that's all. Perhaps the stony flat of Ataga'hi was a mirage--" He hesitated: "Well, if some other things the ancestors mentioned turn up, I'll shift sides and take your version of that Gobi affair."

"That lake was the mirage. I'm telling you."

He shook his head, stubbornly.

"Maybe. But maybe what we see down there now is mirage, too. Maybe both are mirage. And if so, then, how deep is the real floor, and can we make our way over it?"

He stood staring silently at the valley. He shivered, and again I was aware of the curiously intense quality of the cold. I stooped and caught hold of my pack. My hands were numb.

"Well, whatever it is--let's find out."

A quiver ran through the valley floor. Abruptly it became again the shimmering blue lake. And as abruptly turned again to nibbled rock.

But not before I had seemed to see within that lake of illusion--if illusion it were--a gigantic shadowy shape, huge black tentacles stretching out from a vast and nebulous body...a body which seemed to vanish back into immeasurable distances...vanishing into the void... as the Kraken of the Gobi cavern had seemed to vanish into the void... into that void which was--Khalk'ru!

We crept between, scrambled over and slid down the huge broken fragments. The further down we went, the more intense became the cold. It had a still and creeping quality that seeped into the marrow. Sometimes we dropped the packs ahead of us, sometimes dragged them after us. And ever more savagely the cold bit into our bones.

By the frequent glimpses of the valley floor, I was more and more assured of its reality. Every mirage I had ever beheld--and in Mongolia I had seen many--had retreated, changed form, or vanished as I drew near. The valley floor did none of these things. It was true that the stones seemed to be squatter as we came closer; but I attributed that to the different angle of vision.

We were about a hundred feet above the end of the slide when I began to be less sure. The travelling had become peculiarly difficult. The slide had narrowed. At our left the rock was clean swept, stretching down to the valley as smoothly as though it had been brushed by some titanic broom. Probably an immense fragment had broken loose at this point, shattering into the boulders that lay heaped at its termination. We veered to the right, where there was a ridge of rocks, pushed to the side by that same besom of stone. Down this ridge we picked our way.

Because of my greater strength, I was carrying both our rifles, swung by a thong over my left shoulder. Also I was handling the heavier pack. We came upon an extremely awkward place. The stone upon which I was standing suddenly tipped beneath my weight. It threw me sideways. The pack slipped from my hands, toppled, and fell over on the smooth rock. Automatically I threw myself forward, catching at it. The thong holding the two rifles broke. They went slithering after the escaping pack.

It was one of those combinations of circumstances that makes one believe in a God of Mischance. The thing might have happened anywhere else on our journey without any result whatever. And even at that moment I didn't think it mattered.

"Well," I said, cheerfully, "that saves me carrying them. We can pick them up when we get to the bottom."

"That is," said Jim, "if there is a bottom."

I cocked my eye down the slide. The rifles had caught up with the pack and the three were now moving fast.

"There they stop," I said. They were almost on the rubble at the end.

"The hell they do," said Jim. "There they go!"

I rubbed my eyes, and looked and looked again. The pack and the pushing rifles should have been checked by that barrier at the slide's end. But they had not been. They had vanished.

VI. THE SHADOWED-LAND

There had been a queer quivering when rifles and pack had touched the upthrust of rock. Then they had seemed to melt into it.

"I'd say they dropped into the lake," said Jim.

"There's no lake. They dropped into some break in the rock. Come on--"

He gripped my shoulder.

"Wait, Leif. Go slow."

I followed his pointing finger. The barrier of stones had vanished. Where they had been, the slide ran, a smooth tongue of stone, far out into the valley.

"Come on," I said.

We went down, testing every step. With each halt, the nibbled plain became flatter and flatter, the boulders squatted lower and lower. A cloud drifted over the sun. There were no boulders. The valley floor stretched below us, a level slate-grey waste!

The slide ended abruptly at the edge of this waste. The rocks ended as abruptly, about fifty feet ahead. They stood at the edge with the queer effect of stones set in place when the edge had been viscous. Nor did the waste appear solid; it, too, gave the impression of viscosity; through it ran a slight but constant tremor, like waves of heat over a sun-baked road--yet with every step downward the bitter, still cold increased until it was scarcely to be borne.

There was a narrow passage between the shattered rocks and the cliff at our right. We crept through it. We stood upon an immense flat stone at the very edge of the strange plain. It was neither water nor rock; more than anything, it had the appearance of a thin opaque liquid glass, or a gas that had been turned semi-liquid.

I stretched myself out on the slab, and reached out to touch it. I did touch it--there was no resistance; I felt nothing. I let my hand sink slowly in. I saw my hand for a moment as though reflected in a distorting mirror, and then I could not see it at all. But it was pleasantly warm down there where my hand had disappeared. The chilled blood began to tingle in my numbed fingers. I leaned far over the stone and plunged both arms in almost to the shoulders. It felt damned good.

Jim dropped beside me and thrust in his arms.

"It's air," he said.

"Feels like it--" I began, and then a sudden realization came to me--"the rifles and the pack! If we don't get them we're out of luck!"

He said: "If Khalk'ru is--guns aren't going to get us away from him."

"You think this--" I stopped, memory of the shadowy shape in the lake of illusion coming back to me.

"Usunhi'yi, the Darkening-land. The Shadowed-land your old priest called it, didn't he? I'd say this fits either description."

I lay quiet; no matter what the certainty of a coming ordeal a man may carry in his soul, he can't help a certain shrinking when he knows his foot is at the threshold of it. And now quite clearly and certainly I knew just that. All the long trail between Khalk'ru's Gobi temple and this place of mirage was wiped out. I was stepping from that focus of Khalk'ru's power into this one--where what had been begun in the Gobi must be ended. The old haunting horror began to creep over me. I fought it.

I would take up the challenge. Nothing on earth could stop me now from going on. And with that determination, I felt the horror sullenly retreat, leave me. For the first time in years I was wholly free of it.

"I'm going to see what's down there." Jim drew up his arms. "Hold on to my feet, Leif, and I'll slip over the edge of the stone. I felt along its edge and it seems to go on a bit further."

"I'll go first." I said. "After all, it's my party."

"And a fine chance I'd have to pull you up if you fell over, you human elephant. Here goes--catch hold."

I had just time to grip his ankles as he wriggled over the stone, and his head and shoulders passed from sight. On he went, slowly writhing along the slanting rock until my hands and arms were hidden to the shoulders. He paused--and then from the mysterious opacity in which he had vanished came a roar of crazy laughter.

I felt him twist and try to jerk his feet away from me. I pulled him, fighting against me every inch of the way, out upon the stone. He came out roaring that same mad laughter. His face was red, and his eyes were shining drunkenly; he had in fact all the symptoms of a laughing drunk. But the rapidity of his respiration told me what had happened.

"Breathe slowly," I shouted in his ear. "Breathe slowly, I tell you."

And then, as his laughter continued and his struggles to tear loose did not abate, I held him down with one arm and closed his nose and mouth with my hand. In a moment or two he relaxed. I released him; and he sat up groggily.

"Funniest things," he said, thickly. "Saw funniest faces..."

He shook his head, took a deep breath or two, and lay back on the stone.

"What the hell happened to me, Leif?"

"You had an oxygen burn, Indian," I said. "A nice cheap jag on air loaded with carbon-dioxide. And that explains a lot of things about this place. You came up breathing three to the second, which is what carbon-dioxide does to you. Works on the respiratory centres of the brain and speeds up respiration. You took in more oxygen than you could use, and you got drunk on it. What did you see before the world became so funny?"

"I saw you," he said. "And the sky. It was like looking up out of water. I looked down and around. A little below me was something like a floor of pale green mist. I couldn't see through it. It's warm in there, good and plenty warm, and it smells like trees and flowers. That's all I managed to grasp before I went goofy. Oh, yes, this rock fall keeps right on going down. Maybe we can get to the bottom of it-- if we don't laugh ourselves off. I'm going right out and sit in that mirage up to my neck--my God, Leif, I'm freezing!"

I looked at him with concern. His lips were blue, his teeth chattering. The transition from the warmth to the bitter cold was having its effect, and a dangerous one.

"All right," I said, rising. "I'll go first. Breathe slowly, take deep, long breaths as slowly as you can, and breathe out just as slowly. You'll soon get used to it. Come on."

I slung the remaining pack over my back, craw-fished over the side of the stone, felt solid rock under my feet, and drew myself down within the mirage.

It was warm enough; almost as warm as the steam-room of a Turkish bath. I looked up and saw the sky above me like a circle of blue, misty at its edges. Then I saw Jim's legs dropping down toward me, his body bent back from them at an impossible angle. I was seeing him, in fact, about as a fish does an angler wading in its pool. His body seemed to telescope and he was squatting beside me.

"God, but this feels good!"

"Don't talk," I told him. "Just sit here and practise that slow breathing. Watch me."

We sat there, silently, for all of half an hour. No sound broke the stillness around us. It smelled of the jungle, of fast-growing vigorous green life, and green life falling as swiftly into decay; and there were elusive, alien fragrances. All I could see was the circle of blue sky above, and perhaps a hundred feet below us the pale green mist of which Jim had spoken. It was like a level floor of cloud, impenetrable to the vision. The rock-fall entered it and was lost to sight. I felt no discomfort, but both of us were dripping with sweat. I watched with satisfaction Jim's deep, unhurried breathing.

"Having any trouble?" I asked at last.

"Not much. Now and then I have to put the pedal down. But I think I'm getting the trick."

"All right," I said. "Soon we'll be moving. I don't believe it will get any worse as we go down."

"You talk like an old-timer. What's your idea of this place any-way, Leif?"

"Simple enough. Although the combination hasn't a chance in millions to be duplicated. Here is a wide, deep valley entirely hemmed in by precipitous cliffs. It is, in effect, a pit. The mountains enclosing it are seamed with glaciers and ice streams and there is a constant flow of cold air into this pit, even in summer. There is probably volcanic activity close beneath the valley's floor, boiling springs and the like. It may be a miniature of the Valley of Ten Thousand Smokes over to the west. All this produces an excess of carbon-dioxide. There is most probably a lush vegetation which adds to the product. What we are going into is likely to be a little left-over fragment of the Carbonifer-ous Age--about ten million years out of its time. The warm, heavy air fills the pit until it reaches the layer of cold air we've just come from. The mirage is produced where the two meet, by approximately the same causes which produce every mirage. How long it's been this way, God alone knows. Parts of Alaska never had a Glacial Age--the ice for some reason or another didn't cover them. When what is New York was under a thousand feet of ice, the Yukon Flats were an oasis filled with all sorts of animal and plant life. If this valley existed then, we're due to see some strange survivals. If it's comparatively recent, we'll probably run across some equally interesting adaptations. That's about all, except there must be an outlet of some kind somewhere at about this level, otherwise the warm air would fill the whole valley to the top, as gas does a tank. Let's be going."

"I begin to hope we find the guns," said Jim, thoughtfully.

"As you pointed out, they'd be no good against Khalk'ru--what, who, if and where he is," I said. "But they'd be handy against his attendant devils. Keep an eye out for them--I mean the guns."

We started down the rock-fall, toward the floor of green mist. The going was not very difficult. We reached the mist without having seen anything of rifles or packs. The mist looked like a heavy fog. We entered it, and that was precisely what it was. It closed around us, thick and warm. The rocks were reeking wet and slippery, and we had to feel for every foot of the way. Twice I thought our numbers were up. How deep that mist was, I could not tell, perhaps two or three hundred feet--a condensation brought about by the peculiar atmospheric conditions that produced the mirage.

The mist began to lighten. It maintained its curious green tint, but I had the idea that this was due to reflection from below. Suddenly it thinned to nothing. We came out of it upon a breast where the falling rocks had met some obstruction and had piled up into a barrier about thrice my height. We climbed that barrier.

We looked upon the valley beneath the mirage.

It lay a full thousand feet beneath us. It was filled with pale green light like that in a deep forest glade. That light was both lucent and vaporous, lucent where we stood, but hiding the distance with misty curtains of pallid emerald. To the north and on each side as far as I could see, and melting into the vaporous emerald curtains, was a vast carpet of trees. Their breath came pulsing up to me, jungle-strong, laden with the unfamiliar fragrances. At left and right, the black cliffs fell sheer to the forest edge.

"Listen!" Jim caught my arm.

At first only a faint tapping, then louder and louder, we heard from far away the beating of drums, scores of drums, in a strange staccato rhythm--shrill, mocking, jeering! But they were no drums of Khalk'ru! In them was nothing of that dreadful trampling of racing feet upon a hollow world.

They ceased. As though in answer, and from an entirely different direction, there was a fanfarade of trumpets, menacing, warlike. If brazen notes could curse, these did. Again the drums broke forth, still mocking, taunting, defiant.

43

"Little drums," Jim was whispering. "Drums of--" He dropped down from the rocks, and I followed. The barrier led to the east, dipping steadily downward. We followed its base. It stood like a great wall between us and the valley, barring our vision. We heard the drums no more. We descended five hundred feet at least before the barrier ended. At its end was another rock slide like that down which the rifles and pack had fallen.

We stood studying it. It descended at an angle of about forty-five degrees, and while not so smooth as the other, it had few enough foot-holds.

The air had steadily grown warmer. It was not an uncomfortable heat; there was a queer tingling life about it, an exhalation of the crowding forest or of the valley itself, I thought. It gave me a feeling of rampant, reckless life, a heady exaltation. The pack had grown tiresome. If we were to negotiate the slide, and there seemed nothing else to do, I couldn't very well carry it. I unslung it.

"Letter of introduction" I said, and sent it slithering down the rock.

"Breathe deep and slow, you poor ass," said Jim, and laughed.

His eyes were bright; he looked happy, like a man from whom some burden of fear and doubt has fallen. He looked, in fact, as I had felt when I had taken up that challenge of the unknown not so long before. And I wondered.

The slithering pack gave a little leap, and dropped completely out of sight. Evidently the slide did not go all the way to the valley floor, or, if so, it continued at a sharper angle at the point of the pack's disappearance.

I let myself over cautiously, and began to worm down the slide flat on my belly, Jim following. We had negotiated about three-quarters of it when I heard him shout. Then his falling body struck me. I caught him with one hand, but it broke my own precarious hold. We went rolling down the slide and dropped into space. I felt a jarring shock, and abruptly went completely out.

VII. THE LITTLE PEOPLE

I came to myself to find Jim pumping the breath back into me. I was lying on something soft. I moved my legs gingerly, and sat up. I looked around. We were on a bank of moss--in it, rather, for the tops of the moss were a foot or more above my head. It was an exceedingly overgrown moss, I thought, staring at it stupidly. I had never seen moss as big as this. Had I shrunk, or was it really so overgrown? Above me was a hundred feet of almost sheer cliff. Said Jim:

"Well, we're here."

"How did we get here?" I asked, dazed. He pointed to the cliff.

"We fell down that. We struck a ledge. You did, rather. I was on top. It bumped us right out on this nice big moss mattress. I was still on top. That's why I've been pumping breath back into you for the last five minutes. Sorry, Leif, but if it had been the other way about, you'd certainly have had to proceed on your pilgrimage alone. I haven't your resilience."

He laughed. I stood up, and looked about us. The bed of giant moss on which we had landed formed a mound between us and the forest. At the base of the cliff was piled the debris of the fall that had made the slide. I looked at these rocks and shivered. If we had struck them we would have been a jumble of broken bones and mangled flesh. I felt myself over. I was intact.

"Everything, Indian," I said piously, "is always for the best."

"God, Leif! You had me worried for awhile!" He turned abruptly. "Look at the forest."

The mound of moss was a huge and high oval, hemmed almost to the base of the cliffs by gigantic trees. They were somewhat like the sequoias of California, and quite as high. Their crowns towered; their enormous boles were columns carved by Titans. Beneath them grew graceful ferns, tall as palm trees, and curious conifers with trunks thin as bamboos, scaled red and yellow. Over them, hanging from the boles and branches of the trees, were vines and dusters of flowers of every shape and colour; there were cressets of orchids, and chandeliers of lilies; strange symmetrical trees, the tips of whose leafless branches held up flower cups as though they were candelabra; chimes of flower bells swayed from boughs and there were long ropes and garlands of small starry flowers, white and crimson and in all the blues of the tropic seas. Bees dipped into them. There was a constant flashing of great dragon-flies all in lacquered mail of green and scarlet. And mysterious shadows drifted through the forest, like the shadows of the wings of hovering unseen guardians.

It was no forest of the Carboniferous Age, at least none such as I had ever seen reconstructed by science. It was a forest of enchantment. Out of it came heady fragrances. Nor was it, for all its strangeness, in the least sinister, or forbidding. It was very beautiful.

Jim said:

"The woods of the gods! Anything might live in a place like that. Anything that is lovely--"

Ah, Tsantawu, my brother--had that but been true!

All I said was:

"It's going to be damned hard to get through."

"I was thinking that," he answered. "Maybe the best thing is to skirt the cliffs. We may run across easier going farther on. Which way--right or left?"

We tossed a coin. The coin spun right. I saw the pack not far away, and walked over to retrieve it. The moss was as unsteady as a double spring-mattress. I wondered how it came to be there; thought that probably a few of the giant trees had been felled by the rock fall and the moss had fed upon their decay. I slung the pack over my shoulders, and we tramped, waist-deep in the spongy growth, to the cliffs.

We skirted the cliffs for about a mile. Sometimes the forest pressed so closely that we had trouble clinging to the rock. Then it began to change. The giant trees retreated. We entered a brake of the immense ferns. Except for the bees and the lacquered dragon-flies, there was no sign of life amid the riotous vegetation. We passed out of the ferns and into a most singular small meadow. It was almost like a clearing. At each side were the ferns; the forest formed a palisade at one end; at the other was a sheer cliff whose black face was spangled with large cup-shaped white flowers which hung from short, reddish, rather repellantly snake-like vines whose roots I supposed were fixed in crevices in the rock.

No trees or ferns of any kind grew in the meadow. It was carpeted by a lacy grass upon whose tips were minute blue flowerlets. From the base of the cliff arose a thin veil of steam which streamed up softly high in the air, bathing the cup-shaped white blossoms.

A boiling spring, we decided. We drew closer to examine it.

We heard a wailing--despairing, agonized...Like the wail of a heart-broken, tortured child, yet neither quite human nor quite animal. It had come from the cliff, from somewhere behind the veils of steam. We stopped short, listening. The wailing began again, within it something that stirred the very depths of pity, and it did not cease. We ran toward the cliff. The steam curtain at its base was dense. We skirted it and reached its farther end.

At the base of the cliff was a long and narrow pool, like a small closed stream. Its water was black and bubbling, and from these bubbles came the steam. From end to end of the boiling pool, across the face of the black rock, ran a yard-wide ledge. Above it, spaced at regular intervals, were niches cut within the cliff, small as cradles.

In two of these niches, half-within them and half-upon the ledge, lay what at first glance seemed two children. They were outstretched upon their backs, their tiny hands and feet fastened to the stone by staples of bronze. Their hair streamed down their sides; their bodies were stark naked.

And now I saw that they were not children. They were mature--a little man and a little woman. The woman had twisted her head and was staring at the other pygmy. It was she who was wailing. She did not see us. Her eyes were intent upon him. He lay rigid, his eyes closed. Upon his breast, over his heart, was a black corrosion, as though acid had been dropped upon it.

There was a movement on the cliff above him. One of the cup-shaped white flowers was there. Could it have been that which had moved? It hung a foot above the little man's breast, and on its scarlet pistils was a slowly gathering drop which I took for nectar.

It had been the flower whose movement had caught my eye! As I looked the reddish vine trembled. It writhed like a sluggish worm an inch down the rock. The flower shook its cup as though it were a mouth trying to shake loose the gathering drop. And the flower mouth was directly over the little man's heart and the black corrosion on his breast.

I stepped out upon the narrow path, reached up and grasped the vine and tore it loose. It squirmed in my hand like a snake. Its roots dug to my fingers, and like a snake's head the flower raised itself as

47

though to strike. Its rim was thick and fleshy, like a round white mouth. The drop of nectar fell upon my hand and a fiery agony bit into it, running up my arm like a flame. I hurled the squirming thing into the boiling pool.

Close above the little woman was another of the crawling vines. I tore it loose as I had the other. It, too, strove to strike me with its head of flower, but either there was none of that dreadful nectar in its cup, or it missed me. I threw it after the other.

I bent over the little man. His eyes were open; he was glaring up at me. Like his skin, his eyes were yellow, tilted, Mongolian. They seemed to have no pupils, and they were not wholly human; no more than had been the wailing of his woman. There was agony in them, and there was bitter hatred. His gaze wandered to my hair, and I saw amazement banish the hatred.

The flaming torment of my hand and arm was almost intolerable. By it, I knew what the pygmy must be suffering. I tore away the staples that fettered him. I lifted the little man, and passed him over to Jim. He weighed no more than a baby.

I snapped the staples from the slab on which lay the little woman. There was no fear nor hatred in her eyes. They were filled with wonder and unmistakable gratitude. I carried her over and set her beside her man.

I looked back, up the face of the black cliff. There was movement all over it; the reddish ropes of the vines writhing, the white flowers swaying, raising and lowering their cups.

It was rather hideous...

The little man lay quietly, yellow eyes turning from me to Jim and back to me again. The woman spoke, in trilling, bird-like syllables. She darted away across the meadow, into the forest.

Jim was staring down upon the golden pygmy like a man in a dream. I heard him whisper:

"The Yunwi Tsundi! The Little People! It was all true then! All true!"

The little woman came running out of the fern brake. Her hands were full of thick, heavily veined leaves. She darted a look at me, as of apology. She bent over her man. She squeezed some of the leaves over his breast. A milky sap streamed through her fingers and dropped upon the black, corroded spot. It spread over the spot like a film. The little man stiffened and groaned, relaxed and lay still.

The little woman took my hand. Where the nectar had touched, the skin had turned black. She squeezed the juice of the leaves upon it.

A pang, to which all the torment that had gone before was nothing, ran through hand and arm. Then, almost instantly, there was no pain.

I looked at the little man's breast. The black corrosion had disappeared. There was a wound like an old burn, red and normal. I looked at my hand. It was inflamed, but the blackness was no longer there.

The little woman bowed before me. The little man arose. He looked at my eyes and ran his gaze along my bulk. I watched suspicion grow, and the return of bitter hate. He spoke to his woman. She answered at some length, pointing to the cliff, to my inflamed hand, and to the ankles and wrists of both of them. The little man beckoned to me; by gesture asked me to bend down to him. I did, and he touched my yellow hair; he ran it through his tiny fingers. He laid his hand on my heart... then laid his head on my heart, listening to its beat.

He struck me with his small hand across my mouth. It was no blow; I knew it for a caress.

The little man smiled at me, and trilled. I could not understand, and shook my head helplessly. He looked up at Jim and trilled another question. Jim tried him in the Cherokee. This time it was the little man who shook his head. He spoke again to his woman. Clearly I caught the word ev-ah-lee in the bird-like sounds. She nodded.

Motioning us to follow, they ran across the meadow, toward the further brake of fern. How little they were--hardly to my thighs. They were beautifully formed. Their long hair was chestnut brown, fine and silky. Their hair floated behind them like cobwebs.

They ran like small deer. We were hard put to keep up with them. They entered the fern brake toward which we had been heading, and here they slowed their pace. On and on we went through the giant ferns. I could see no path, but the golden pygmies knew their way.

We came out of the ferns. Before us was a wide sward covered with the flowerets whose blue carpet ran to the banks of a wide river, to the banks of a strange river, a river all milky white, over whose placid surface hovered swirls of opalescent mist. Through the swirls I caught glimpses of green, level plains upon the white river's further side, and of green scarps.

The little man halted. He bent his ear to the ground. He leaped back into the brake, motioning us to follow. In a few minutes we came across a half-ruined watch tower. Its entrance gaped open. The pygmies slipped within it, beckoning.

Inside the tower was a crumbling flight of stones leading to its top. The little man and woman danced up them, with us close behind

49

them. There was a small chamber at the tower's top through the chinks of whose stones the green light streamed. I peered through one of the crevices, down upon the blue sward and the white river. I heard the faint trampling of horses' feet and the low chanting of women; closer they drew, and closer.

A woman came riding down the blue sward. She was astride a great black mare. She wore, like a hood, the head of a white wolf. Its pelt covered her shoulders and back. Over that silvery pelt her hair fell in two thick braids of flaming red. Her high, round breasts were bare, and beneath them the paws of the white wolf were clasped like a girdle. Her eyes were blue as the cornflower and set wide apart under a broad, low forehead. Her skin was milky-white flushed with soft rose. Her mouth was full-lipped, crimson, and both amorous and cruel.

She was a strong woman, tall almost as I. She was like a Valkyrie, and like those messengers of Odin she carried on her saddle before her, held by one arm, a body. But it was no soul of a slain warrior snatched up for flight to Valhalla. It was a girl. A girl whose arms were bound to her sides by stout thongs, with head bent hopelessly on her breast. I could not see her face; it was hidden under the veil of her hair. But the hair was russet red and her skin as fair as that of the woman who held her.

Over the Wolf-woman's head flew a snow-white falcon, dipping and circling and keeping pace with her as she rode.

Behind her rode a half-score other women, young and strong-thewed, pink-skinned and blue-eyed, their hair of copper-red, rust-red, bronzy-red, plaited around their heads or hanging in long braids down their shoulders. They were bare-breasted, kirtled and buskined. They carried long, slender spears and small round targes. And they, too, were like Valkyries, each of them a shield-maiden of the Aesir. As they rode, they sang, softly, muted, a strange chant.

The Wolf-woman and her captive passed around a bend of the sward and out of sight. The chanting women followed and were hidden.

There was a gleam of silver from the white falcon's wing as it circled and dropped, circled and dropped. Then it, too, was gone.

50

VIII. EVALIE

The golden pygmies hissed; their yellow eyes were molten with hatred.

The little man touched my hand, talking in the rapid trilling syllables, and pointing over the white river. Clearly he was telling me we must cross it. He stopped, listening. The little woman ran down the broken stairs. The little man twittered angrily, darted to Jim, beat at his legs with his fists as though to arouse him, then shot after the woman.

"Snap out of it, Indian!" I said, impatiently. "They want us to hurry."

He shook his head, like a man shaking away the last cobwebs of some dream.

We sped down the broken steps. The little man was waiting for us; or at least he had not run away, for, if waiting for us, he was doing so, in a most singular manner. He was dancing in a small circle, waving his arms and hands oddly, and trilling a weird melody upon four notes, repeated over and over in varying progressions. The woman was nowhere in sight.

A wolf howled. It was answered by other wolves farther away in the flowered forest--like a hunting pack whose leader has found the scent.

The little woman came racing through the fern brake; the little man stopped dancing. Her hands were filled with small purplish fruits resembling fox-grapes. The little man pointed toward the white river, and they set off through the screening brake of ferns. We followed.

We came out of the brake, crossed the blue sward and stood on the bank of the river.

The howl of the wolf sounded again, answered by the others, and closer.

The little man leaped upon me, twittering frantically; he twined his legs about my waist and strove to tear my shirt from me. The woman was trilling at Jim, waving in her hands the bunches of purple fruit.

"They want us to take off our clothes," said Jim. "They want us to be quick about it."

We stripped, hastily. There was a crevice in the bank into which I pushed the pack. Quickly we rolled up our clothes and boots, and threw a strap around them and slung them over our shoulders.

The little woman threw a handful of the purple fruit to her man. She motioned Jim to bend, and as he did so she squeezed the berries over his head and hands, his breasts and thighs and feet. The little man was doing the same for me. The fruit had an oddly pungent odour that made my eyes water.

I straightened up and looked out over the white river.

The head of a serpent broke through its milky surface; then another and another. Their heads were as large as those of the anaconda, and were scaled in vivid emerald. They were crested by brilliant green spines which continued along their backs and were revealed as they swirled and twisted in the white water. Quite definitely, I did not like plunging into that water, but now I thought I knew the purpose of our anointing, and that most certainly the golden pygmies intended us no harm. And just as certainly, I assumed, they knew what they were about.

The howling of the wolves came once more, not only much nearer, but from the direction along which had gone the troop of women.

The little man dived into the water, motioning me to follow. I obeyed, and heard the small splash of the woman and the louder one of Jim. The little man glanced back at me, nodded, and began to swim across like an eel, at a speed that I found difficult to emulate.

The crested serpents did not molest us. Once I felt the slither of scales across my loins; once I shook the water from my eyes to find one of them swimming beside me, matching in play my speed, or so it seemed; racing me.

The water was warm, as warm as the milk it resembled, and curiously buoyant. The river at this point was about a thousand feet wide. I had covered half of it when I heard a shrill shriek and felt the buffeting of wings about my head. I rolled over, beating up with my hands to drive off whatever it was that had attacked me.

It was the white falcon of the Wolf-woman, hovering, dropping, rising again, threshing me with its pinions!

I heard a cry from the bank, a bell-like contralto, vibrant, imperious--in archaic Uighur:

"Come back! Come back. Yellow-hair!"

I swung round to see. The falcon ceased its bufferings. Upon the farther bank was the Wolf-woman upon her great black mare, the captive girl still clasped in her ann. The Wolf-woman's eyes were like sapphire stars, her free hand was raised in summons.

And all around her, heads lowered, glaring at me with eyes as green as hers were blue, was a pack of snow-white wolves!

"Come back!" she cried again.

She was very beautiful--the Wolf-woman. It would not have been hard to have obeyed. But no--she was not a Wolf-woman! What was she? Into my mind came a Uighur word, an ancient word that I had not blown I knew. She was the Salur'da--the Witch-woman. And with it came angry resentment of her summons. Who was she--the Salur'da--to command me! Me, Dwayanu, who in olden time long forgot would have had her whipped with scorpions for such insolence!

I raised myself high above the white water.

"Back to your den, Salur'da!" I shouted. "Does Dwayanu come to your call? When I summon you, then see that you obey!"

She stared at me, stark amazement in her eyes; the strong arm that held the girl relaxed so that the captive almost dropped from the mare's high pommel. I struck out across the water to the farther shore.

I heard the Witch-woman whistle. The falcon circling round my head screamed, and flew. I heard the white wolves snarling; I heard the thud of the black mare's hoofs racing over the blue sward. I reached the bank and climbed it. Only then did I turn. Witch-woman, falcon and white wolves--all of them were gone.

Across my wake the emerald-headed, emerald-crested serpents swam and swirled and dived.

The golden pygmies had climbed upon the bank.

Jim asked:

"What did you say to her?"

"The Witch-woman comes to my call--not I to hers," I answered, and wondered as I did so what it was that compelled the words.

"Still very much--Dwayanu, aren't you, Leif? What touched the trigger on you this time?"

"I don't know." The inexplicable resentment against the woman was still strong, and, because I could not understand it, irritating to a degree. "She ordered me to come back, and a little fire-cracker went off in my brain. Then I--I seemed to know her for what she is, and that her command was rank insolence. I told her so. She was no more surprised by what I said than I am. It was like someone else speaking. It was like--" I hesitated--"well, it was like when I started that cursed ritual and couldn't stop."

He nodded, then began to put on his clothes. I followed suit. They were soaking wet. The pygmies watched us wriggle into them with frank amazement. I noticed that the angry red around the wound on the little man's breast had paled, and that while the wound itself was raw, it was not deep and had already begun to heal. I looked at my own hand; the red had almost disappeared, and only a slight tenderness betrayed where the nectar had touched it.

When we had laced our boots, the golden pygmies trotted off, away from the river toward a line of cliffs about a mile ahead. The vaporous green light half hid them, as it had wholly hidden our view to the north when we had first looked over the valley. For half the distance the ground was level and covered with the blue-flowered grass. Then ferns began, steadily growing higher. We came upon a trail little wider than a deer path which threaded into a greater brake. Into this we turned.

We had eaten nothing since early morning, and I thought regretfully of the pack I had left behind. However, it is my training to eat heartily when I can, and philosophically go without when I must. So I tightened my belt and glanced back at Jim, close upon my heels.

"Hungry?" I asked.

"No. Too busy thinking."

"Indian--what brought the red-headed beauty back?"

"The wolves. Didn't you hear them howling after her? They found our track and gave her the signal."

"I thought so--but it's incredible! Hell--then she is a Witch-woman."

"Not because of that. You're forgetting your Mowgli and the Grey Companions. Wolves aren't hard to train. But she's a Witch-woman, nevertheless. Don't hold back Dwayanu when you deal with her, Leif."

The little drums again began to beat. At first only a few, then steadily more and more until there were scores of them. This time the cadences were lilting, gay, tapping out a dancing rhythm that lifted all weariness. They did not seem far away. But now the ferns were high over our heads and impenetrable to the sight, and the narrow path wove in and out among them like a meandering stream

The pygmies hastened their pace. Suddenly the trail came out of the ferns, and the pair halted. In front of us the ground sloped sharply upward for three or four hundred feet. The slope, except where the path ran, was covered from bottom to top with a tangle of thick green vines studded along all their lengths with wicked three-inch thorns; a living chevaux-de-frise which no living creature would penetrate. At the end of the path was a squat tower of stone, and from this came the glint of spear-heads.

In the tower a shrill-voiced drum chattered an unmistakable alarm. Instantly the lilting drums were silent. The same shrill chatter was taken up and repeated from point to point, diminishing in the far distance; and now I saw that the slope was like an immense circular fortification, curving far out toward the unbroken palisade of the giant ferns, and retreating at our right toward the sheer wall of black cliff, far away. Everywhere upon it was the thicket of thorn.

The little man twittered to his woman, and walked up the trail toward the tower. He was met by other pygmies streaming out of it. The little woman stayed with us, nodding and smiling and patting our knees reassuringly.

Another drum, or a trio of them, began to beat from the tower. I thought there were three because their burden was on three different notes, soft, caressing, yet far-carrying. They sang a word, a name, those drums, as plainly as though they had lips, the name I had heard in the trilling of the pygmies...

Ev-ah-lee... Ev-ah-lee...Ev-ah-lee...Over and over and over. The drums in the other towers were silent.

The little man beckoned us. We went forward, avoiding with difficulty the thorns. We came to the top of the path beside the small tower. A score of the little men stepped out and barred our way. None was taller than the one I had saved from the white flowers. All had the same golden skin, the same half-animal yellow eyes; like his, their hair was long and silky, floating almost to their tiny feet, They wore twisted loin-cloths of what appeared to be cotton; around their waists were broad girdles of silver, pierced like lace-work in intricate de-signs. Their spears were wicked weapons for all their apparent frailty, long-handled, hafted in some black wood, and with foot-deep points of red metal, and barbed like a muskalonge hook from tip to base. Swung on their backs were black bows with long arrows barbed in similar manner; and in their metal girdles were slender sickle-shaped knives of the red metal, like scimitars of gnomes.

They stood staring at us, like small children. They made me feel as Gulliver must have felt among the Lilliputians. Also, there was that about them which gave me no desire to tempt them to use their weapons. They looked at Jim with curiosity and interest and with no trace of unfriendliness. They looked at me with little faces that grew hard and fierce. Only when their eyes roved to my yellow hair did I see wonder and doubt lighten suspicion--but they never dropped the points of the spears turned toward me.

Ev-ah-lee...Ev-ah-lee...Ev-ah-lee...sang the drums.

There was an answering roll from beyond, and they were silent.

I heard a sweet, low-pitched voice at the other side of the tower trilling the bird-like syllables of the Little People--And then--I saw Evalie.

Have you watched a willow bough swaying in spring above some clear sylvan pool, or a slender birch dancing with the wind in a secret woodland and covert, or the flitting green shadows in a deep forest glade which are dryads half-tempted to reveal themselves? I thought of them as she came toward us.

She was a dark girl, and a tall girl. Her eyes were brown under long black lashes, the clear brown of the mountain brook in autumn; her hair was black, the jetty hair that in a certain light has a sheen of darkest blue. Her face was small, her features certainly neither classic nor regular--the brows almost meeting in two level lines above her small, straight nose; her mouth was large but finely cut, and sensitive. Over her broad, low forehead the blue-black hair was braided like a coronal. Her skin was clear amber. Like polished fine amber it shone under the loose, yet clinging, garment that clothed her, knee-long, silvery, cobweb fine and transparent. Around her hips was the white loincloth of the Little People. Unlike them, her feet were sandalled.

But it was the grace of her that made the breath catch in your throat as you looked at her, the long flowing line from ankle to shoulder, delicate and mobile as the curve of water flowing over some smooth breast of rock, a liquid grace of line that changed with every movement.

It was that--and the life that burned in her like the green flame of the virgin forest when the kisses of spring are being changed for the warmer caresses of summer. I knew now why the old Greeks had believed in the dryads, the naiads, the nereids--the woman souls of trees, of brooks and waterfalls and fountains, and of the waves.

I could not tell how old she was--hers was the pagan beauty which knows no age.

She examined me, my clothes and boots, in manifest perplexity; she glanced at Jim, nodded, as though to say there was nothing in him to be disturbed about; then turned back to me, studying me. The small soldiers ringed her, their spears ready.

The little man and his woman had stepped forward. They were both talking at once, pointing to his breast, to my hand, to my yellow hair. The girl laughed, drew the little woman to her and covered her lips with a hand. The little man went on trilling and twittering.

Jim had been listening with a puzzled intensity whenever the girl had done the talking. He caught my arm.

"It's Cherokee they're speaking! Or something like it-- Listen...there was a word...it sounded like 'Yun'-wini'giski'...it means 'Man-eaters.' Literally, 'They eat people'...if that's what it was... and look...he's showing how the vines crawled down the cliffs..."

The girl began speaking again. I listened intently. The rapid enunciation and the trilling made understanding difficult, but I caught sounds that seemed familiar--and now I heard a combination that I certainly knew.

"It's some kind of Mongolian tongue, Jim. I got a word just then that means 'serpent-water' in a dozen different dialects."

"I know--she called the snake 'aha'nada' and the Cherokees say 'inadu'--but it's Indian, not Mongolian."

"It might be both. The Indian dialects are Mongolian. Maybe it's the ancient mother-tongue. If we could only get her to speak slower, and tune down on the trills."

"It might be that. The Cherokees called themselves 'the oldest people' and their language 'the first speech'--wait--"

He stepped forward, hand upraised; he spoke the word which in the Cherokee means, equally, friend or one who comes with good intentions. He said it several times. Wonder and comprehension crept into the girl's eyes. She repeated it as he had spoken it, then turned to the pygmies, passing the word on to them--and I could distinguish it now plainly within the trills and pipings. The pygmies came closer, staring up at Jim.

He said, slowly: "We come from outside. We know nothing of this place. We know none within it."

Several times he had to repeat this before she caught it. She looked gravely at him, and at me doubtfully--yet as one who would like to believe. She answered haltingly.

"But Sri"--she pointed to the little man--"has said that in the water he spoke the tongue of evil."

"He speaks many tongues," said Jim--then to me:

"Talk to her. Don't stand there like a dummy, admiring her. This girl can think--and we're in a jam. Your looks make no hit with the dwarfs, Leif, in spite of what you did."

"Is it any stranger that I should have spoken that tongue than that I now speak yours, Evalie?" I said. And asked the same question in two of the oldest dialects of the Mongolian that I knew. She studied me, thoughtfully.

"No," she said at last--"no; for I, too, know something of it, yet that does not make me evil."

And suddenly she smiled, and trilled some command to the guards. They lowered their spears, regarding me with something of the friendly interest they had showed toward Jim. Within the tower, the drums began to roll a cheerful tattoo. As at a signal, the other unseen drums which the shrill alarm had silenced, resumed their lilting rhythm.

The girl beckoned us. We walked behind her, the little soldiers ringing us, between a portcullis of thorn and the tower.

We passed over the threshold of the Land of the Little People and of Evalie.

IX.

The green light that filled the Shadowed-land was darkening. As the green forest darkens at dusk. The sun must long since have dipped beneath the peaks circling that illusory floor which was the sky of the Shadowed-land. Yet here the glow faded slowly, as though it were not wholly dependent upon the sun, as though the place had some luminosity of its own.

We sat beside the tent of Evalie. It was pitched on a rounded knoll not far from the entrance of her lair within the cliff. All along the base of the cliff were the lairs of the Little People, tiny openings through which none larger than they could creep into the caves that were their homes, their laboratories, their workshops, their storehouses and granaries, their impregnable fortresses.

It had been hours since we had followed her over the plain between the watch-tower and her tent. The golden pygmies had swarmed from every side, curious as children, chattering and trilling, questioning Evalie, twittering her answers to those on the outskirts of the crowd. Even now there was a ring of them around the base of the knoll, dozens of little men and little women, staring up at us with their yellow eyes, chirping and laughing. In the arms of the women were babies like tiniest dolls, and like larger dolls were the older children who clustered at their knees.

Child-like, their curiosity was soon satisfied; they went back to their occupations and their play. Others, curiosity not yet quenched, took their places.

I watched them dancing upon the smooth grass. They danced in circling measures to the lilting rhythm of their drums. There were other knolls upon the plain, larger and smaller than that on which we were, and all of them as rounded and as symmetrical. Around and over them the golden pygmies danced to the throbbing of the little drums.

They had brought us little loaves of bread, and oddly sweet but palatable milk and cheese, and unfamiliar delicious fruits and melons. I was ashamed of the number of platters I had cleaned. The little people had only watched, and laughed, and urged the women to bring me more.

Jim said, laughingly:"It's the food of the Yunwi Tsundsi you're eating. Fairy food, Leif! You can never eat mortal food again."

I looked at Evalie, and at the wine and amber beauty of her. Well, I could believe Evalie had been brought up on something more than mortal food.

I studied the plain for the hundredth time. The slope on which stood the squat towers was an immense semi-circle, the ends of whose arcs met the black cliffs. It must enclose, I thought, some twenty square miles. Beyond the thorned vines were the brakes of the giant fern; beyond them, on the other side of the river, I could glimpse the great trees. If there were forests on this side, I could not tell. Nor what else there might be of living things. There was something to be guarded against, certainly, else why the fortification, the defences?

Whatever else it might be, this guarded land of the golden pygmies was a small Paradise, with its stands of grain, its orchards, its vines and berries and its green fields.

I thought over what Evalie had told us of herself, carefully and slowly tuning down the trilling syllables of the little people into vocables we could understand. It was an ancient tongue she spoke--one whose roots struck far deeper down in the soil of Time than any I knew, unless it were the archaic Uighur itself. Minute by minute I found myself mastering it with ever greater ease, but not so rapidly as Jim. He had even essayed a few trills, to the pygmies' delight. More than that, however, they had understood him. Each of us could follow Evalie's thought better than she could ours.

Whence had the Little People come into the Shadowed-land? And where had they learned that ancient tongue? I asked myself that, and answered that as well ask how it came that the Sumerians, whose great city the Bible calls Ur of the Chaldees, spoke a Mongolian language. They, too, were a dwarfish race, masters of strange sorceries, students of the stars. And no man knows whence they came into Mesopotamia with their science full-blown. Asia is the Ancient Mother, and to how many races she has given birth and watched blown away in dust none can say.

The transformation of the tongue into the bird-like speech of the Little People, I thought I understood. Obviously, the smaller the throat, the higher are the sounds produced. Unless by some freak, one never hears a child with a bass voice. The tallest of the Little People was no bigger than a six-year-old child. They could not, perforce, sound the gutturals and deeper tones; so they had to substitute other sounds. The natural thing, when you cannot strike a note in a lower octave, is to strike that same note in a higher. And so they had, and in time this had developed into the overlying pattern of trills and pipings, beneath which, however, the essential structure persisted.

She remembered, Evalie had told us, a great stone house. She thought she remembered a great water. She remembered a land of trees which had become "white and cold". There had been a man and a woman...then there was only the man...and it was all like mist. All she truly remembered was the Little People...she had forgotten there had ever been anything else... until we had come. She remembered when she had been no bigger than the Little People...and how frightened she was when she began to be bigger than they. The Little People, the Rrrllya--it is the closest I can come to the trill--loved her; they did as she told them to do. They had fed and clothed and taught her, especially the mother of Sri, whose life I had saved from the Death Flower. Taught her what? She looked at us oddly, and only repeated--"taught me." Sometimes she danced with the Little People and sometimes she danced for them--again the oddly secretive, half-amused glance. That was all. How long ago had she been as small as the Little People? She did not know--long and long ago. Who had named her Evalie? She did not know.

I studied her, covertly. There was not one thing about her to give a clue to her race. Foundling, I knew, she must have been, the vague man and woman her father and mother. But what had they been--of what country? No more than could her lips, did her eyes or hair, colouring or body hint at answer.

She was more changeling than I. A changeling of the mirage! Nurtured on food from Goblin Market!

I wondered whether she would change back again into everyday woman if I carried her out of the Shadowed-land.

I felt the ring touch my breast with the touch of ice.

Carry her away! There was Khalk'ru to meet first--and the Witch-woman!

The green twilight deepened; great fire-flies began to flash lanterns of pale topaz through the flowering trees; a little breeze stole over the fern brakes, laden with the fragrances of the far forest. Evalie sighed.

"You will not leave me, Tsantawu?"

If he heard her, he did not answer. She turned to me.

"You will not leave me--Leif?"

61

"No!" I said...and seemed to hear the drums of Khalk'ru beating down the lilting tambours of the Little People like far-away mocking laughter.

The green twilight had deepened into darkness, a luminous darkness, as though a full moon were shining behind a cloud-veiled sky. The golden pygmies had stilled their lilting drums; they were passing into their cliff lairs. From the distant towers came the tap-tap-tap of the drums of the guards, whispering to each other across the thorn-covered slopes. The fire-flies' lights were like the lanterns of a goblin watch; great moths floated by on luminous silvery wings, like elfin planes.

"Evalie," Jim spoke. "The Yunwi Tsundsi--the Little People-- how long have they dwelt here?"

"Always, Tsantawu--or so they say."

"And those others--the red-haired women?"

We had asked her of those women before, and she had not answered, had tranquilly ignored the matter, but now she replied without hesitation.

"They are of the Ayjir--it was Lur the Sorceress who wore the wolfskin. She rules the Ayjir with Yodin the High Priest and Tibur-- Tibur the Laugher, Tibur the Smith. He is not so tall as you, Leif, but he is broader of shoulder and girth, and he is strong--strong! I will tell you of the Ayjir. Before it was as though a hand were clasped over my lips--or was it my heart? But now the hand is gone.

"The Little People say the Ayjir came riding here long and long and long ago. Then the Rrrllya held the land on each side of the river. There were many of the Ayjir--and many. Far more than now, many men and women where now are mainly women and few men. They came as though in haste from far away, or so the little people say their fathers told them. They were led by a--by a--I have no word! It has a name, but that name I will not speak--no, not even within me! Yet it has a shape...I have seen it on the banners that float from the towers of Karak...and it is on the breasts of Lur and Tibur when they..."

She shivered and was silent. A silver-winged moth dropped upon her hand, lifting and dropping its shining wings; gently she raised it to her lips, wafted it away.

"All this the Rrrllya--whom you call the Little People--did not then know. The Ayjir rested. They began to build Karak, and to cut within the cliff their temple to--to what had led them here. They built quickly at first, as though they feared pursuit; but when none came, they built more slowly. They would have made my little ones their

62

servants, their slaves. The Rrrllya would not have it so. There was war. The Little Ones lay in wait around Karak, and when the Ayjir came forth, they killed them; for the Little Ones know all the--the life of the plants, and so they know how to make their spears and arrows slay at once those whom they only touch. And so, many of the Ayjir died.

"At last a truce was made, and not because the Little People were being beaten, for they were not. But for another reason. The Ayjir were cunning; they laid traps for the little ones, and caught a number. Then this they did--they carried them to the temple and sacrificed them to--to that which had led them here. By sevens they took them to the temple, and one out of each seven they made watch that sacrifice, then released him to carry to the Rrrllya the tale of what he had seen.

"The first they would not believe, so dreadful was the story of that sacrifice--but then came the second and third and fourth with the same story. And a great dread and loathing and horror fell upon the Little People. They made a covenant. They would dwell upon this side of the river; the Ayjir should have the other. In return the Ayjir swore by what had led them that never more should one of the Little People be given in sacrifice to it. If one were caught in Ayjirland, he would be killed--but not by the Sacrifice. And if any of the Ayjir should flee Karak, seek refuge among the Rrrllya, they must kill that fugitive. To all of this, because of that great horror, the Little People agreed. Nansur was broken, so none could cross--Nansur, that spanned Nanbu, the white river, was broken. All boats both of the Ayjir and the Rrrllya were destroyed, and it was agreed no more should be built. Then, as further guard, the Little People took the dalan'usa and set them in Nanbu, so none could cross by its waters. And so it has been--for long and long and long."

"Dalan'usa, Evalie--you mean the serpents?"

"Tlanu'se--the leech," said Jim.

"The serpents--they are harmless. I think you would not have stopped to talk to Lur had you seen one of the dalan'usa, Leif," said Evalie, half-maliciously.

I filed that enigma for further reference.

"Those two we found beneath the death flowers. They had broken the truce?"

"Not broken it. They knew what to expect if found, and were ready to pay. There are plants that grow on the farther side of white Nanbu--and other things the Little Ones need, and they are not to be found on this side. And so they swim Nanbu to get them--the dalan'usa are their friends--and not often are they caught there. But this day Lur was hunting a runaway who was trying to make her way to Sirk, and she crossed their trail and ran them down, and laid them beneath the Death Flowers."

"But what had the girl done--she was one of them?"

"She had been set apart for the Sacrifice. Did you not see--she was taluli...with child...ripening for...for..."

Her voice trailed into silence. A chill touched me.

"But, of course, you know nothing of that," she said. "Nor will I speak of it--now. If Sri and Sra had found the girl before they, themselves, had been discovered, they would have guided her past the dalan'usa--as they guided you; and here she would have dwelt until the time came that she must pass-out of herself. She would have passed in sleep, in peace, without pain...and when she awakened it would have been far from here...perhaps with no memory of it...free. So it is that the Little People who love life send forth those who must be sent."

She said it tranquilly, with clear eyes, untroubled.

"And are many sent forth so?"

"Not many, since few may pass the dalan'usa--yet many try."

"Both men and women, Evalie?"

"Can men bear children?"

"What do you mean by that?" I asked, roughly enough; there had been something in the question that somehow touched me in the raw.

"Not now," she answered. "Besides, men are few in Karak, as I told you. Of children born, not one in twenty is a man child. Do not ask me why, for I do not know."

She arose, stood looking at us dreamily.

"Enough for to-night. You shall sleep in my tent. On the morrow you shall have one of your own, and the Little People will cut you a lair in the cliff next mine. And you shall look on Karak, standing on broken Nansur--and you shall see Tibur the Laugher, since he always comes to Nansur's other side when I am there. You shall see it all...on the morrow...or the morrow after...or on another morrow. What does it matter, since every morrow shall be ours, together. Is it not so?"

And again Jim made no answer.

"It is so, Evalie," I said.

She smiled at us, sleepily. She turned from us and floated toward the darker shadow on the cliff which was the door to her cave. She merged into the shadow, and was gone.

X. IF A MAN COULD USE ALL HIS BRAIN

The drums of the sentinel dwarfs beat on softly, talking to one another along the miles of circling scarp. And suddenly I had a desperate longing for the Gobi. I don't know why, but its barren and burning, wind-swept and sand-swept body was more desirable than any woman's. It was like strong homesickness. I found it hard to shake it off. I spoke at last in sheer desperation. "You've been acting damned queer, Indian." "Tsi Tsa'lagi--I told you--I'm all Cherokee." "Tsantawu--It is I, Degata, who speaks to you now." I had dropped into the Cherokee; he answered:

"What is it my brother desires to know?"

"What it was the voices of the dead whispered that night we slept beneath the spruces? What it was you knew to be truth by the three signs they gave you. I did not hear the voices, brother--yet by the blood rite they are my ancestors as they are yours; and I have the right to know their words."

He said: "Is it not better to let the future unroll itself without giving heed to the thin voices of the dead? Who can tell whether the voices of ghosts speak truth?"

"Tsantawu points his arrow in one direction while his eyes look the other. Once he called me dog slinking behind the heels of the hunter. Since it is plain he still thinks me that..."

"No, no, Lief," he broke in, dropping the tribal tongue. "I only mean I don't know whether it's truth. I know what Barr would call it--natural apprehensions put subconsciously in terms of racial superstitions. The voices--we'll call them that, anyway--said great danger lay north. The Spirit that was north would destroy them for ever and for ever if I fell in its hands. They and I would be 'as though we never had been.' There was some enormous difference between ordinary death and this peculiar death that I couldn't understand. But the voices did. I would know by three signs that they spoke truth, by Ataga'hi, by

Usunhi'yi and by the Yunwi Tsundi. I could meet the first two and still go back. But if I went on to the third--it would be too late. They begged me not to--this was peculiarly interesting, Leif--not to let them be--dissolved."

"Dissolved!" I exclaimed. "But--that's the same word I used. And it was hours after!"

"Yes, that's why I felt creepy when I heard you. You can't blame me for being a little preoccupied when we came across the stony flat that was like Ataga'hi, and more so when we struck the coincidence of the Shadowed-land, which is pretty much the same as Usunhi'yi, the Darkening-land. It's why I said if we ran across the third, the Yunwi Tsundi, I'd take your interpretation rather than Barr's. We did strike it. And if you think all those things aren't a good reason for acting damned queer, as you put it, well--what would you think a good one?"

Jim in the golden chains...Jim with the tentacle of that Dark Power creeping, creeping toward him...my lips were dry and stiff...

"Why didn't you tell me all that! I'd never have let you go on!"

"I know it. But you'd have come back, wouldn't you, old-timer?"

I did not answer; he laughed.

"How could I be sure until I saw all the signs?"

"But they didn't say you would be--dissolved," I clutched at the straw. "They only said there was the danger."

"That's all."

"And what would I be doing? Jim--I'd kill you with my own hand before I'd let what I saw happen in the Gobi happen to you."

"If you could," he said, and I saw he was sorry he had said it.

"If I could? What did they say about me--those damned ances-tors?"

"Not a damned thing," he answered, cheerfully. "I never said they did. I simply reasoned that if we went on, and I was in danger, so would you be. That's all."

"Jim--it isn't all. What are you keeping back?"

He arose, and stood over me.

"All right. They said that even if the Spirit didn't get me, I'd never get out. Now you have the whole works."

"Well," I said, a burden rolling off me, "that's not so bad. And, as for getting out--that may be as may be. One thing's sure--if you stay, so do I."

He nodded, absently. I went on to something else that had been puzzling me.

"The Yunwi Tsundi, Jim, what were they? You never told me anything about them that I remember. What's the legend?"

"Oh--the Little People," he squatted beside me, chuckling, wide awake from his abstraction. "They were in Cherokee-land when the Cherokees got there. They were a pygmy race, like those in Africa and Australia to-day. Only they weren't blacks. These small folk fit their description. Of course, the tribes did some embroidering. They had them copper-coloured and only two feet high. These are golden-skinned and average three feet. At that, they may have faded some here and put on height. Otherwise they square with the accounts--long hair, perfect shape, drums and all."

He went on to tell of the Little People. They had lived in caves, mostly in the region now Tennessee and Kentucky. They were earth-folk, worshippers of life; and as such at times outrageously Rabelaisian. They were friendly toward the Cherokees, but kept rigorously to themselves and seldom were seen. They frequently aided those who had got lost in the mountains, especially children. If they helped any-one, and took him into their caves, they warned him he mustn't tell where the caves were, or he would die. And, ran the legends, if he told, he did die. If anyone ate their food he had to be very careful when he returned to his tribe, and resume his old diet slowly, or he would also die.

The Little People were touchy. If anyone followed them in the woods, they cast a spell on him so that for days he had no sense of lo-cation. They were expert wood and metal workers, and if a hunter found in the forest a knife or arrow-head or any kind of trinket, before he picked it up he had to say: "Little People, I want to take this." If he didn't ask, he never killed any more game and another misfortune came upon him. One which distressed his wife.

They were gay, the Little People, and they spent half their time in dancing and drumming. They had every kind of drum--drums that would make trees fall, drums that brought sleep, drums that drove to madness, drums that talked and thunder drums. The thunder drums sounded just like thunder, and when the Little People beat on them soon there was a real thunderstorm, because they sounded so much like the actuality that it woke up the thunderstorms, and one or more storms was sure to come poking around to gossip with what it sup-posed a wandering member of the family...

I remembered the roll of thunder that followed the chanting; I wondered whether that had been the Little People's defiance to Khalk'ru...

"I've a question or two for you, Leif."

"Go right ahead, Indian."

"Just how much do you remember of--Dwayanu?"

I didn't answer at once; it was the question I had been dreading ever since I had cried out to the Witch-woman on the white river's bank.

"If you're thinking it over, all right. If you're thinking of a way to stall, all wrong. I'm asking for a straight answer."

"Is it your idea that I'm that ancient Uighur, re-born? If it is, maybe you have a theory as to where I've been during the thousands of years between this time and now."

"Oh, so the same idea has been worrying you, has it? No, reincarnation isn't what I had in mind. Although at that, we know so damned little I wouldn't rule it out. But there may be a more reasonable explanation. That's why I ask--what do you remember of Dwayanu?"

I determined to make a clean breast of it.

"All right, Jim," I said. "That same question has been riding my mind right behind Khalk'ru for three years. And if I can't find the answer here, I'll go back to the Gobi for it--if I can get out. When I was in that room of the oasis waiting the old priest's call, I remembered perfectly well it had been Dwayanu's. I knew the bed, and I knew the armour and the weapons. I stood looking at one of the metal caps and I remembered that Dwayanu--or I--had got a terrific clout with a mace when wearing it. I took it down, and there was a dent in it precisely where I remembered it had been struck. I remembered the swords, and recalled that Dwayanu--or I--had the habit of using a heavier one in the left hand than in the right. Well, one of them was much heavier than the other. Also, in a fight I use my left hand better than I do my right. These memories, or whatever they were, came in flashes. For a moment I would be Dwayanu, plus myself, looking with amused interest on old familiar things--and the next moment I would be only myself and wondering, with no amusement, what it all meant."

"Yes, what else?"

"Well, I wasn't entirely frank about the ritual matter," I said, miserably. "I told you it was as though another person had taken charge of my mind and gone on with it. That was true, in a way--but God help me, I knew all the time that other person was--myself! It was like being two people and one at the same time. It's hard to make clear...you know how you can be saying one thing and thinking another. Suppose you could be saying one thing and thinking two things at once. It was like that. One part of me was in revolt, horror-stricken, terrified. The other part was none of those things; it knew it had power and was enjoying exercising that power--and it had control of my will. But both were--I. Unequivocally, unmistakably--I. Hell, man--if I'd really believed it was somebody, something, besides myself, do you suppose I'd feel the remorse I do? No, it's because I knew it was I--the same part of me that knew the helm and the swords, that I've gone hag-ridden ever since."

"Anything else?"

"Yes. Dreams."

He leaned over, and spoke sharply.

"What dreams?"

"Dreams of battles--dreams of feasts...a dream of war against yellow men, and of a battlefield beside a river and of arrows flying overhead in clouds...of hand-to-hand fights in which I wield a weapon like a huge hammer against big yellow-haired men I know are like myself... dreams of towered cities through which I pass and where white, blue-eyed women toss garlands down for my horse to trample...When I wake the dreams are vague, soon lost. But always I know that while I dreamed them, they were clear, sharp-cut--real as life..."

"Is that how you knew the Witch-woman was Witch-woman-- through those dreams?"

"If so, I don't remember. I only knew that suddenly I recognized her for what she was--or that other self did."

He sat for a while in silence.

"Leif," he asked, "in those dreams do you ever take any part in the service of Khalk'ru? Have anything at all to do with his worship?"

"I'm sure I don't. I'd remember that, by God! I don't even dream of the temple in the Gobi!"

He nodded, as though I had confirmed some thought in his own mind; then was quiet for so long that I became jumpy.

"Well, Old Medicine Man of the Tsalagi', what's the diagnosis? Reincarnation, demonic possession, or just crazy?"

"Leif, you never had any of those dreams before the Gobi?"

"I did not."

"Well--I've been trying to think as Barr would, and squaring it with my own grey matter. Here's the result. I think that everything you've told me is the doing of your old priest. He had you under his control when you saw yourself riding to the Temple of Khalk'ru--and wouldn't go in. You don't know what else he might have suggested at that time, and have commanded you to forget consciously when you came to yourself. That's a simple matter of hypnotism. But he had another chance at you. When you were asleep that night. How do you know he didn't come in and do some more suggesting? Obviously, he wanted to believe you were Dwayanu. He. wanted you to 'remember'-- but having had one lesson, he didn't want you to remember what went on with Khalk'ru. That would explain why you dreamed about the pomp and glory and the pleasant things, but not the unpleasant. He was a wise old gentleman--you say that yourself. He knew enough of your psychology to foresee you would balk at a stage of the ritual. So you did--but he had tied you well up. Instantly the post-hypnotic command to the subconscious operated. You couldn't help going on. Although your conscious self was wide-awake, fully aware, it had no control over your will. I think that's what Barr would say. And I'd agree with him. Hell, there are drugs that do all that to you. You don't have to go into migrations of the soul, or demons, or any medieval matter to account for it."

"Yes," I said, hopefully but doubtfully. "And how about the Witch-woman?"

"Somebody like her in your dreams, but forgotten. I think the explanation is what I've said. If it is, Leif, it worries me."

"I don't follow you there," I said.

"No? Well, think this over. If all these things that puzzle you come from suggestions the old priest made--what else did he suggest? Clearly, he knew something of this place. Suppose he foresaw the possibility of your finding it. What would he want you to do when you did find it? Whatever it was, you can bet your chances of getting out that he planted it deep in your subconscious. All right--that being a reasonable deduction, what is it you will do when you come in closer contact with those red-headed ladies we saw, and with the happy few gentlemen who share their Paradise? I haven't the slightest idea--nor have you. And if that isn't something to worry about, tell me what is. Come on--let's go to bed."

We went into the tent. We had been in it before with Evalie. It had been empty then except for a pile of soft pelts and silken stuffs at one side. Now there were two such piles. We shed our clothes in the pale green darkness and turned in. I looked at my watch.

"Ten o'clock," I said. "How many months since morning?"

"At least six. If you keep me awake I'll murder you. I'm tired."

So was I; but I lay long, thinking. I was not so convinced by Jim's argument, plausible as it was. Not that I believed I had been lying dormant in some extra-spatial limbo for centuries. Nor that I had

70

ever been this ancient Dwayanu. There was a third explanation, although I didn't like it a bit better than that of reincarnation; and it had just as many unpleasant possibilities as that of Jim's.

Not long ago an eminent American physician and psychologist had said he had discovered that the average man used only about one-tenth of his brain; and scientists generally agreed he was right. The ablest thinkers, all-round geniuses, such as Leonardo da Vinci and Michelangelo were, might use a tenth more. Any man who could use all his brain could rule the world--but probably wouldn't want to. In the human skull was a world only one-fifth explored at the most.

What was in the terra incognita of the brain--the unexplored eight-tenths?

Well, for one thing there might be a storehouse of ancestral memories, memories reaching back to those of the hairy, ape-like ancestors who preceded man, reaching beyond them even to those of the flippered creatures who crawled out of the ancient seas to begin their march to men--and further back to their ancestors who had battled and bred in the steaming oceans when the continents were being born.

Millions upon millions of years of memories! What a reservoir of knowledge if man's consciousness could but tap it!

There was nothing more unbelievable in this than that the physical memory of the race could be contained in the two single cells which start the cycle of birth. In them are all the complexities of the human body--brain and nerves, muscles, bone and blood. In them, too, are those traits we call hereditary--family resemblances, resemblances not only of face and body but of thought, habits, emotions, reactions to environment: grandfather's nose, great-grandmother's eyes, great-great-grandfather's irascibility, moodiness or what not. If all this can be carried in those seven and forty, and eight and forty, microscopic rods within the birth cells which biologists call the chromosomes, tiny mysterious gods of birth who determine from the beginning what blend of ancestors a boy or girl shall be, why could they not carry, too, the accumulated experiences, the memories of those ancestors?

Somewhere in the human brain might be a section of records, each neatly graven with lines of memories, waiting only for the needle of consciousness to run over them to make them articulate.

Maybe the consciousness did now and then touch and read them. Maybe there were a few people who by some freak had a limited power of tapping their contents.

If that were true, it would explain many mysteries. Jim's ghostly voices, for example. My own uncanny ability of picking up languages.

71

Suppose that I had come straight down from this Dwayanu. And that in this unknown world of my brain, my consciousness, that which now was I, could and did reach in and touch those memories that had been Dwayanu. Or that those memories stirred and reached my consciousness? When that happened--Dwayanu would awaken and live. And I would be both Dwayanu and Leif Langdon!

Might it not be that the old priest had known something of this? By words and rites and by suggestion, even as Jim had said, had reached into that terra incognita and wakened these memories that were--Dwayanu?

They were strong--those memories. They had not been wholly asleep; else I would not have learned so quickly the Uighur...nor experienced those strange, reluctant flashes of recognition before ever I met the old priest...

Yes, Dwayanu was strong. And in some way I knew he was ruthless. I was afraid of Dwayanu--of those memories that once had been Dwayanu. I had no power to arouse them, and I had no power to control them. Twice they had seized my will, had pushed me aside.

What if they grew stronger?

What if they became--all of me?

XI. DRUMS OF THE LITTLE PEOPLE

Six times the green light of the Shadowed-land had darkened into the pale dusk that was its night, and I had heard nothing, seen nothing of the Witch-woman or of any of those who dwelt on the far side of the white river. They had been six days and nights of curious interest. We had gone with Evalie among the golden pygmies over all their guarded plain; and we had gone at will among them, alone.

We had watched them at their work and at their play, listened to their drumming and looked on in wonder at their dances--dances so intricate, so extraordinary, that they were more like complex choral harmonies than steps and gestures. Sometimes the Little People danced in small groups of a dozen or so, and then it was like some simple song. But sometimes they were dancing by the hundreds, interlaced, over a score of the smooth-turfed dancing greens; and then it was like symphonies translated into choreographic measures.

They danced always to the music of their drums; they had no other music, nor did they need any. The drums of the Little People were of many shapes and sizes, in range covering all of ten octaves, and producing not only the semitones of our own familiar scale, but quarter and eighth-tones and even finer gradations that oddly affect the listener--at least, they did me. They ranged in pitch from the pipe organ's deepest bass to a high staccato soprano. Some, the pygmies played with thumbs and fingers, and some with palms of their hands, and some with sticks. There were drums that whispered, drums that hummed, drums that laughed, and drums that sang.

Dances and drums, but especially the drums, were evocative of strange thoughts, strange pictures; the drums beat at the doors of another world--and now and then opened them wide enough to give a glimpse of fleeting, weirdly beautiful, weirdly disturbing, images.

There must have been between four and five thousand of the Little People in the approximately twenty square miles of cultivated, fertile plain enclosed by their wall; how many outside of it, I had no means of knowing. There were a score or more of small colonies, Evalie told us. These were like hunting or mining posts from which came the pelts, the metals and other things the horde fashioned to their uses. At Nansur Bridge was a strong warrior post. Some balance of nature, so far as I could learn from her, kept them at about the same constant; they grew quickly into maturity and their lives were not long.

She told us of Sirk, the city of those who had fled from the Sacrifice. From her description an impregnable place, built against the cliffs; walled; boiling springs welling up at the base of its battlements and forming an impassable moat. There was constant warfare between the people of Sirk and the white wolves of Lur, lurking in the encompassing forest, keeping watch to intercept those fleeing to it from Karak. I had the feeling that there was furtive intercourse between Sirk and the golden pygmies, that perhaps the horror of the Sacrifice which both shared, and the revolt of those in Sirk against the worshippers of Khalk'ru was a bond. And that when they could, the Little People helped them, and would even join hands with them, were it not for the deep ancient fear of what might follow should they break the compact their forefathers had made with the Ayjir.

It was a thing Evalie said that made me think that.

"If you had turned the other way, Leif--and if you had escaped the wolves of Lur--you would have come to Sirk. And a great change might have grown from that, for Sirk would have welcomed you, and who knows what might have followed, with you as their leader. Nor would my Little People then..."

She stopped there, nor would she complete the sentence, for all my urging. So I told her there were too many ifs about the matter, and I was content that the dice had fallen as they had. It pleased her.

I had one experience not shared by Jim. Its significance I did not then recognize. The Little People were as I have said--worshippers of life. That was their whole creed and faith. Here and there about the plain were small cairns, altars in fact, upon which, cut from wood or stone or fossil ivory, were the ancient symbols of fertility; sometimes singly, sometimes in pairs, and sometimes in a form curiously like that same symbol of the old Egyptians--the looped cross, the crux ansata which Osiris, God of the Resurrection, carried in his hand and touched, in the Hall of the Dead, those souls which had passed all tests and had earned immortality.

It happened on the third day. Evalie bade me go with her, and alone. We walked along the well-kept path that ran along the base of the cliffs in which the pygmies had their lairs. The tiny golden-eyed women peeped out at us and trilled to their dolls of children as we passed. Groups of elders, both men and women, came dancing toward us and fell in behind us as we went on. Each and all carried drums of a type I had not yet seen. They did not beat them, nor did they talk; group by group they dropped in behind us, silently.

After awhile I noticed that there were no more lairs. At the end of half an hour we turned a bastion of the dins. We were at the edge of a small meadow carpeted with moss, fine and soft as the pile of a silken carpet. The meadow was perhaps five hundred feet wide and about as many feet deep. Opposite me was another bastion. It was as though a rounded chisel had been thrust down, cutting out a semicircle in the precipice. At the far end of the meadow was what, at first glance, I thought a huge domed building, and then saw was an excrescence from the cliff itself.

In this rounded rock was an oval entrance, not much larger than an average door. As I stood, wondering, Evalie took my hand and led me toward it. We went through it.

The domed rock was hollow.

It was a temple of the Little People--I knew that, of course, as soon as I had crossed the threshold. Its walls of some cool, green stone curved smoothly up. It was not dark within the temple. The rocky dome had been pierced as though by the needle of a lace-maker, and through hundreds of the frets light streamed. The walls caught it, and dispersed it from thousands of crystalline angles within the stone. The floor was carpeted with the thick, soft moss, and this was faintly luminous, adding to the strange pellucid light; it must have covered at least two acres.

Evalie drew me forward. In the exact centre of the floor was a depression, like an immense bowl. Between it and me stood one of the looped-cross symbols, thrice the height of a tall man. It was polished, and glimmered as though cut from some enormous amethystine crystal. I glanced behind me. The pygmies who had followed us were pouring through the oval doorway.

They crowded close behind us as Evalie again took my hand and led me toward the cross. She pointed, and I peered down into the bowl.

I looked upon the Kraken!

There it lay, sprawled out within the bowl, black tentacles spread fanwise from its bloated body, its huge black eyes staring inscrutably up into mine!

Resurgence of the old horror swept me. I jumped back with an oath.

The pygmies were crowding around my knees, staring up at me intently. I knew that my horror was written plain upon my face. They began an excited trilling, nodding to one another, gesticulating. Evalie watched them gravely, and then I saw her own face lighten as though with relief.

She smiled at me, and pointed again to the bowl. I forced myself to look. And now I saw that the shape within it had been cunningly carved. The dreadful, inscrutable eyes were of jet-like jewel. Through the end of each of the fifty-foot-long tentacles had been driven one of the crux ansatas, pinioning it like a spike; and through the monstrous body had been driven a larger one. I read the meaning: life fettering the enemy of life; rendering it impotent; prisoning it with the secret, ancient and holy symbol of that very thing it was bent upon destroying. And the great looped-cross above--watching and guarding like the god of life.

I heard a rippling and rustling and rushing from the drums. On and on it went in quickly increasing tempo. There was triumph in it-- the triumph of onrushing conquering waves, the triumph of the free rushing wind; and there was peace and surety of peace in it--like the rippling song of little waterfalls chanting their faith that "they will go on and on for ever," the rippling of little waves among the sedges of the river-bank, and the rustling of the rain bringing life to all the green things of earth.

Round the amethystine cross Evalie began to dance, circling it slowly to the rippling, the rustling and the rushing music of the drums. And she was the spirit of that song they sang, and the spirit of all those things of which they sang.

Three times she circled it. She came dancing to me, took my hand once more and led me away, out through the portal. From behind us, as we passed through, there came a sustained rolling of the little drums, no longer rippling, rustling, rushing--defiant now, triumphal.

But of that ceremony, or of its reasons, or of the temple itself she would speak no word thereafter, question her as I might.

And we still had to stand upon Nansur Bridge and look on towered Karak.

"On the morrow," she would say; and when the morrow came, again she would say--"on the morrow." When she answered me, she would drop long lashes over the clear brown eyes and glance at me from beneath them, strangely; or touch my hair and say that there were

76

many morrows and what did it matter on which of them we went, since Nansur would not run away. There was some reluctance I could not fathom. And day by day her sweetness and her beauty wound a web around my heart until I began to wonder whether it might become a shield against the touch of what I carried on my breast.

But the Little People still had their doubts about me, temple ceremony or none; that was plain enough. Jim, they had taken to their hearts; they twittered and trilled and laughed with him as though he were one of them. They were polite and friendly enough to me, but they watched me. Jim could take up the tiny doll-like children and play with them. The mothers didn't like me to do that and showed it very clearly. I received direct confirmation of how they felt about me that morning.

"I'm going to leave you for two or three days, Leif," he told me when we had finished breakfasting. Evalie had floated away on some call from her small folk.

"Going to leave me!" I gaped at him in astonishment. "What do you mean? Where are you going?"

He laughed.

"Going to look at the tlanusi--what Evalie calls the dalanusa--the big leeches. The river guards she told us the pygmies put on the job when the bridge was broken."

She had not spoken about them again, and I had forgotten all about them.

"What are they, Indian?"

"That's what I'm going to find out. They sound like the great leech of Tianusi'yi. The tribes said it was red with white stripes and as big as a house. The Little People don't go that far. They only say they're as big as you are."

"Listen, Indian--I'm going along."

"Oh, no, you're not."

"I'd like to know why not."

"Because the Little People won't let you. Now listen to me, old-timer--the plain fact is that they're not entirely satisfied about you. They're polite, and they wouldn't hurt Evalie's feelings for the world, but--they'd much rather be without you."

"You're telling me nothing new," I said.

"No, but here is something new. A party that's been on a hunting trip down the other end of the valley came in yesterday. One of them remembered his grandfather had told him that when the Ayjir came riding into this place they all had yellow hair like yours. Not the red they have now. It's upset them."

"I thought they'd been watching me pretty damned close the last twenty-four hours," I said. "So that's the reason, is it?"

"That's the reason, Leif. It's upset them. It's also the reason for this expedition to the tianusi. They're going to increase the river guard. It involves some sort of ceremony, I gather. They want me to go along. I think it better that I do."

"Does Evalie know all this?"

"Sure she does. And she wouldn't let you go, even if the pygmies would."

Jim left with a party of about a hundred of the pygmies about noon. I bade him a cheerful good-bye. If it puzzled Evalie that I took his departure so calmly, and asked her no questions she did not show it. But she was very quiet that day, speaking mostly in monosyllables abstractedly. Once or twice I caught her looking at me with a curious wonder in her eyes. And once I had taken her hand, and she had quivered and leaned toward me, and then snatched it away, half-angrily. And once when she had forgotten her moodiness and had rested against my shoulder, I had fought hard against taking her in my arms.

The worst of it was that I could find no cogent argument why I shouldn't take her. A voice within my mind was whispering that if I so desired, why should I not? And there were other things besides that whisper which sapped my resistance. It had been a queer day even for this queer place. The air was heavy, as though a storm brooded. The heady fragrances from the far forest were stronger, clinging amorously, confusing. The vaporous veils that hid the distances had thickened; at the north they were almost smoke colour, and they marched slowly but steadily nearer.

We sat, Evalie and I, beside her tent. She broke a long silence.

"You are sorrowful, Leif--and why?"

"Not sorrowful, Evalie--just wondering."

"I, too, am wondering. Is it what you wonder?"

"How do I know--who know nothing of your mind?"

She stood up, abruptly.

"You like to watch the smiths. Let us go to them."

I looked at her, struck by the anger in her voice. She frowned down upon me, brows drawn to a straight line over bright, half-contemptuous eyes.

"Why are you angry, Evalie? What have I done?"

78

"I am not angry. And you have done nothing." She stamped her foot. "I say you have done--nothing! Let us watch the smiths."

She walked away. I sprang up, and followed her. What was the matter with her? I had done something to irritate her, that was certain. But what? Well, I'd know, sooner or later. And I did like to watch the smiths. They stood beside their small anvils beating out the sickled knives, the spear and arrowheads, shaping the earrings and bracelets of gold for their tiny women.

Tink-a-tink, tink-a-clink, cling-clang, clink-a-tink went their little hammers.

They stood beside their anvils like gnomes, except that there was no deformity about them. Miniature men they were, perfectly shaped, gleaming golden in the darkening light, long hair coiled about their heads, yellow eyes intent upon their forgings. I forgot Evalie and her wrath, watching them as ever, fascinated.

Tink-a-tink! Cling-clang! Clink--

The little hammers hung suspended in air; the little smiths stood frozen. Speeding from the north came the horn of a great gong, a brazen stroke that seemed to break overhead. It was followed by another and another and another. A wind wailed over the plain; the air grew darker, the vaporous smoky veils quivered and marched closer.

The clangour of the gongs gave way to a strong chanting, the singing of many people; the chanting advanced and retreated, rose and waned as the wind rose and fell, rose and fell in rhythmic pulse. From all the walls the drums of the guards roared warning.

The little smiths dropped their hammers and raced to the lairs. Over all the plain there was turmoil, movement of the golden pygmies racing to the cliffs and to the circling slope to swell the garrisons there.

Through the strong chanting came the beat of other drums. I knew them--the throb of the Uighur kettle-drums, the war drums. And I knew the chant--it was the war song, the battle song of the Uighurs. Not the Uighurs, no--not the patched and paltry people I had led from the oasis! War song of the ancient race! The great race--the Ayjir!

The old race! My people! I knew the song--well did I know it! Often and often had I heard it in the olden days...when I had gone forth to battle...By Zarda of the Thirsty Spears...by Zarda God of Warriors, but it was like drink to a parched throat to hear it again!

My blood drummed in my ears...I opened my throat to roar that song... "Leif! Leif! What is the matter?" Evalie's hands were on my shoulders, shaking me! I glared at her, uncomprehending for a moment. I felt a strange, angry bafflement. Who was this dark girl that

79

checked me on my way to war? And abruptly the obsession left me. It left me trembling, shaken at though by some brief wild tempest of the mind. I put my own hands upon those on my shoulders, drew reality from the touch. I saw that there was amazement in Evalie's eyes, and something of fear. And around us was a ring of the Little People, staring up at me. I shook my head, gasping for breath, "Leif! What is the matter?" Before I could answer, chanting and drums were drowned in a bellow of thunder. Peal upon peal of thunder roared and echoed over the plain, beating back, beating down the sounds from the north-- roaring over them, rolling over them, sweeping them back.

I stared stupidly around me. All along the cliffs were the golden pygmies, scores of them, beating upon great drums high as their waists. From those drums came the pealing of thunder, claps and shattering strokes of the bolt's swift fall, and the shouting reverberations that follow it.

The Thunder Drums of the Little People!

On and on roared the drums, yet through their rolling diapason beat ever the battle chant and those other drums...like thrusts of lances... like trampling of horses and of marching men...by Zarda, but the old race still was strong...

A ring of the Little People was dancing around me. Another ring joined them. Beyond them I saw Evalie, watching me with wide, astonished eyes. And around her was another ring of the golden pygmies, arrows at readiness, sickled knives in hand.

Why was she watching me...why were the arms of the Little People turned against me...and why were they dancing? That was a strange dance...it made you sleepy to look at it...what was this lethargy creeping over me...God, but I was sleepy! So sleepy that my dull ears could hardly hear the Thunder Drums...so sleepy I could hear nothing else...so sleepy...I knew, dimly, that I had dropped to my knees, then had fallen prone upon the soft turf...then slept.

I awakened, every sense alert. The drums were throbbing all around me. Not the Thunder Drums, but drums that sang, drums that throbbed and sang to some strange lilting rhythm that set the blood racing through me in tune and in time with its joyousness. The throbbing, singing notes were like tiny, warm, vital blows that whipped my blood into ecstasy of life.

I leaped to my feet. I stood upon a high knoll, round as a woman's breast. Over all the plain were lights, small fires burning, ringing the little altars of the pygmies. And around the fires the Little People were dancing to the throbbing drums. Around the fires and the altars they danced and leaped like little golden flames of life made animate.

Circling the knoll on which I stood was a triple ring of the dwarfs, women and men, weaving, twining, swaying.

They and the burden of the drums were one.

A soft and scented wind was blowing over the knoll. It hummed as it streamed by--and its humming was akin to dance and drum.

In and out, and round about and out and in and back again, the golden pygmies danced around the knoll. And round and round and back again they circled the fire-ringed altars.

I heard a sweet low voice singing--singing to the cadence, singing the song of the drums, singing the dancing of the Little People.

Close by was another knoll like that on which I was--like a pair of woman's high breasts they stood above the plain. It, too, was circled by the dancing dwarfs.

On it sang and danced Evalie.

Her singing was the soul of drum song and dance--her dancing was the sublimation of both. She danced upon the knoll--cobweb veils and girdle gone, clothed only in the silken, rippling cloak of her blue-black hair.

She beckoned, and she called to me--a high-pitched, sweet call.

The fragrant, rushing wind pushed me toward her as I ran down the mound.

The dancing pygmies parted to let me through. The throbbing of the drums grew swifter; their song swept into a higher octave.

Evalie came dancing down to meet me...she was beside me, her arms round my neck, her lips pressed to mine...The drums beat faster. My pulses matched them.

The two rings of little yellow living flames of life joined. They became one swirling circle that drove us forward. Round and round and round us they swirled, driving us on and on to the pulse of the drums. I ceased to think--drum-throb, drum-song, dance-song were all of me.

Yet still I knew that the fragrant wind thrust us on and on, caressing, murmuring, laughing.

We were beside an oval doorway. The silken, scented tresses of Evalie streamed in the wind and kissed me. Beyond and behind us sang the drums. And ever the wind pressed us on...

Drums and wind drove us through the portal of the domed rock.

They drove us into the temple of the Little People...

The soft moss glimmered...the amethystine cross gleamed...

Evalie's arms were around my neck . I held her close...the touch of her lips to mine was like the sweet, secret fire of life...

It was silent in the temple of the Little People. Their drums were silent. The glow of the looped cross above the pit of the Kraken was dim.

Evalie stirred, and cried out in her sleep. I touched her lips and she awoke.

"What is the matter, Evalie?"

"Leif, beloved--I dreamed a white falcon tried to dip its beak into my heart!"

"It was but a dream, Evalie."

She shuddered; she raised her head and bent over me so that her hair covered our faces.

"You drove the falcon away--but then a white wolf came...and leaped upon me."

"It was only a dream, Evalie--bright flame of my heart."

She bent closer to me under the tent of her hair, lips close to mine.

"You drove the wolf away. And I would have kissed you...but a face came between ours..."

"A face, Evalie?"

She whispered:

"The face of Lur! She laughed at me...and then you were gone... with her...and I was alone..."

"It was a lying dream, that! Sleep, beloved."

She sighed. There was a long silence; then drowsily:

"What is it you carry round your neck, Leif? Something from some woman that you treasure?"

"Nothing of woman, Evalie. That is truth."

She kissed me--and slept.

Fool that I was not to have told her then, under the shadow of the ancient symbol...Fool that I was--I did not!

XII. ON NANSUR BRIDGE

When we went out of the temple into the morning there were half a hundred of the elders, men and women, patiently awaiting our appearance. I thought they were the same who had followed into the domed rock when I had first entered it.

The little women clustered around Evalie. They had brought wraps and swathed her from head to feet. She walked off among them with never a glance nor a word for me. There was something quite ceremonial about it all; she looked for all the world like a bride being led away by somewhat mature elfin bridesmaids.

The little men clustered around me. Sri was there. I was glad of that, for, whatever the doubts of the others about me, I knew he had none. They bade me go with them, and I obeyed without question.

It was raining, and it was both jungle-wet and jungle-warm. The wind was blowing in the regular, rhythmic gusts of the night before. The rain seemed less to fall than to condense in great drops from the air about, except when the wind blew and then the rain drove by in almost level lines. The air was like fragrant wine. I felt like singing and dancing. There was thunder all around--not the drums, but real thunder.

I had been wearing only my shirt and my trousers. I had discarded my knee-high boots for sandals. It was only a minute or two before I was soaking wet. We came to a steaming pool. and there we halted. Sri told me to strip and plunge in.

The pool was hot and invigorating and as I splashed around in it I kept feeling better and better. I reflected that whatever had been in the minds of the Little People when they had driven Evalie and me into the temple, their fear of me had been exorcised--for the time at any rate. But I thought I knew what had been in their minds. They suspected that Khalk'ru had some hold on me, as over the people I resembled. Not much of a hold maybe--but still it was not to be ignored. Very well--the remedy, since they couldn't kill me without breaking Evalie's heart, was to spike me down as they had the Kraken which was Khalk'ru's symbol. So they had spiked me down with Evalie.

I climbed out of the pool, more thoughtful than I had gone into it. They wrapped a loin cloth around me, in curious folds and knots. Then they trilled and twittered and laughed, and danced.

Sri had my clothes and belt. I didn't want to lose them, so when we started off I kept close behind him. Soon we stopped--in front of Evalie's lair.

After a while there was a great commotion, singing and beating of drums, and along came Evalie with a crowd of the little women dancing around her. They led her to where I was waiting. Then all of them danced away.

That was all there was to it. The ceremony, if ceremony it was, was finished. But, somehow, I felt very much married.

I looked down at Evalie. She looked up at me, demurely. Her hair was no longer free, but braided cunningly around head and ears and neck. The swathings were gone. She wore the little apron of the pygmy matrons and the silvery cobweb veils. She laughed, and took my hand, and we went into the lair.

Next day, late in the afternoon, we heard a fanfare of trumpets that sounded rather close. They blew long and loudly, as though summoning someone. We stepped out into the rain, to listen better. I noted that the wind had changed from north to west, and was blowing steadily and strongly. By this time I knew that the acoustics of the land under the mirage were peculiar and that there was no way of telling just how close the trumpets were. They were on the far side of the river bank of course, but how far away the pygmies' guarded slope was from the river, I did not know. There was some bustling on the wall, but no excitement.

There came a final trumpet blast, raucous and derisive. It was followed by a roar of laughter more irritatingly mocking because of its human quality. It brought me out of my indifference with a jump. It made me see red.

"That," said Evalie, "was Tibur. I suppose he has been hunting with Lur. I think he was laughing at--you, Leif."

Her delicate nose was turned up disdainfully, but there was a smile at the corner of her lips as she watched my quick anger flare up.

"See here, Evalie, just who is this Tibur?"

"I told you. He is Tibur the Smith, and he rules the Ayjir with Lur. Always does he come when I stand on Nansur. We have talked together--often. He is very strong--oh, strong."

"Yes?" I said, still more irritated. "And why does Tibur come when you are there?"

"Why, because he desires me, of course," she said tranquilly.

My dislike for Tilbur the Laugher increased.

"He'll not laugh if I ever get an opening at him," I muttered.

"What did you say?" she asked. I translated, as best t could. She nodded and began to speak--and then I saw her eyes open wide and stark terror fill them. I heard a whirring over my head.

Out of the mists had flown a great bird. It hovered fifty feet over us, glaring down with baleful yellow eyes. A great bird--a white bird...

The white falcon of the Witch-woman!

I thrust Evalie back into the lair, and watched it. Thrice it circled over me, and then, screaming, hurtled up into the mists and vanished.

I went in to Evalie. She was crouched on the couch of skins. She had undone her hair and it streamed over her head and shoulders, hiding her like a cloak. I bent over her, and parted it. She was crying. She put her arms around my neck, and held me close, close. I felt her heart beating like a drum against mine.

"Evalie, beloved--there's nothing to be afraid of."

"The--white falcon, Leif!"

"It is only a bird."

"No--Lur sent it."

"Nonsense, dark sweetheart. A bird flies where it wills. It was hunting--or it had lost its way in the mists."

She shook her head.

"But, Leif, I--dreamed of a white falcon..."

I held her tight, and after a while she pushed me away and smiled at me. But there was little of gaiety the remainder of that day. And that night her dreams were troubled, and she held me close to her, and cried and murmured in her sleep.

The next day Jim came back. I had been feeling a bit uncomfortable about his return. What would he think of me? I needn't have worried. He showed no surprise at all when I laid the cards before him. And then I realized that of course the pygmies must have been talking to one another by their drums, and that they would have gone over matters with him.

"Good enough," said Jim, when I had finished. "If you don't get out, it's the best thing for both of you. If you do get out, you'll take Evalie with you--or won't you?"

That stung me.

"Listen, Indian--I don't like the way you're talking! I love her."

"All right. I'll put it another way. Does Dwayanu love her?"

That question was like a slap on my mouth. While I struggled for an answer, Evalie ran out. She went over to Jim and kissed him. He patted her shoulder and hugged her like a big brother. She glanced at me, and came to me, and drew my head down to her and kissed me too, but not exactly the way she had kissed him.

I glanced over her head at Jim. Suddenly I noticed that he looked tired and haggard.

"You're, feeling all right, Jim?"

"Sure. Only a bit weary. I've--seen things."

"What do you mean?"

"Well," he hesitated, "well--the tlanusi--the big leeches--for one thing. I'd never have believed it if I hadn't seen them, and if I had seen them before we dived into the river, I'd have picked the wolves as cooing doves in comparison."

He told me they had camped at the far end of the plain that night.

"This place is bigger than we thought, Leif. It must be, because I've gone more miles than would be possible if it were only as large as it looked before we went through the mirage. Probably the mirage foreshortened it--confused us."

The next day they had gone through forest and jungle and canebrake and marsh. They had come at last to a steaming swamp. A raised path ran across it. They had taken that path, and eventually came to another transecting it. Where the two causeways met, there was a wide, circular and gently rounded mound rising from the swamp. Here the pygmies had halted. They had made fires of fagots and leaves. The fires sent up a dense and scented smoke which spread slowly out from the mound over the swamp. When the fires were going well, the pygmies began drumming--a queerly syncopated beat. In a few moments he had seen a movement in the swamp, close by the mound.

"There was a ring of pygmies between me and the edge," he said, "and when I saw the thing that crawled out I was glad of it. First there was an upheaval of the mud, and then up came the back of what I thought was an enormous red slug. The slug raised itself, and crept out on land. It was a leech all right, and that was all it was--but it made me more than a bit sick. It was its size that did that. It must have been seven feet long, and it lay there, blind and palpitating, its mouth gaping, listening to the drums and luxuriating in that scented smoke. Then another and another came out. After a while there were a hundred of the things grouped around in a semi-circle, eyeless heads all turned to us--sucking in the smoke, palpitating to the drums.

"Some of the pygmies got up, took burning sticks from the fire and started off on the intersecting causeway, drumming as they went. The others quenched the fires. The leeches writhed along after the torch-bearers. The other pygmies fell in behind, herding them. I stuck in the rear. We went along until we came to the bank of the river. Those in the lead stopped drumming. They threw their smoking, blazing sticks into the water, and they cast into it handfuls of crushed berries--not the ones Sri and Sra rubbed on us. Red berries. The big leeches went writhing over the bank and into the river, following, I suppose, the smoke and the scent of the berries. Anyway, they went in--each and all of them.

"We went back, and out of the marsh. We camped on its edge. All that night they talked with the drums.

"They had talked the night before, and were uneasy; but I took it that it was the same worry they had when we started. They must have known what was going on, but they didn't tell me then. Yesterday morning, though, they were happy and care-free. I knew something must have happened--that they must have got good news in the night. They were so good-natured that they told me why they were. Not just as you have--but the sense was the same--"

He chuckled.

"That morning we herded up a couple of hundred more of the tianusi and put them where the Little People think they'll do the most good. Then we started back--and here I am."

"Yes," I asked suspiciously. "And is that all?"

"All for to-night, anyway," he said "I'm sleepy. I'm going to turn in. You go with Evalie and leave me strictly alone till to-morrow."

I left him to sleep, determined to find out in the morning what he was holding back; I didn't think it was entirely the journey and the leeches that accounted for his haggardness.

But in the morning I forgot all about it.

In the first place, when I awoke, Evalie was missing. I went over to the tent, looking for Jim. He was not there. The Little People had long since poured out of the cliffs, and were at work; they always worked in the morning--afternoons and nights they played and drummed and danced. They said Evalie and Tsantawu had gone into council with the elders. I went back to the tent.

In a little while Evalie and Jim came up. Evalie's face was white and her eyes were haunted. Also they were misty with tears. Also, she was madder than hell. Jim was doing his best to be cheerful.

"What's the matter?" I asked.

"You're due for a little trip," said Jim. "You've been wanting to see Nansur Bridge, haven't you?"

"Yes." I said.

"Well," said Jim. "That's where we're going. Better put on your travelling clothes and your boots. If the trail is anything like what I've just gone over, you'll need them. The Little People can slip through things--but we're built different."

I studied them, puzzled. Of course I'd wanted to see Nansur Bridge--but why should the fact we were to go there make them behave so oddly? I went to Evalie, and turned her face up to mine.

"You've been crying, Evalie. What's wrong?"

She shook her head, slipped out of my arms and into the lair. I followed her. She was bending over a coffer, taking yards and yards of veils out of it. I swung her away from it and lifted her until her eyes were level with mine.

"What's wrong, Evalie?"

A thought struck me. I lowered her to her feet.

"Who suggested going to Nansur Bridge?"

"The Little People...the elders...I fought against it...I don't want you to go...they say you must..."

"I must go?" The thought grew clearer. "Then you need not go-- nor Tsantawu. Unless you choose?"

"Let them try to keep me from going with you." She stamped a foot furiously.

The thought was crystal clear, and I began to feel a bit irritated by the Little People. They were thorough to the point of annoyance. I now understood perfectly why I was to go to Nansur Bridge. The pygmies were not certain that their magic--including Evalie--had thoroughly taken. Therefore I was to look upon the home of the enemy-- and be watched for my reactions. Well, that was fair enough, at that. Maybe the Witch-woman would be there. Maybe Tibur--Tibur who desired Evalie--Tibur who had laughed at me. Suddenly I was keen for going to Nansur Bridge. I began to put on my old clothes. As I was tying the high shoes, I glanced over at Evalie. She had coiled her hair and covered it with a cap; she had swathed her body from neck to knees in the veils and she was lacing high sandals that covered her feet and legs as completely as my boots did mine. She smiled faintly at my look of wonder.

"I do not like Tibur to look on me--not now!" she said.

I bent over her and took her in my arms. She set her lips to mine in a kiss that bruised them...When we came out, Jim and about fifty of the pygmies were waiting.

We struck diagonally across the plain away from the cliffs, heading north toward the river. We went over the slope, past one of the towers, and put feet on a narrow path like that which we had trod when coming into the land of the Little People. It wound through a precisely similar fern-brake. We went along it single file, and, perforce, in silence. We came out of it into a forest of close-growing, coniferous trees, through which the trail wound tortuously. We went through this for an hour or more, without once resting, the pygmies trotting along tirelessly. I looked at my watch. We had been going for four hours and had covered, I calculated, about twelve miles. There was no sign of bird or animal life.

Evalie seemed deep in thought and Jim had fallen into one of his fits of Indian taciturnity. I didn't feel much like talking. It was a silent journey; not even the golden pygmies chattered, as was their habit. We came to a sparkling spring, and drank. One of the dwarfs swung a small cylindrical drum in front of him and began to tap out some message. It was answered at length from far ahead by other tappings.

We swung into our way once more. The conifers began to thin. At our left and far below us I began to catch glimpses of the white river and of the dense forest on its opposite bank. The conifers ceased and we came out upon a rocky waste. Just ahead of us was an outthrust of cliff along whose base streamed the white river. The outthrust cut off our view of what lay beyond. Here the pygmies halted and sent another drum message. The answer was startlingly close. Then around the edge of the cliff, half-way up, spear tips glinted. A group of little warriors stood there, scrutinizing us. They signalled, and we marched forward, over the waste.

There was a broad road up the side of the cliff, wide enough for six horses abreast. We climbed it. We came to the top, and I looked on Nansur Bridge and towered Karak.

Once, thousands or hundreds of thousands of years ago, there had been a small mountain here, rising from the valley floor. Nanbu, the white river, had eaten it away--all except a vein of black adamantine rock.

89

Nanbu had fallen, fallen, steadily gnawing at the softer stone until at last it was spanned by a bridge that was like a rainbow of jet. That gigantic bow of black rock winged over the abyss with the curved flight of an arrow.

Its base, on each side, was a mesa--sculptured as Nansur had been from the original mount.

The mesa, at whose threshold I stood, was flat-topped. But on the opposite side of the river, thrusting up from the mesa-top, was a huge, quadrangular pile of the same black rock as the bow of Nansur. It looked less built from than cut out of that rock. It covered I judged about half a square mile. Towers and turrets both square and round sprang up from it. It was walled.

There was something about that immense ebon citadel that struck me with the same sense of fore-knowledge that I had felt when I had ridden into the ruins of the Gobi oasis. Also I thought it looked like that city of Dis which Dante glimpsed in Hades. And its antiquity hung over it like a sable garment.

Then I saw that Nansur was broken. Between the arch that winged from the side on which we stood and the arch that swept up and out from the side of the black citadel, there was a gap. It was as though a gigantic hammer had been swung down on the soaring bow, shattering it at its centre. I thought of Bifrost Bridge over which the Valkyries rode, bearing the souls of the warriors to Valhalla; and I thought it had been as great a blasphemy to have broken Nansur Bridge as it would have been to have broken Bifrost.

Around the citadel were other buildings, hundreds of them outside its walls--buildings of grey and brown stone, with gardens; they stretched over acres. And on each side of this city were fertile fields and flowering groves. There was a wide road stretching far, far away to cliffs shrouded in the green veils. I thought I saw the black mouth of a cavern at its end.

"Karak!" whispered Evalie. "And Nansur Bridge! And Oh, Leif, beloved...but my heart is heavy...so heavy!"

I hardly heard her, looking at Karak. Stealthy memories had begun to stir. I trod on them, and put my arm around Evalie. We went on, and now I saw why Karak had been built where it was, for on the far side the black citadel commanded both ends of the valley, and when Nansur had been unbroken, it had commanded this approach as well.

Suddenly I felt a feverish eagerness to run out upon Nansur and look down on Karak from the broken end. I was restive at the slowness of the pygmies. I started forward. The garrison came crowding around me, staring up at me, whispering to one another, studying me with their yellow eyes. Drums began to beat.

They were answered by trumpets from the citadel.

I walked ever more rapidly toward Nansur. The fever of eagerness had become consuming. I wanted to run. I pushed the golden pygmies aside impatiently. Jim's voice came to me, warningly:

"Steady, Leif--steady!"

I paid no heed. I went out upon Nansur. Vaguely, I realized that it was wide and that low parapets guarded its edges, and that the stone was ramped for the tread of horses and the tread of marching men. And that if the white river had shaped it, the hands of men had finished its carving.

I reached the broken end. A hundred feet below me the white river raced smoothly. There were no serpents. A dull red body, slug-like, monstrous, lifted above the milky current; then another and another, round mouths gaping--the leeches of the Little People, on guard.

There was a broad plaza between the walls of the dark citadel and the end of the bridge. It was empty. Set in the walls were massive gates of bronze. I felt a curious quivering inside me, a choking in my throat. I forgot Evalie; I forgot Jim; I forgot everything in watching those gates.

There was a louder blaring of the trumpets, a clanging of bars, and the gates swung open. Through them galloped a company, led by two riders, one on a great black horse, the other upon a white. They raced across the plaza, dropped from their mounts and came walking over the bridge. They stood facing me across the fifty-foot gap.

The one who had ridden the black horse was the Witch-woman, and the other I knew for Tibur the Smith--Tibur the Laugher. I had no eyes just then for the Witch-woman or her followers. I had eyes only for Tibur.

He was a head shorter than I, but strength great or greater than mine spoke from the immense shoulders, the thick body. His red hair hung sleekly straight to his shoulders. He was red-bearded. His eyes were violet-blue and lines of laughter crinkled at their corners; and the wide, loose mouth was a laughing mouth. But the laughter which had graven those lines on Tibur's face was not the kind to make the bearer merry.

He wore a coat of mail. At his left side hung a huge war hammer. He looked me over from head to foot and back again with narrowed, mocking eyes. If I had hated Tibur before I had seen him, it was nothing to what I felt now.

I looked from him to the Witch-woman. Her cornflower-blue eyes were drinking me in; absorbed, wondering--amused. She, too, wore a coat of mail, over which streamed her red braids. Those who were clustered behind Tibur and the Witch-woman were only a blur to me.

Tibur leaned forward.

"Welcome--Dwayanu!" he jeered. "What has brought you out of your skulking place? My challenge?"

"Was it you I heard baying yesterday?" I said. "Hai--you picked a safe distance ere you began to howl, red dog!"

There was a laugh from the group around the Witch-woman, and I saw that they were women, fair and red-haired like herself, and that there were two tall men with Tibur. But the Witch-woman said nothing, still drinking me in, a curious speculation in her eyes.

Tibur's face grew dark. One of the men leaned, and whispered to him. Tibur nodded, and swaggered forward. He called out to me:

"Have you grown soft during your wanderings, Dwayanu? By the ancient custom, by the ancient test, we must learn that before we acknowledge you--great Dwayanu. Stand fast--"

His hand dropped to the battle-hammer at his side. He hurled it at me.

The hammer was hurtling through the air at me with the speed of a bullet--yet it seemed to come slowly. I could even see the thong that held it to Tibur's arm slowly lengthening as it flew...

Little doors were opening in my brain...the ancient test... Hai! but I knew that play...I waited motionless as the ancient custom prescribed...but they should have given me a shield...no matter...how slowly the great sledge seemed to come...and it seemed to me that the hand I thrust out to catch it moved as slowly...

I caught it. Its weight was all of twenty pounds, yet I caught it squarely, effortlessly, by its metal shaft. Hai! but did I not know the trick of that?...The little doors were opening faster now...and I knew another. With my other hand I gripped the thong that held the battle-hammer to Tibur's arm and jerked him toward me.

The laugh was frozen on Tibur's face. He tottered on Nansur's broken edge. I heard behind me the piping shout of the pygmies...

The Witch-woman sliced down a knife and severed the thong. She jerked Tibur back from the verge. Rage swept me...that was not in the play...by the ancient test it was challenger and challenged alone...I swung the great hammer around my head and around, and hurled it back at Tibur; it whistled as it flew and the severed thong streamed rigid in its wake. He threw himself aside, but not quickly enough. The sledge struck him on a shoulder. A glancing blow, but it dropped him.

And now I laughed across the gulf.

The Witch-woman leaned forward, incredulity flooding the speculation in her eyes. She was no longer amused. No! And Tibur jerked himself up on one knee, glaring at me, his laughter lines twisted into nothing like mirth of any kind.

Still other doors, tiny doors, opening in my brain...They wouldn't believe I was Dwayanu...Hai! I would show them. I dipped into the pocket of my belt. Ripped open the buckskin pouch. Drew out the ring of Khalk'ru. I held it up. The green light glinted on it. The yellow stone seemed to expand. The black octopus to grow...

"Am I Dwayanu? Look on this! Am I Dwayanu?"

I heard a woman scream--I knew that voice. And I heard a man calling, shouting to me--and that voice I knew too. The little doors clicked shut, the memories that had slipped through them darted back before they closed...

Why, it was Evalie who was screaming! And Jim who was shouting at me! What was the matter with them? Evalie was facing me, arms outstretched. And there was stark unbelief and horror--and loathing--in the brown eyes fastened on me. And rank upon rank, the Little People were closing around the pair of them--barring me from them. Their spears and arrows were levelled at me. They were hissing like a horde of golden snakes, their faces distorted with hatred, their eyes fastened on the ring of Khalk'ru still held high above my head.

And now I saw that hatred reflected upon the face of Evalie--and the loathing deepen in her eyes.

"Evalie!" I cried, and would have leaped toward her...Back went the hands of the pygmies for the throwing cast; the arrows trembled in their bows.

"Don't move, Leif! I'm coming!" Jim jumped forward. Instantly the pygmies swarmed round and upon him. He swayed and went down under them.

"Evalie!" I cried again.

I saw the loathing fade, and heart-break come into her face. She called some command.

A score of pygmies shot by her, on each side, casting down their bows and spears as they raced toward me. Stupidly, I watched them come; among them I saw Sri.

They struck me like little living battering rams. I was thrust backward. My foot struck air--

MERRITT

The pygmies clinging to my legs, harrying me like terriers, I toppled over the edge of Nansur.

BOOK OF THE
WITCH-WOMAN

XIII. KARAK

I had sense enough to throw my hands up over my head, and so I went down feet first. The pygmies hanging to my legs helped that, too. When I struck the water I sank deep and deep. The old idea is that when a man drowns his whole past life runs through his mind in a few seconds, like a reversed cinema reel. I don't know about that, but I do know that in my progress into Nanbu's depths and up again I thought faster than ever before in my life.

In the first place I realized that Evalie had ordered me thrown off the bridge. That made me white-hot mad. Why hadn't she waited and given me a chance to explain the ring! Then I thought of how many chances I'd had to explain--and hadn't taken one of them. Also that the pygmies had been in no mood for waiting, and that Evalie had held back their spears and arrows and given me a run for my life, even though it might be a brief one. Then I thought of my utter folly in flashing the ring at that particular moment, and I couldn't blame the Little People for thinking me an emissary of Khalk'ru. And I saw again the heart-break in Evalie's eyes, and my rage vanished in a touch of heart-break of my own.

After that, quite academically, the idea came to me that Tibur's hammer-play explained old God Thor of the Norse and his hammer Mjolnir, the Smasher, which always returned to his hand after he had thrown it-- to make it more miraculous the skalds had left out that practical detail of the thong; here was still another link between the Uighur or Ayjir and the Aesir--I'd talk to

Jim about it. And then I knew I couldn't get back to Jim to talk to him about that or anything else because the pygmies would certainly be waiting for me, and would quite as certainly drive me back among the leeches, even if I managed to get as far as their side of Nanbu. At that thought, if a man entirely immersed in water can break into a cold sweat I did it. I would much rather pass out by way of the Little People's spears and darts or even Tibur's smasher than be drained dry by those sucking mouths.

Just then I broke through the surface of Nanbu, trod water for a moment, clearing my eyes, and saw the red-slug back of a leech gliding toward me not twenty feet away. I cast a despairing glance around me. The current was swift and had borne me several hundred yards below the bridge. Also it had carried me toward the Karak side, which seemed about five hundred feet away. I turned to face the leech. It came slowly, as though sure of me. I planned to dive under it and try to make for the shore...if--only there were no others...

I heard a chattering shout. Sri shot past me. He raised an arm and pointed at Karak. Clearly he was telling me to get there as quickly as I could. I had forgotten all about him, except for a momentary flash of wrath that he had joined my assailants. Now I saw what an injustice I had done him. He swam straight to the big leech and slapped it alongside its mouth. The creature bent toward him, actually it nuzzled him. I waited to see no more, but struck out as fast as my boots would let me for the river bank.

That was no pleasant swim, no! The place was thick with the gliding red backs. Without question it was only Sri that saved me from them. He came scuttering back, and he circled round and round me as I ploughed on; he drove the leeches away. I touched bottom, and scrambled over rocks to the safety of the bank. The golden pygmy sent one last call to me. What he said I could not hear. I stood there, gasping for breath, and saw him shooting across the white water like a yellow flying fish, a half-dozen of the red slug-backs gliding in his wake.

I looked up at Nansur Bridge. The Little People's end of it and the parapets were crowded with pygmies, watching me. The other side was empty. I looked around me. I was in the shadow of the walls of the black citadel. They arose, smooth, impregnable, for a hundred feet. Between me and them was a wide plaza, similar to that over which Tibur and the Witch-woman had ridden from the bronze gates. It was bordered with squat, one-storied houses of stone; there were many small flowering trees. Beyond the bordering houses were others, larger, more pretentious, set farther apart. Not so far away and covering part of the plaza was an everyday, open-air market.

From the bordering houses and from the market, scores of people were pouring down upon me. They came swiftly, but they came silently, not calling to one another, not signalling nor summoning-- intent upon me. I felt for my automatic and swore, remembering that I had not worn it for days. Something flashed on my hand...

The ring of Khalk'ru! I must have slipped it on my thumb when the pygmies had rushed me. Well, the ring had brought me here.

Surely its effect would not be less upon these people, than it had been upon those who had faced me from the far side of the broken bridge. At any rate, it was all I had. I turned it so that the stone was hidden in my hand.

They were close now, and mostly women and girls and girl children. They all wore much the same kind of garment, a smock that came down to their knees and which left the right breast bare. Without exception, they were red-haired and blue-eyed, their skins creamy-white and delicate rose, and they were tall and strong and beautifully formed. They might have been Viking maids and mothers come to welcome home some dragon-ship from its sea-faring. The children were little blue-eyed angels. I took note of the men; there were not many of them, a dozen perhaps. They, too, had the red polls and blue eyes. The older wore short beards, the younger were clean-shaven. They were not so tall by several inches as the run of the women. None, men nor women, came within half a head of my height. They bore no weapons.

They halted a few yards from me, looking at me in silence. Their eyes ran over me and stopped at my yellow hair, and rested there.

There was a bustle at the edge of the crowd. A dozen women pushed through and walked toward me. They wore short kirtles; there were short swords in their girdles and they carried javelins in their hands; unlike the others, their breasts were covered. They ringed me, javelins raised, so close that the tips almost touched me.

The leader's bright blue eyes were bold, more soldier's than woman's.

"The yellow-haired stranger! Luka has smiled on us this day!"

The woman beside her leaned and whispered, but I caught the words:

"Tibur would give us more for him than Lur."

The leader shook her head.

"Too dangerous. We'll enjoy Lur's reward longer."

She looked me over, quite frankly.

"It's a shame to waste him," she said.

"Lur won't," the other answered, cynically.

The leader gave me a prod of her javelin, and motioned toward the citadel wall.

"Onward, Yellow Hair," she said. "It's a pity you can't understand me. Or I'd tell you something for your own good--at a price, of course."

98

She smiled at me, and prodded me again. I felt like grinning back at her; she was so much like a hard-boiled sergeant I'd known in the War. I spoke, instead, sternly:

"Summon Lur to me with fitting escort, O! woman whose tongue rivals the drum stick."

She gaped at me, her javelin dropping from her hand. Quite evidently, although an alarm had been sounded for me, the fact that I could speak the Uighur had not been told.

"Summon Lur at once," I said. "Or, by Khalk'ru--"

I did not complete the sentence. I turned the ring and held up my hand.

There was a gasp of terror from the crowd. They went down on their knees, heads bent low. The soldier-woman's face whitened, and she and the others dropped before me. And then there was a grating of bars. An immense block opened in the wall of the citadel not far away.

Out of the opening, as though my words had summoned them, rode the Witch-woman with Tibur beside her, and at their heels the little troop who had watched me from Nansur Bridge.

They waited, staring at the kneeling crowd. Then Tibur spurred his horse; the Witch-woman thrust out a hand and stayed him, and they spoke together. The soldier touched my foot.

"Let us rise,. Lord," she said. I nodded, and she jumped up with a word to her women. Again they ringed me. I read the fear in the leader's eyes, and appeal. I smiled at her.

"Don't fear. I heard nothing," I whispered.

"Then you have a friend in Dara," she muttered. "By Luka--they would boil us for what we said!"

"I heard nothing," I repeated.

"A gift for a gift," she breathed. "Watch Tibur's left hand should you fight him."

The little troop was in motion; they came riding slowly toward me. As they drew near I could see that Tibur's face was dark, and that he was holding in his temper with an effort. He halted his horse at the edge of the crowd. His rage fell upon them; for a moment I thought he was going to ride them down.

"Up, you swine!" he roared. "Since when has Karak knelt to any but its rulers?"

They arose, huddled together with frightened faces as the troop rode through them. I looked up at the Witch-woman and the Laugher.

Tibur glowered down on me, his hand fumbling at his hammer; the two big men who had flanked him on the bridge edged close to me, long swords in hand. The Witch-woman said nothing, studying me intently yet with a certain cynical impersonality I found disquieting; evidently she still had not made up her mind about me and was waiting for some word or move of mine to guide her. I didn't like the situation very much. If it came to a dog fight I would have little chance with three mounted men, to say nothing of the women. I had the feeling that the Witch-woman did not want me killed out-of-hand, but then she might be a bit late in succouring me--and beyond that I had no slightest wish to be beaten up, trussed up, carried into Karak a prisoner.

Also I began to feel a hot and unreasoning resentment against these people who dared bar my way, dared hold me back from whatever way I chose to go, an awakening arrogance--a stirring of those mysterious memories that had cursed me ever since I had carried the ring of Khalk'ru...

Well, those memories had served me on Nansur Bridge when Tibur cast the hammer at me...and what was it Jim had said?...to let Dwayanu ride when I faced the Witch-woman...well, let him...it was the only way...the bold way...the olden way...It was as though I heard the words! I threw my mind wide open to the memories, or to--Dwayanu.

There was a tiny tingling shock in my brain, and then something like the surging up of a wave toward that consciousness which was Leif Langton. I managed to thrust it back before it had entirely submerged that consciousness. It retreated, but sullenly--nor did it retreat far. No matter, so long as it did not roll over me...I pushed the soldiers aside and walked to Tibur. Something of what had occurred must have stamped itself on my face, changed me. Doubt crept into the Witch-woman's eyes. Tibur's hand fell from his hammer, and he backed his horse away. I spoke, and my wrathful voice fell strangely on my own ears.

"Where is my horse? Where are my arms? Where are my standard and my spearsmen? Why are the drums and the trumpets silent? Is it thus Dwayanu is greeted when he comes to a city of the Ayjir! By Zarda, but this is not to be home!"

Now the Witch-woman spoke, mockery in the clear, deep bell-toned voice, and I felt that whatever hold I had gained over her had in some way slipped.

"Hold your hand, Tibur! I will speak to--Dwayanu. And you--if you are Dwayanu--scarcely can hold us to blame. It has been long and long since human eyes rested on you--and never in this land. So how could we know you? And when first we saw you, the little yellow dogs ran you away from us. And when next we saw you, the little yellow dogs ran you to us. If we have not received you as Dwayanu has a right to expect from a city of the Ayjir, equally is it true that no city of the Ayjir has ever before been so visited by Dwayanu."

Well, that was true enough, admirable reasoning, lucid and all of that. The part of me that was Lief Langdon, and engaged in rather desperate struggle to retain control, recognized it. Yet the unreasoning anger grew. I held up the ring of Khalk'ru.

"You may not know Dwayanu--but you know this."

"I know you have it," she said, levelly. "But I do not know how you came by it. In itself it proves nothing."

Tibur leaned forward, grinning.

"Tell us where you did come from. Are you by-blow of Sirk?"

There was a murmur from the crowd. The Witch-woman leaned forward, frowning. I heard her murmur, half-contemptuously:

"Your strength was never in your head, Tibur!"

Nevertheless, I answered him.

"I come," I said bleakly, "from the Mother-land of the Ayjir. From the land that vomited your shivering forefathers, red toad!"

I shot a glance at the Witch-woman. That had jolted her all right. I saw her body stiffen, her cornflower eyes distend and darken, her red lips part; and her women bent to each other, whispering, while the murmur of the crowd swelled.

"You lie!" roared Tibur. "There is no life in the Mother-land. There is no life elsewhere than here. Khalk'ru has sucked earth dry of Life. Except here. You lie!"

His hand dropped to his hammer.

And suddenly I saw red; all the world dissolved in a mist of red. The horse of the man closest to me was a noble animal. I had been watching it--a roan stallion, strong as the black stallion that had carried me from the Gobi oasis. I reached up, caught at its jaw, and pulled it down to its knees. Taken unaware, its rider toppled forward, somersaulted over its head and fell at my feet. He was up again like a cat, sword athrust at me. I caught his arm before he could strike and swung up my left fist. It cracked on his jaw; his head snapped back, and he dropped. I snatched up the sword, and swung myself on the rising horse's back. Before Tibur could move I had the point of the sword at his throat.

"Stop! I grant you Dwayanu! Hold your hand!" It was the Witch-woman's voice, low, almost whispering.

I laughed. I pressed the point of the sword deeper into Tiber's throat.

"Am I Dwayanu? Or by-blow of Sirk?"

"You are--Dwayanu!" he groaned.

I laughed again.

"I am Dwayanu! Then guide me into Karak to make amends for your insolence, Tibur!"

I drew the sword away from his throat.

Yes, I drew it back--and by all the mad mixed gods of that mad mixed mind of mine at that moment I would that I had thrust it through his throat!

But I did not, and so that chance passed. I spoke to the Witch-woman:

"Ride at my right hand. Let Tibur ride before."

The man I had struck down was on his feet, swaying unsteadily. Lur spoke to one of her women. She slipped from her horse, and with Tibur's other follower helped him upon it.

We rode across the plaza, and through the walls of the black citadel.

XIV. IN THE BLACK CITADEL

The bars that held the gate crashed down behind us. The passage through the walls was wide and long and lined with soldiers, most of them women. They stared at me; their discipline was good, for they were silent, saluting us with upraised swords.

We came out of the walls into an immense square, bounded by the towering black stone of the citadel. It was stone-paved and bare, and there must have been half a thousand soldiers in it, again mostly women and one and all of the strong-bodied, blue-eyed, red-haired type. It was a full quarter-mile to the side--the square. Opposite where we entered, there was a group of people on horses, of the same class as those who rode with us, or so I judged. They were clustered about a portal in the farther walls, and toward these we trotted.

About a third of the way over, we passed a circular pit a hundred feet wide in which water boiled and bubbled and from which steam arose. A hot spring, I supposed; I could feel its breath. Around it were slender stone pillars from each of which an arm jutted like that of a gallows, and from the ends of them dangled thin chains. It was, indefinably, an unpleasant and ominous place. I didn't like the look of it at all. Something of this must have shown on my face, for Tibur spoke, blandly.

"Our cooking pot."

"No easy one from which to ladle broth," I said. I thought him jesting.

"Ah--but the meat we cook there is not the kind we eat," he answered, still more blandly. And his laughter roared out.

I felt a little sick as his meaning reached me. It was tortured human flesh which those chains were designed to hold, lowering it slowly inch by inch into that devil's cauldron. But I only nodded indifferently, and rode on.

The Witch-woman had paid no attention to us; her russet head bent, she went on deep in thought, though now and then I caught her oblique glance at me. We drew near the portal. She signalled those who awaited there, a score of the red-haired maids and women and a half-dozen men; they dismounted. The Witch-woman leaned to me and whispered:

"Turn the ring so its seal will be covered."

I obeyed her, asking no question.

We arrived at the portal. I looked at the group there. The women wore the breast-revealing upper garment; their legs were covered with loose baggy trousers tied in at the ankles; they had wide girdles in which were two swords, one long and one short. The men were clothed in loose blouses, and the same baggy trousers; in their girdles beside the swords--or rather, hanging from their girdles--were hammers like that of the Smith, but smaller. The women who had gathered around me after I had climbed out of Nanbu had been fair enough, but these were far more attractive, finer, with a stamp of breeding the others had not had. They stared at me as frankly, as appraisingly, as had the soldier woman and her lieutenant; their eyes rested upon my yellow hair and stopped there, as though fascinated. On all their faces was that suggestion of cruelty latent in the amorous mouth of Lur.

"We dismount here," said the Witch-woman, "to go where we may become--better acquainted."

I nodded as before, indifferently. I had been thinking that it was a foolhardy thing I had done, thus to thrust myself alone among these people; but I had been thinking, too, that I could have done nothing else except have gone to Sirk, and where that was I did not know; and that if I had tried I would have been a hunted outlaw on this side of white Nanbu, as I would be on the other. The part of me that was Leif Langdon was thinking that--but the part of me that was Dwayanu was not thinking like that at all. It was fanning the fire of recklessness, the arrogance, that had carried me thus far in safety; whispering that none among the Ayjir had the right to question me or to bar my way, whispering with increasing insistence that I should have been met by dipping standards and roll of drums and fanfare of trumpets. The part that was Leif Langdon answered that there was nothing else to do but continue as I had been doing, that it was the game to play, the line to take, the only way. And that other part, ancient memories, awakening of Dwayanu, post-hypnotic suggestion of the old Gobi priest, impatiently asked why I should question even myself, urging that it was no game--but truth! And that it would brook little more insolence from these degenerate dogs of the Great Race--and little more cowardice from me!

So I flung myself from my horse, and stood looking arrogantly down upon the faces turned to me, literally looking down, for I was four inches or more taller than the tallest of them. Lur touched my arm. Between her and Tibur I strode through the portal and into the black citadel.

It was a vast vestibule through which we passed, and dimly lighted by slits far up in the polished rock. We went by groups of silently saluting soldier-women; we went by many transverse passages. We came at last to a great guarded door, and here Lur and Tibur dismissed their escorts. The door rolled slowly open; we entered and it rolled shut behind us.

The first thing I saw was the Kraken.

It sprawled over one wall of the chamber into which we had come. My heart leaped as I saw it, and for an instant I had an almost ungovernable impulse to turn and run. And now I saw that the figure of the Kraken was a mosaic set in the black stone. Or rather, that the yellow field in which it lay was a mosaic and that the Black Octopus had been cut from the stone of the wall itself. Its unfathomable eyes of jet regarded me with that suggestion of lurking malignity the yellow pygmies had managed to imitate so perfectly in their fettered symbol inside the hollow rock.

Something stirred beneath the Kraken. A face looked out on me from under a hood of black. At first I thought it the old priest of the Gobi himself, and then I saw that this man was not so old, and that his eyes were clear deep blue and that his face was unwrinkled, and cold and white and expressionless as though carved from marble. Then I remembered what Evalie had told me, and knew this must be Yodin the High Priest. He sat upon a throne-like chair behind a long low table on which were rolls like the papyrus rolls of the Egyptians, and cylinders of red metal which were, I supposed, their containers. On each side of him was another of the thrones.

He lifted a thin white hand and beckoned me.

"Come to me--you who call yourself Dwayanu."

The voice was cold and passionless as the face, but courteous. I seemed to hear again the old priest when he had called me to him. I walked over, more as one who humours another a little less than equal than as though obeying a summons. And that was precisely the way I felt. He must have read my thought, for I saw a shadow of anger pass over his face. His eyes searched me.

"You have a certain ring, I am told."

With the same feeling of humouring one slightly inferior, I turned the bevel of the Kraken ring and held my hand out toward him. He looked at the ring, and the white face lost its immobility. He thrust a hand into his girdle, and drew from it a box, and out of it another ring, and placed it beside mine. I saw that it was not so large, and that the setting was not precisely the same. He studied the two rings, and then with a hissing intake of breath he snatched my hands and turned them over, scanning the palms. He dropped them and leaned back in his chair.

"Why do you come to us?" he asked.

A surge of irritation swept me.

"Does Dwayanu stand like a common messenger to be questioned?" I said harshly.

I walked around the table and dropped into one of the chairs beside him.

"Let drink be brought, for I am thirsty. Until my thirst is quenched, I will not talk."

A faint flush stained the white face; there was a growl from Tibur. He was glaring at me with reddened face; the Witch-woman stood, gaze intent upon me, no mockery in it now; the speculative interest was intensified. It came to me that the throne I had usurped was Tibur's. I laughed.

"Beware, Tibur," I said. "This may be an omen!"

The High Priest intervened, smoothly.

"If he be indeed Dwayanu, Tibur, then no honour is too great for him. See that wine is brought."

The look that the Smith shot at Yodin seemed to me to hold a question. Perhaps the Witch-woman thought so too. She spoke quickly.

"I will see to it."

She walked to the door, opened it and gave an order to a guard. She waited; there was silence among us while she waited. I thought many things. I thought, for example, that I did not like the look that had passed between Yodin and Tibur, and that while I might trust Lur for the present--still she would drink first when the wine came. And I thought that I would tell them little of how I came to the Shadowed-land. And I thought of Jim--and I thought of Evalie. It made my heart ache so that I felt the loneliness of nightmare; and then I felt the fierce contempt of that other part of me, and felt it strain against the fetters I had put on it. Then the wine came.

The Witch-woman carried ewer and goblet over to the table and set them before me. She poured yellow wine into the goblet and handed it to me. I smiled at her.

"The cup-bearer drinks first," I said. "So it was in the olden days, Lur. And the olden customs are dear to me."

Tibur gnawed his lip and tugged at his beard at that, but Lur took up the goblet and drained it. I refilled it, and raised it to Tibur. I had a malicious desire to bait the Smith.

"Would you have done that had you been the cup-bearer, Tibur?" I asked him and drank.

That was good wine! It tingled through me, and I felt the heady recklessness leap up under it as though lashed. I filled the goblet again and tossed it off.

"Come up, Lur, and sit with us," I said. "Tibur, join us."

The Witch-woman quietly took the third throne. Tibur was watching me, and I saw a new look in his eyes, something of that furtive speculation I had surprised in Lur's. The white-faced priest's gaze was far away. It occurred to me that the three of them were extremely busy with their own thoughts, and that Tibur at least, was becoming a bit uneasy. When he answered me his voice had lost all truculency.

"Well and good--Dwayanu!" he said, and, lifting a bench, carried it to the table, and set it where he could watch our faces.

"I answer your question," I turned to Yodin. "I came here at the summons of Khalk'ru."

"It is strange," he said, "that I, who am High Priest of Khalk'ru, knew nothing of any summons."

"The reasons for that I do not know," I said, casually. "Ask them of him you serve."

He pondered over that.

"Dwayanu lived long and long and long ago," he said. "Before--"

"Before the Sacrilege. True." I took another drink of the wine. "Yet--I am here."

For the first time his voice lost its steadiness.

"You--you know of the Sacrilege!" His fingers clutched my wrist. "Man--whoever you are--from whence do you come?"

"I come," I answered, "from the Mother-land."

His fingers tightened around my wrist. He echoed Tibur.

"The Mother-land is a dead land. Khalk'ru in his anger destroyed its life. There is no life save here, where Khalk'ru hears his servants and lets life be."

He did not believe that; I could tell it by the involuntary glance he had given the Witch-woman and the Smith. Nor did they.

"The Mother-land," I said, "is bleached bones. Its cities lie covered in shrouds of sand. Its rivers are waterless, and all that runs within their banks is sand driven by the arid winds. Yet still is there life in the Mother-land, and although the ancient blood is thinned--still it runs. And still is Khalk'ru worshipped and feared in the place from whence I came--and still in other lands the earth spawns life as always she has done."

I poured some more wine. It was good wine, that.

Under it I felt my recklessness increase...under it Dwayanu was stronger...well, this was a tight box I was in, so let him be...

"Show me the place from whence you came," the High Priest spoke swiftly. He gave me a tablet of wax and a stylus. I traced the outline of Northern Asia upon it and of Alaska. I indicated the Gobi and approximately the location of the oasis, and also the position of the Shadowed-land.

Tibur got up to look at it; their three heads bent over it. The priest fumbled among the rolls, picked one, and they compared it with the tablet. It appeared like a map, but if so the northern coast line was all wrong. There was a line traced on it that seemed to be a route of some sort. It was overscored and underscored with symbols. I wondered whether it might not be the record of the trek those of the Old Race had made when they had fled from the Gobi.

They looked up at last; there was perturbation in the priest's eyes, angry apprehension in Tibur's, but the eyes of the Witch-woman were clear and untroubled--as though she had made up her mind about something and knew precisely what she was going to do.

"It is the Mother-land!" the priest said. "Tell me--did the black-haired stranger who fled with you across the river and who watched you hurled from Nansur come also from there?"

There was sheer malice in that question. I began to dislike Yodin.

"No," I answered. "He comes from an old land of the Rrrllya."

That brought the priest up standing; Tibur swore incredulously; and even the Witch-woman was shaken from her serenity.

"Another land--of the Rrrllya! But that cannot be!" whispered Yodin.

"Nevertheless it is so," I said.

He sank back, and thought for a while.

"He is your friend?"

"My brother by the ancient blood rite of his people."

"He would join you here?"

"He would if I sent for him. But that I will not do. Not yet. He is well off where he is."

I was sorry I had said that the moment I had spoken. Why--I did not know. But I would have given much to have recalled the words.

Again the priest was silent.

"These are strange things you tell us," he said at last. "And you have come to us strangely for--Dwayanu. You will not mind if for a little we take counsel?"

I looked in the ewer. It was still half-full. I liked that wine--most of all because it dulled my sorrow over Evalie.

"Speak as long as you please," I answered, graciously. They went off to a corner of the room. I poured myself another drink, and another. I forgot about Evalie. I began to feel I was having a good time. I wished Jim was with me, but I wished I hadn't said he would come if I sent for him. And then I took another drink and forgot about Jim. Yes, I was having a damned good time...well, wait till I let Dwayanu loose a bit more! I'd have a better one...I was sleepy...I wondered what old Barr would say if he could be here with me...

I came to myself with a start. The High Priest was standing at my side, talking. I had a vague idea he had been talking to me for some time but I couldn't remember what about. I also had the idea that someone had been fumbling with my thumb. It was clenched stubbornly in my palm, so tightly that the stone had bruised the flesh. The effect of the wine had entirely worn off I looked around the room. Tibur and the Witch-woman were gone. Why hadn't I seen them go? Had I been asleep? I studied Yodin's face. There was a look of strain about it, of bafflement; and yet I sensed some deep satisfaction. It was a queer composite of expression. And I didn't like it.

"The others have gone to prepare a fitting reception for you," he said. "To make ready a place for you and fitting apparel."

I arose and stood beside him.

"As Dwayanu?" I asked.

"Not as yet," he answered urbanely. "But as an honoured guest. The other is too serious a matter to decide without further proof."

"And that proof?"

He looked at me a long moment before answering.

"That Khalk'ru will appear at your prayer!"

A little shudder went through me at that. He was watching me so closely that he must have seen it.

"Curb your impatience," his voice was cold honey. "You will not have long to wait. Until then I probably shall not see you. In the meantime--I have a request to make."

"What is it?" I asked.

"That you will not wear the ring of Khalk'ru openly--except, of course, at such times as may seem necessary to you."

It was the same thing Lur had asked me. Yet scores had seen me with the ring--more must know I had it. He read my indecision.

"It is a holy thing," he said. "I did not know another existed until word was brought me that you had shown it on Nansur. It is not well to cheapen holy things. I do not wear mine except when I think it-- necessary."

I wondered under what circumstances he considered it-- necessary. And I wished fervently I knew under what circumstances it would be helpful to me. His eyes were searching me, and I hoped he had not read that thought.

"I see no reason to deny that request," I said. I slipped the ring off my thumb and into my belt pocket.

"I was sure you would not," he murmured.

A gong sounded lightly. He pressed the side of the table, and the door opened. Three youths clothed in the smocks of the people entered and stood humbly waiting.

"They are your servants. They will take you to your place," Yodin said. He bent his head. I went out with the three young Ayjirs. At the door was a guard of a dozen women with a bold-eyed young captain. They saluted me smartly. We marched down the corridor and at length turned into another. I looked back.

I was just in time to see the Witch-woman slipping into the High Priest's chamber.

We came to another guarded door. It was thrown open and into it I was ushered, followed by the three youths.

"We are also your servants. Lord," the bold-eyed captain spoke. "If there is anything you wish, summon me by this. We shall be at the door."

She handed me a small gong of jade, saluted again and marched out.

The room had an odd aspect of familiarity. Then I realized it was much like that to which I had been taken in the oasis. There were the same oddly shaped stools, and chairs of metal, the same wide, low di-van bed, the tapestried walls, the rugs upon the floor. Only here there were no signs of decay. True, some of the tapestries were time-faded, but exquisitely so; there were no rags or tatters in them. The others were beautifully woven but fresh as though just from the loom. The ancient hangings were threaded with the same scenes of the hunt and war as the haggard drapings of the oasis; the newer ones bore scenes of the land under the mirage. Nansur Bridge sprang unbroken over one, on another was a battle with the pygmies, on another a scene of the fantastically lovely forest--with the white wolves of Lur slinking through the trees. Something struck me as wrong. I looked and looked before I knew what it was. The arms of its olden master had been in the chamber of the oasis, his swords and spears, helmet and shield; in this one there was not a weapon. I remembered that I had carried the sword of Tibur's man into the chamber of the High Priest. I did not have it now.

A disquietude began to creep over me. I turned to the three young Ayjirs, and began to unbutton my shirt. They came forward silently, and started to strip me. And suddenly I felt a consuming thirst.

"Bring me water," I said to one of the youths. He paid not the slightest attention to me.

"Bring me water," I said again, thinking he had not heard. "I am thirsty."

He continued tranquilly taking off a boot. I touched him on the shoulder.

"Bring me water to drink," I said, emphatically.

He smiled up at me, opened his mouth and pointed. He had no tongue. He pointed to his ears. I understood that he was telling me he was both dumb and deaf. I pointed to his two comrades. He nodded.

My disquietude went up a point or two. Was this a general custom of the rulers of Karak; had this trio been especially adapted not only for silent service but unhearing service on special guests? Guests or-- prisoners?

I tapped the gong with a finger. At once the door opened, and the young captain stood there, saluting.

"I am thirsty," I said. "Bring water."

For answer she crossed the room and pulled aside one of the hangings. Behind it was a wide, deep alcove.

Within the floor was a shallow pool through which clean water was flowing, and close beside it was a basin of porphyry from which sprang a jet like a tiny fountain. She took a goblet from a niche, filled it under the jet and handed it to me. It was cold and sparkling.

"Is there anything more, Lord?" she asked. I shook my head, and she marched out.

I went back to the ministrations of the three deaf-mutes. They took off the rest of my clothes and began to massage me, with some light, volatile oil. While they were doing it, my mind began to function rather actively. In the first place, the sore spot in my palm kept reminding me of that impression someone had been trying to get the ring off my thumb. In the second place, the harder I thought the more I was sure that before I awakened or had come out of my abstraction or drink or whatever it was, the white-faced priest had been talking, talking, talking to me, questioning me, probing into my dulled mind. And in the third place, I had lost almost entirely all the fine carelessness of consequences that had been so successful in putting me where I was-- in fact, I was far too much Leif Langdon and too little Dwayanu. What had the priest been at with his talking, talking, questioning--and what had I said?

I jumped out of the hands of my masseurs, ran over to my trousers and dived into my belt. The ring was there right enough. I searched for my old pouch. It was gone. I rang the gong. The captain answered. I was mother-naked, but I hadn't the slightest sense of her being a woman.

"Hear me," I said. "Bring me wine. And bring with it a safe, strong case big enough to hold a ring. Bring with that a strong chain with which I can hang the case around my neck. Do you understand?"

"Done at once, Lord," she said. She was not long in returning. She set down the ewer she was carrying and reached into her blouse. She brought out a locket suspended from a metal chain. She snapped it open.

"Will this do, Lord?"

I turned from her, and put the ring of Khalk'ru into the locket. It held it admirably.

"Most excellently," I told her, "but I have nothing to give you in return."

She laughed.

"Reward enough to have beheld you, Lord," she said, not at all ambiguously, and marched away. I hung the locket round my neck. I poured a drink and then another. I went back to my masseurs and began to feel better. I drank while they were bathing me, and I drank while they were trimming my hair and shaving me. And the more I drank the more Dwayanu came up, coldly wrathful and resentful.

My dislike for Yodin grew. It did not lessen while the trio were dressing me. They put on me a silken under-vest. They covered it with a gorgeous tunic of yellow shot through with metallic threads of blue;

they covered my long legs with the baggy trousers of the same stuff; they buckled around my waist a broad, gem-studded girdle, and they strapped upon my feet sandals of soft golden leather. They had shaved me, and now they brushed and dressed my hair which they had shorn to the nape of my neck.

By the time they were through with me, the wine was done. I was a little drunk, willing to be more so, and in no mood to be played with. I rang the gong for the captain. I wanted some more wine, and I wanted to know when, where and how I was going to eat. The door opened, but it was not the captain who came in.

It was the Witch-woman.

XV. THE LAKE OF THE GHOSTS

Lur paused, red lips parted, regarding me. Plainly she was startled by the difference the Ayjir trappings and the ministrations of the mutes had made in the dripping, bedraggled figure that had scrambled out of the river not long before. Her eyes glowed, and a deeper rose stained her cheeks. She came. close.

"Dwayanu--you will go with me?"

I looked at her, and laughed.

"Why not, Lur--but also, why?"

She whispered:

"You are in danger--whether you are Dwayanu or whether you are not. I have persuaded Yodin to let you remain with me until you go to the temple. With me you shall be safe--until then."

"And why did you do this for me, Lur?"

She made no answer--only set one hand upon my shoulder and looked at me with blue eyes grown soft; and though common sense told me there were other reasons for her solicitude than any quick passion for me, still at that touch and look the blood raced through my veins, and it was hard to master my voice and speak.

"I will go with you, Lur."

She went to the door, opened it.

"Ouarda, the cloak and cap." She came back to me with a black cloak which she threw over my shoulders and fastened round my neck; she pulled down over my yellow hair a close-fitting cap shaped like the Phyrgian and she tucked my hair into it. Except for my height it made me like any other Ayjir in Karak.

"There is need for haste, Dwayanu."

"I am ready. Wait--"

I went over to where my old clothes lay, and rolled them up around my boots. After all--I might need them. The Witch-woman made no comment, opened the door and we went out. The captain and her guard were in the corridor, also a half-dozen of Lur's women, and handsome creatures they were. Then I noticed that each of them wore the light coat of mail and, besides the two swords, carried throwing hammers. So did Lur. Evidently they were ready for trouble, whether with me or with someone else; and whichever way it was, I didn't like it.

"Give me your sword," I said abruptly to the captain. She hesitated.

"Give it to him," said Lur.

I weighed the weapon in my hand; not so heavy as I would have liked, but still a sword. I thrust it into my girdle, and bunched the bundle of my old clothes beneath my left arm, under the cloak. We set off down the corridor, leaving the guard at the door.

We went only a hundred yards, and then into a small bare chamber. We had met no one. Lur drew a breath of relief, walked over to a side, and a slab of stone slid open, revealing a passage. We went into that and the slab closed, leaving us in pitch-darkness. There was a spark, produced I don't know how, and the place sprang into light from torches in the hands of two of the women. They burned with a clear, steady and silvery flame. The torch-bearers marched ahead of us. After a while we came to the end of that passage, the torches were extinguished, another stone slid away and we stepped out. I heard whispering, and after the glare of the flambeaux had worn away, I saw that we were at the base of one of the walls of the black citadel, and that close by were half a dozen more of Lur's women, with horses. One of them led forward a big grey stallion.

"Mount, and ride beside me," said Lur.

I fixed my bundle on the pommel of the high saddle, and straddled the grey. We set off silently. It was never wholly dark at night in the land under the mirage; there was always a faint green luminescence, but to-night it was brighter than I had ever seen it. I wondered whether there was a full moon shining down over the peaks of the valley. I wondered if we had far to go. I was not as drunk as I had been when Lur had come in on me, but in a way I was drunker. I had a queer, light-headed feeling that was decidedly pleasant, a carefree irresponsibility. I wanted to keep on feeling that way. I hoped that Lur had plenty of wine wherever she was taking me. I wished I had a drink right now.

We were going through the city beyond the citadel, and we went fast. The broad street we were on was well paved. There were lights in the houses and in the gardens and people singing and drums and pipes playing. Sinister the black citadel might be, but it did not seem to cast any shadow on the people of Karak. Or so I thought then.

115

We passed out of the city into a smooth road running between thick vegetation. The luminous moths like fairy planes were flitting about, and for a moment I felt a pang of memory, and Evalie's face floated up before me. It didn't last a second. The grey went sweetly and I began to sing an old Kirghiz song about a lover who rode in the moonlight to his maid and what he found when he got there. Lur laughed, and put her hand over my mouth.

"Quiet, Dwayanu! There still is danger." Then I realized that I hadn't been singing the Kirghiz at all, but the Uighur, which was probably where the Kirghiz got it from. And then it occurred to me that I had never heard the song in the Uighur. It started the old problem going in my mind--and that lasted no longer than the memory of Evalie.

Now and then I caught a glimpse of the white river. And then we went over a long stretch where the road narrowed so that we rode single file between verdure-covered cliffs. When we came out of them, the road forked. One part of it ran right on, the other turned sharply to the left. We rode along this for three or four miles, apparently directly through the heart of the strange forest. The great trees spread their arms out far overhead; the candelabras and cressets and swaying ropes of blooms gleamed like ghosts of flowers in the pallid light; the scaled trees were like men-at-arms on watch. And the heady fragrances, the oddly stimulating exhalations were strong--strong. They throbbed from the forest, rhythmically, as though they were the pulse of its life-drunken heart.

And as we came to the end of that road and I looked down upon the Lake of the Ghosts.

Never, I think, in all the world was there such a place of breath-taking, soul-piercing, unearthly beauty as that lake beneath the mirage in which Lur the Witch-woman had her home. And had she not been Witch-woman before she dwelt there, it must have made her so.

It was shaped like an arrow-head, its longer shores not more than a mile in length. It was enclosed by low hills whose sides were covered with the tree-ferns; their feathery fronds clothed them as though they were the breasts of gigantic birds of Paradise; threw themselves up from them like fountains; soared over them like vast virescent wings. The colour of its water was pale emerald, and like an emerald it gleamed, placid, untroubled. But beneath that untroubled surface there was movement--luminous circles of silvery green that spread swiftly and vanished, rays that laced and interlaced in fantastic yet ordered, geometric forms; luminous spirallings, none of which ever came quite to the surface to disturb its serenity. And here and there were clusters of soft lights, like vaporous rubies, misted sapphires and opals and glimmering pearls--witch-lights. The luminous lilies of the Lake of the Ghosts.

Where the point of the arrow-head touched, there were no ferns. A broad waterfall spread itself like a veil over the face of the cliff, whispering as it fell. Mists rose there, mingling with the falling water, dancing slowly with the falling water, swaying toward it and reaching up with ghostly hands as though to greet it. And from the shores of the lake, other wraiths of mist would rise, and glide swiftly over the emerald floor and join those other dancing, welcoming wraiths of the waterfall. Thus first I saw the Lake of the Ghosts under the night of the mirage, and it was no less beautiful in the mirage day.

The road ran out into the lake like the shaft of an arrow. At its end was what once, I supposed, had been a small island. It lay two-thirds of the way across. Over its trees were the turrets of a small castle.

We walked our horses down the steep to the narrowing of the road where it became the shaft of the arrow. Here there were no ferns to hide the approach; they had been cleared away and the breast of the hill was covered with the blue flowerets. As we reached the narrow part, I saw that it was a causeway, built of stone. The place to which we were going was still an island. We came to the end of the causeway, and there was a forty-foot gap between it and a pier on the opposite shore. Lur drew from her girdle a small horn and sounded it. A drawbridge began to creak, and to drop down over the gap. We rode across that and into a garrison of her women. We cantered up a winding road, and I heard the creak of the lifting bridge as we went. We drew up before the house of the Witch-woman.

I looked at it with interest, not because it was unfamiliar, for it was not, but I was thinking I had never seen a castle of its sort built of that peculiar green stone nor with so many turrets. Yes, I knew them well. "Lady castles," we had called them; lana'rada, bowers for favourite women, a place to rest, a place to love after war or when weary of statecraft.

Women came and took the horses. Wide doors of polished wood swung open. Lur led me over the threshold.

Girls came forward with wine. I drank thirstily. The queer light-headedness, and the sense of detachment were growing. I seemed to have awakened from a long, long sleep, and was not thoroughly awake and troubled by memories of dreams. But I was sure that they had not all been dreams. That old priest who had awakened me in the desert which once had been fertile Ayjirland--he had been no dream. Yet the people among whom I had awakened had not been Ayjirs. This was not Ayjirland, yet the people were of the ancient breed! How had I gotten here? I must have fallen asleep again in the temple after--after--by Zarda, but I must feel my way a bit! Be cautious. Then would follow a surge of recklessness that swept away all thought of caution, a roaring relish of life, a wild freedom as of one who, long in prison, sees suddenly the bars broken and before him the table of life spread with all he has been denied, to take as he wills. And on its heels a flash of recognition that I was Leif Langdon and knew perfectly well how I came to be in this place and must some way, somehow, get back to Evalie and to Jim. Swift as the lightning were those latter flashes, and as brief.

I became aware that I was no longer in the castle's hall but in a smaller chamber, octagonal, casemented, tapestried. There was a wide, low bed. There was a table glistening with gold and crystal; tall candles burned upon it. My blouse was gone, and in its place a light silken tunic. The casements were open and the fragrant air sighed through them. I leaned from one.

Below me were the lesser turrets and the roof of the castle. Far below was the lake. I looked through another. The waterfall with its beckoning wraiths whispered and murmured not a thousand feet away.

I felt the touch of a hand on my head; it slipped down to my shoulder; I swung round. The Witch-woman was beside me.

For the first time I seemed to be realizing her beauty, seemed for the first time to be seeing her clearly. Her russet hair was braided in a thick coronal; it shone like reddest gold, and within it was twisted a strand of sapphires. Her eyes outshone them. Her scanty robe of gossamer blue revealed every lovely, sensuous line of her. White shoulders and one of the exquisite breasts were bare. Her full red lips promised--anything, and even the subtle cruelty stamped upon them, lured.

There had been a dark girl...who had she been...Ev--Eval--the name eluded me...no matter...she was like a wraith beside this woman...like one of the mist wraiths swaying at the feet of the waterfall...

The Witch-woman read what was in my eyes. Her hand slipped from my shoulder and rested on my heart. She bent closer, blue eyes languorous--yet strangely intent.

"And are you truly Dwayanu?"

"I am he--none else, Lur."

"Who was Dwayanu--long and long and long ago?"

"I cannot tell you that, Lur--I who have been long asleep and in sleep forgotten much. Yet--I am he."

"Then look--and remember."

Her hand left my heart and rested on my head; she pointed to the waterfall. Slowly its whispering changed. It became the beat of drums, the trample of horses, the tread of marching men. Louder and louder they grew. The waterfall quivered, and spread across the black cliff like a gigantic curtain. From every side the mist wraiths were hurrying, melting into it. Clearer and nearer sounded the drums. And suddenly the waterfall vanished. In its place was a great walled city. Two armies were fighting there and I knew that the forces which were attacking the city were being borne back. I heard the thunder of the hoofs of hundreds of horses. Down upon the defenders raced a river of mounted men. Their leader was clothed in shining mail. He was helmetless, and his yellow hair streamed behind him as he rode. He turned his face. And that face was my own! I heard a roaring shout of "Dwayanu!" The charge struck like a river in spate, rolled over the defenders, submerged them.

I saw an army in rout, and smashed by companies with the throwing hammers.

I rode with the yellow-haired leader into the conquered city. And I sat with him on a conquered throne while ruthlessly, mercilessly, he dealt death to men and women dragged before him, and smiled at the voices of rapine and pillage rising from without. I rode and sat with him, I say, for now it was no longer as though I were in the Witch-woman's chamber but was with this yellow-haired man who was my twin, seeing as he did, hearing as he did--yes, and thinking as he thought.

Battle upon battle, tourneys and feasts and triumphs, hunts with the falcons and hunts with great dogs in fair Ayjirland, hammer-play and anvil-play--I saw them, standing always beside Dwayanu like an unseen shadow. I went with him to the temples when he served the gods. I went with him to the Temple of the Dissolver--Black Khalk'ru, the Greater-than-Gods--and he wore the ring which rested on my breast. But when he passed within Khalk'ru's temple, I held back. The same deep, stubborn resistance which had halted me when I had visioned the portal of the oasis temple halted me now. I listened to two voices. One urged me to enter with Dwayanu.

The other whispered that I must not. And that voice I could not disobey.

And then, abruptly, Ayjirland was no more! I was staring out at the waterfall and gliding mist wraiths. But--I was Dwayanu!

I was all Dwayanu! Leif Langdon had ceased to exist!

Yet he had left memories--memories which were like half-remembered dreams, memories whose source I could not fathom but realized that, even if only dreams, were true ones. They told me the Ayjirland I had ruled had vanished as utterly as had the phantom Ayjirland of the waterfall, that dusty century upon century had passed since them, that other empires had risen and fallen, that here was an alien land with only a dying fragment of the ancient glory.

Warrior-king and warrior-priest I had been, holding in my hands empire and the lives and destinies of a race.

And now--no more!

XVI. KISSES OF LUR

Black sorrow and the bitter ashes were in my heart when I turned from the window. I looked at Lur. From long slim feet to shining head I looked at her, and the black sorrow lightened and the bitter ashes blew away.

I put my hands on her shoulders and laughed. Luka had spun her wheel and sent my empire flying off its rim like dust from the potter's. But she had left me something. In all old Ayjirland there had been few women like this.

Praise Luka! A sacrifice to her next morning if this woman proves what I think her!

My vanished empire! What of it? I would build another. Enough that I was alive!

Again I laughed. I put my hand under Lur's chin, raised her face to mine, set my lips against hers. She thrust me from her. There was anger in her eyes--but there was doubt under the anger.

"You bade me remember. Well, I have remembered. Why did you open the gates of memory. Witch-woman, unless you had made up your mind to abide by what came forth? Or did you know less of Dwayanu than you pretended?"

She took a step back; she said, furiously:

"I give my kisses. None takes them."

I caught her in my arms, crushed her mouth to mine, then released her.

"I take them."

I struck down at her right wrist. There was a dagger in her hand. I was amused, wondering where she had hidden it. I wrenched it from her grip and slipped it my girdle.

"And draw the stings from those I kiss. Thus did Dwayanu in the days of old and thus he does to-day."

She stepped back and back, eyes dilated. Ai! but I could read her! She had thought me other than I was, thought me hare-brain, imposter, trickster. And it had been in her mind to trick me, to bend me to her will. To beguile me. Me--Dwayanu, who knew women as I knew war! And yet--

She was very beautiful...and she was all I had in this alien land to begin the building of my rule. I summed her up as she stood staring at me. I spoke, and my words were as cold as my thoughts.

"Play no more with daggers--nor with me. Call your servants. I am hungry and I thirst. When I have eaten and drunk we will talk."

She hesitated, then clapped her hands. Women came in with steaming dishes, with ewers of wine, with fruits. I ate ravenously. I drank deeply. I ate and drank, thinking little of Lur--but thinking much of what her sorcery had made me see, drawing together what I remembered from desert oasis until now. It was little enough. I ate and drank silently. I felt her eyes upon me. I looked into them and smiled. "You thought to make me slave to your will, Lur. Never think it again!"

She dropped her head between her hands and gazed at me across the table.

"Dwayanu died long and long ago. Can the leaf that has withered grow green?"

"I am he, Lur."

She did not answer.

"What was in your thought when you brought me here, Lur?"

"I am weary of Tibur, weary of his laughter, weary of his stupidity."

"What else?"

"I tire of Yodin. You and I--alone--could rule Karak, if--"

"That 'if' is the heart of it. Witch-woman. What is it?"

She arose, leaned toward me.

"If you can summon Khalk'ru!"

"And if I cannot?"

She shrugged her white shoulders, dropped back into her chair. I laughed.

"In which case Tibur will not be so wearisome, and Yodin may be tolerated. Now listen to me, Lur. Was it your voice I heard urging me to enter Khalk'ru's temples? Did you see as I was seeing? You need not answer. I read you, Lur. You would be rid of Tibur. Well, perhaps I can kill him. You would be rid of Yodin. Well, no matter who I am, if I can summon the Greater-than-Gods, there is no need of Yodin. Tibur and Yodin gone, there would be only you and me. You think you could rule me. You could not, Lur."

She had listened quietly, and quietly now she answered.

"All that is true--"

She hesitated; her eyes glowed; a rosy flush swept over bosom and cheeks.

"Yet--there might be another reason why I took you--"

I did not ask her what that other reason might be; women had tried to snare me with that ruse before. Her gaze dropped from me, the cruelty on the red mouth stood out for an instant, naked.

"What did you promise Yodin, Witch-woman?"

She arose, held out her arms to me, her voice trembled--

"Are you less than man--that you can speak to me so! Have I not offered you power, to share with me? Am I not beautiful--am I not desirable?"

"Very beautiful, very desirable. But always I learned the traps my city concealed before I took it."

Her eyes shot blue fires at that. She took a swift step toward the door. I was swifter. I held her, caught the hand she raised to strike me.

"What did you promise the High-priest, Lur?"

I put the point of the dagger at her throat. Her eyes blazed at me, unafraid. Luka--turn your wheel so I need not slay this woman!

Her straining body relaxed; she laughed.

"Put away the dagger, I will tell you."

I released her, and walked back to my chair. She studied me from her place across the table; she said, half incredulously:

"You would have killed me!"

"Yes," I told her.

"I believe you. Whoever you may be. Yellow-hair--there is no man like you here."

"Whoever I may be--Witch?"

She stirred impatiently

"No further need for pretence between us." There was anger in her voice. "I am done with lies--better for both if you be done with them too. Whoever you are--you are not Dwayanu. I say again that the withered leaf cannot turn green nor the dead return."

"If I am not he, then whence came those memories you watched with me not long ago? Did they pass from your mind to mine. Witch-woman--or from my mind to yours?"

She shook her head, and again I saw a furtive doubt cloud her eyes.

"I saw nothing. I meant you to see--something. You eluded me. Whatever it was you saw--I had no part in it. Nor could I bend you to my will. I saw nothing."

"I saw the ancient land, Lur."

She said, sullenly:

"I could go no farther than its portal."

"What was it you sent me into Ayjirland to find for Yodin, Witch-woman?"

"Khalk'ru," she answered evenly.

"And why?"

"Because then I would have known surely, beyond all doubt, whether you could summon him. That was what I promised Yodin to discover."

"And if I could summon him?"

"Then you were to be slain before you had opportunity."

"And if I could not?"

"Then you would be offered to him in the temple."

"By Zarda!" I swore. "Dwayanu's welcome is not like what he had of old when he went visiting--or, if you prefer it, the hospitality you offer a stranger is no thing to encourage travellers. Now do I see eye to eye with you in this matter of eliminating Tibur and the priest. But why should I not begin with you, Witch?"

She leaned back, smiling.

"First--because it would do you no good. Yellow-hair. Look."

She beckoned me to one of the windows. From it I could see the causeway and the smooth hill upon which we had emerged from the forest. There were soldiers all along the causeway and the top of the hill held a company of them. I felt that she was quite right--even I could not get through them unscathed. The old cold rage began to rise within me. She watched me, with mockery in her eyes.

"And second--" she said. "And second--well, hear me. Yellow-hair."

I poured wine, raised the goblet to her, and drank. She said:

"Life is pleasant in this land. Pleasant at least for those of us who rule it. I have no desire to change it--except in the matter of Tibur and Yodin. And another matter of which we can talk later. I know the world has altered since long and long ago our ancestors fled from Ayjirland. I know there is life outside this sheltered place to which Khalk'ru led those ancestors. Yodin and Tibur know it, and some few more. Others guess it. But none of us desires to leave this pleasant place--nor do we desire it invaded. Particularly have we no desire to have our people go from it. And this many would attempt if they knew there were green fields and woods and running water and a teeming world of men beyond us. For through the uncounted years they have been taught that in all the world there is no life save here. That

Khalk'ru, angered by the Great Sacrilege when Ayjirland rose in revolt and destroyed his temples, then destroyed all life except here, and that only by Khalk'ru's sufferance does it here exist--and shall persist only so long as he is offered the ancient Sacrifice. You follow me, Yellow-hair?"

I nodded.

"The prophecy of Dwayanu is an ancient one. He was the greatest of the Ayjir kings. He lived a hundred years or more before the Ayjirs began to turn their faces from Khalk'ru, to resist the Sacrifice--and the desert in punishment began to waste the land. And as the unrest grew, and the great war which was to destroy the Ayjirs brewed, the prophecy was born. That he would return to restore the ancient glory. No new story. Yellow-hair. Others have had their Dwayanus--the Redeemer, the Liberator, the Loosener of Fate--or so I have read in those rolls our ancestors carried with them when they fled. I do not believe these stories; new Dwayanus may arise, but the old ones do not return. Yet the people know the prophecy, and the people will believe anything that promises them freedom from something they do not like. And it is from the people that the sacrifices to Khalk'ru are taken--and they do not like the Sacrifice. But because they fear what might come if there were no more sacrifices--they endure them.

"And now. Yellow-hair--we come to you. When first I saw you, heard you shouting that you were Dwayanu, I took council with Yodin and Tibur. I thought you then from Sirk. Soon I knew that could not be. There was another with you--"

"Another?" I asked, in genuine surprise.

She looked at me, suspiciously.

"You have no memory of him?"

"No. I remember seeing you. You had a white falcon. There were other women with you. I saw you from the river."

She leaned forward, gaze intent.

"You remember the Rrrllya--the Little People? A dark girl who calls herself Evalie?"

Little People--a dark girl--Evalie? Yes, I did remember something of them--but vaguely. They had been in those dreams I had forgotten, perhaps. No--they had been real...or had they?

"Faintly, I seem to remember something of them, Lur. Nothing clearly."

She stared at me, a curious exultation in her eyes.

"No matter," she said. "Do not try to think of them. You were not--awake. Later we will speak of them. They are enemies. No matter--follow me now. If you were from Sirk, posing as Dwayanu, you might be a rallying point for our discontented. Perhaps even the leader they needed. If you were from outside--you were still more dangerous, since you could prove us liars. Not only the people, but the soldiers might rally to you. And probably would. What was there for us to do but to kill you?"

"Nothing," I answered. "I wonder now you did not when you had the chance."

"You had complicated matters," she said. "You had shown the ring. Many had seen it, many had heard you call yourself Dwayanu--"

Ah, yes! I remember now--I had come up from the river. How had I gotten into the river? The bridge--Nansur--something had happened there...it was all misty, nothing clear-cut...the Little People...yes, I remembered something of them...they were afraid of me...but I had nothing against them...vainly I tried to sort the vague visions into some pattern. Lur's voice recalled my wandering thoughts.

"And so," she was saying, "I made Yodin see that it was not well to slay you outright. It would have been known, and caused too much unrest--strengthened Sirk for one thing. Caused unrest among the soldiers. What--Dwayanu had come and we had slain him! 'I will take him,' I told Yodin. 'I do not trust Tibur who, in his stupidity and arrogance, might easily destroy us all. There is a better way. Let Khalk'ru eat him and so prove us right and him the liar and braggart. Then not soon will another come shouting that he is Dwayanu'!"

"So the High-priest does not think me Dwayanu, either?"

"Less even than I do. Yellow-hair," she said, smiling. "Nor Tibur. But who you are, and whence you came, and how and why--that puzzles them as it does me. You look like the Ayjir--it means nothing. You have the ancient marks upon your hands--well, granted you are of the ancient blood. So has Tibur--and he is no Redeemer," again her laughter rang like little bells, "You have the ring. Where did you find it. Yellow-hair? For you know little of its use. Yodin found that out. When you were in sleep. And Yodin saw you turn colour and half turn to flee when first you saw Khalk'ru in his chamber. Deny it not. Yellow-hair. I saw it myself. Ah, no--Yodin has little fear of a rival with the Dissolver. Yet-he is not wholly certain. There is the faintest shadow of doubt. I played on that. And so--you are here."

I looked at her with frankest admiration, again raised the goblet and drank to her. I clapped my hands, and the serving girls entered.

"Clear the table. Bring wine."

They came with fresh ewers and goblets. When they had gone out I went over to the door. There was a heavy bar that closed it. I thrust it down. I picked up one of the ewers and half emptied it.

"I can summon the Dissolver, Witch-woman."

She drew in her breath, sharply; her body trembled; the blue fires of her eyes were bright--bright.

"Shall I show you?"

I took the ring from the locket, slipped it on my thumb, raised my hands in the beginning of the salutation--

A cold breath seemed to breathe through the room. The Witch-woman sprang to me, dragged down my hand. Her lips were white.

"No!--No! I believe--Dwayanu!"

I laughed. The strange cold withdrew, stealthily.

"And now. Witch, what will you tell the priest?"

The blood was slowly coming back into her lips and face. She lifted the ewer and drained it. Her hand was steady. An admirable woman--this Lur!

She said:

"I will tell him that you are powerless."

I said:

"I will summon the Dissolver. I will kill Tibur. I will kill Yodin--what else is there?"

She came to me, stood with breast touching mine.

"Destroy Sirk. Sweep the dwarfs away. Then you and I shall rule--alone."

I drank more wine.

"I will summon Khalk'ru; I will eliminate Tibur and the priest; I will sack Sirk and I will war against the dwarfs--if--"

She looked into my eyes, long and long; her arm stole round my shoulder...I thrust out a hand and swept away the candles. The green darkness of the mirage night seeped through the casements. The whispering of the waterfall was soft laughter.

"I take my pay in advance," I said. "Such was Dwayanu's way of old--and am I not Dwayanu?"

"Yes!" whispered the Witch-woman.

She took the strand of sapphires from her hair, she unbraided her coronal and shook loose its russet-gold. Her arms went round my neck. Her lips sought mine and clung to them.

There was the beat of horses' hoofs on the causeway. A distant challenge. A knocking at the door. The Witch-woman awakened, sat sleepily up under the silken tent of her hair.

"Is it you, Ouarda?"

"Yes, mistress. A messenger from Tibur."

I laughed.

"Tell him you are busy with your gods, Lur."

She bent her head over mine so that the silken tent of it covered us both.

"Tell him I am busy with the gods, Ouarda. He may stay till morning--or return to Tibur with the message."

She sank back, pressed her lips to mine--

By Zarda! But it was as it was of old--enemies to slay, a city to sack, a nation to war with and a woman's soft arms around me.

I was well content!

BOOK OF DWAYANU

XVII. ORDEAL BY KHALK'RU

Twice the green night had filled the bowl of the land beneath the mirage while I feasted and drank with Lur and her women. Sword-play there had been, and the hammer-play and wrestling. They were warriors--these women! Tempered steel under silken skins, they pressed me hard now and again--strong as I was, quick as I might be. If Sirk were soldiered by such as these, it would be no easy conquest.

By the looks they gave me and by soft whispered words I knew I need not be lonely if Lur rode off to Karak. But she did not; she was ever at my side, and no more messengers came from Tibur; or if they did I did not know it. She had sent secret word to the High-priest that he had been right--I had no power to summon the Greater-than-Gods--that I was either imposter or mad. Or so she told me. Whether she had lied to him or, lied now to me I did not know and did not greatly care. I was too busy--living.

Yet no more did she call me Yellow-hair. Always it was Dwayanu. And every art of love of hers--and she was no novice, the Witch-woman--she used to bind me tighter to her.

It was early dawn of the third day; I was leaning from the casement, watching the misty jewel-fires of the luminous lilies fade, the mist wraiths that were the slaves of the waterfall rise slowly and more slowly. I thought Lur asleep. I heard her stir, and turned. She was sitting up, peering at me through the red veils of her hair. She looked all Witch-woman then...

"A messenger came to me last night from Yodin. To-day you pray to Khalk'ru."

A thrill went through me; the blood sang in my ears. Always had I felt so when I must evoke the Dissolver--a feeling of power that surpassed even that of victory. Different--a sense of inhuman power and pride. And with it a deep anger, revolt against this Being which was Life's enemy. This demon that fed on Ayjirland's flesh and blood--and soul. She was watching me. "Are you afraid, Dwayanu?" I sat beside her, parted the veils of her hair. "Was that why your kisses were dou-

bled last night, Lur? Why they were so--tender? Tenderness, Witch-
woman, becomes you--but it sits strangely on you. Were you afraid?
For me? You soften me, Lur!" Her eyes flashed, her face flushed at my
laughter.

"You do not believe I love you, Dwayanu?"

"Not so much as you love power. Witch-woman."

"You love me?"

"Not so much as I love power. Witch-woman," I answered, and
laughed again.

She studied me with narrowed eyes. She said:

"There is much talk in Karak of you. It grows menacing. Yodin
regrets that he did not kill you when he could have--but knows full
well the case might be worse if he had. Tibur regrets he did not kill
you when you came up from the river--urges that no more time be lost
in doing so. Yodin has declared you a false prophet and has promised
that the Greater-than-Gods will prove you so. He believes what I have
told you--or perhaps he has a hidden sword. You"--faint mockery crept
into her voice--"you, who can read me so easily, surely can read him
and guard against it! The people murmur; there are nobles who de-
mand you be brought forth; and the soldiers would follow Dwayanu
eagerly--if they believed you truly he. They are restless. Tales spread.
You have grown exceedingly--inconvenient. So you face Khalk'ru to-
day."

"If all that be true," I said, "it occurs to me that I may not have to
evoke the Dissolver to gain rule."

She smiled.

"It was not your old cunning which sent that thought. You will
be closely guarded. You would be slain before you could rally a dozen
round you. Why not--since there would then be nothing to lose by killing you? And perhaps something to be gained. Besides--what of your
promises to me?"

I thrust my arm around her shoulders, lifted and kissed her.

"As for being slain--well, I would have a thing to say to that. But
I was jesting, Lur. I keep my promises."

There was the galloping of horses on the causeway, the jangle of
accoutrement, the rattle of kettle-drums. I went over to the window.
Lur sprang from the bed and stood beside me. Over the causeway was
coming a troop of a hundred or more horsemen. From their spears
floated yellow pennons bearing the black symbol of Khalk'ru. They
paused at the open drawbridge. At their head I recognized Tibur, his

great shoulders covered by a yellow cloak, and on his breast the Kraken.

"They come to take you to the temple. I must let them pass."

"Why not?" I asked, indifferently. "But I'll go to no temple until I've broken my fast."

I looked again toward Tibur.

"And if I ride beside the Smith, I would you had a coat of mail to fit me."

"You ride beside me," she said. "And as for weapons, you shall have your pick. Yet there is nothing to fear on the way to the temple-- it is within it that danger dwells."

"You speak too much of fear, Witch-woman," I said, frowning. "Sound the horn. Tibur may think I am loath to meet him. And that I would not have him believe."

She sounded the signal to the garrison at the bridge. I heard it creaking as I bathed. And soon the horses were trampling before the door of the castle. Lur's tire-woman entered, and with her she slipped away.

I dressed leisurely. On my way to the great hall I stopped at the chamber of weapons. There was a sword there I had seen and liked. It was of the weight to which I was accustomed, and long and curved and of metal excellent as any I had ever known in Ayjirland. I weighed it in my left hand and took a lighter one for my right. I recalled that someone had told me to beware of Tibur's left hand...ah, yes, the woman soldier. I laughed--well, let Tibur beware of mine. I took a hammer, not so heavy as the Smith's...that was his vanity... there was more control to the lighter sledges...I fastened to my forearm the strong strap that held its thong. Then I went down to meet Tibur.

There were a dozen of the Ayjir nobles in the hall, mostly men. Lur was with them. I noticed she had posted her soldiers at various vantage points, and that they were fully armed. I took that for evidence of her good faith, although it somewhat belied her assurance to me that I need fear no danger until I had reached the temple. I had no fault to find in Tibur's greeting. Nor with those of the others. Except one. There was a man beside the Smith almost as tall as myself. He had cold blue eyes and in them the singular expressionless stare that marks the born killer of men. There was a scar running from left temple to chin, and his nose had been broken. The kind of man, I reflected, whom in the olden days I would have set over some peculiarly rebellious tribe. There was an arrogance about him that irritated me, but I held it down. It was not in my thoughts to provoke any conflict at this moment. I desired to raise no suspicions in the mind of the Smith. My greetings to him and to the others might be said to have had almost a touch of apprehension, of conciliation.

I maintained that attitude while we broke fast and drank. Once it was difficult. Tibur leaned toward the scar-face, laughing.

"I told you he was taller than you, Rascha. The grey stallion is mine!"

The blue eyes ran over me, and my gorge rose.

"The stallion is yours."

Tibur leaned toward me.

"Rascha the Back-breaker, he is named. Next to me, the strongest in Karak. Too bad you must meet the Greater-than-Gods so quickly. A match between you two would be worth the seeing."

Now my rage swelled up at this, and my hand dropped to my sword, but I managed to check it, and answered with a touch of eagerness.

"True enough--perhaps that meeting may be deferred..."

Lur frowned and stared at me, but Tibur snapped at the bait, his eyes gleaming with malice.

"No--there is one that may not be kept waiting. But after--perhaps..."

His laughter shook the table. The others joined in it. The scar-face grinned. By Zarda, but this is not to be borne! Careful, Dwayanu, thus you tricked them in the olden days--and thus you shall trick them now. I drained my goblet, and another. I joined them in their laughter--as though I wondered why they laughed. But I sealed their faces in my memory. We rode over the causeway with Lur at my right and a close half-circle of her picked women covering us.

Ahead of us went Tibur and the Back-breaker with a dozen of Tibur's strongest. Behind us came the troop with the yellow pennons, and behind them another troop of the Witch-woman's guards.

I rode with just the proper touch of dejection. Now and then the Smith and his familiars looked back at me. And I would hear their laughter. The Witch-woman rode as silently as I. She glanced at me askance, and when that happened I dropped my head a little lower.

The black citadel loomed ahead of us. We entered the city. By that time the puzzlement in Lur's eyes had changed almost to contempt, the laughter of the Smith become derisive.

The streets were crowded with the people of Karak. And now I sighed, and seemed to strive to arouse myself from my dejection, but still rode listlessly. And Lur bit her lip, and drew close to me, frowning.

"Have you tricked me, Yellow-hair? You go like a dog already beaten!"

I turned my head from her that she might not see my face. By Luka, but it was hard to stifle my own laughter!

There were whisperings, murmurings, among the crowd. There were no shouts, no greetings. Everywhere were the soldiers, sworded and armed with the hammers, spears and pikes ready. There were archers. The High-priest was taking no chances.

Nor was I.

It was no intention of mine to precipitate a massacre. None to give Tibur slightest excuse to do away with me, turn spears and arrow storm upon me. Lur had thought my danger not on my way to the temple, but when within it. I knew the truth was the exact opposite.

So it was no conquering hero, no redeemer, no splendid warrior from the past who rode through Karak that day. It was a man not sure of himself--or better, too sure of what was in store for him. The people who had waited and watched for Dwayanu felt that--and murmured, or were silent. That well pleased the Smith. And it well pleased me, who by now was as eager to meet Khalk'ru as any bridegroom his bride. And was taking no risks of being stopped by sword or hammer, spear or arrow before I could.

And ever the frown on the face of the Witch-woman grew darker, and stronger the contempt and fury in her eyes.

We skirted the citadel, and took a broad road leading back to the cliffs. We galloped along this, pennons flying, drums rolling. We came to a gigantic doorway in the cliff--many times had I gone through such a door as that! I dismounted, hesitatingly. Half-reluctantly, I let myself be led through it by Tibur and Lur and into a small rock-hewn chamber.

They left me, without a word. I glanced about. Here were the chests that held the sacrificial garments, the font of purification, the vessels for the anointing of the evoker of Khalk'ru.

The door opened. I looked into the face of Yodin.

There was vindictive triumph in it, and I knew he had met the Smith and Witch-woman, and that they had told him how I had ridden. As a victim to the Sacrifice! Well, Lur could tell him honestly what he hoped was the truth. If she had the thought to betray me--had betrayed me--she now believed me liar and braggart with quite as good reason as Tibur and the others. If she had not betrayed me, I had backed her lie to Yodin.

Twelve lesser priests filed in behind him, dressed in the sacred robes. The High-priest wore the yellow smock with the tentacles entwined round him. The ring of Khalk'ru shone on his thumb.

"The Greater-than-Gods awaits your prayer, Dwayanu," he said. "But first you must undergo purification."

I nodded. They busied themselves with the necessary rites. I submitted to them awkwardly, like one not familiar with them, but as one who plainly wished to be thought so. The malice in Yodin's eyes increased.

The rites were finished. Yodin took a smock like his own from a chest and draped it on me. I waited.

"Your ring," he reminded me, sardonically. "Have you forgotten you must wear the ring!"

I fumbled at the chain around my neck, opened the locket and slipped the ring over my thumb. The lesser priests passed from the chamber with their drums. I followed, the High-priest beside me. I heard the clang of a hammer striking a great anvil. And knew it for the voice of Tubalka, the oldest god, who had taught man to wed fire and metal. Tubalka's recognition of, his salutation and his homage to-- Khalk'ru!

The olden exaltation, the ecstasy of dark power, was pouring through me. Hard it was not to betray it. We came out of the passage and into the temple.

Hai! But they had done well by the Greater-than-Gods in this far shrine! Vaster temple I had never beheld in Ayjirland. Cut from the mountain's heart, as all Khalk'ru's abodes must be, the huge pillars which bordered the amphitheatre struck up to a ceiling lost in darkness. There were cressets of twisted metal and out of them sprang smooth spirals of wan yellow flame. They burned steadily and soundlessly; by their wan light I could see the pillars marching, marching away as though into the void itself.

Faces were staring up at me from the amphitheatre--hundreds of them. Women's faces under pennons and bannerets broidered with devices of clans whose men had fought beside and behind me in many a bloody battle. Gods--how few the men were here! They stared up at me, these women faces...women-nobles, women-knights, women-soldiers... They stared up at me by the hundreds...blue eyes ruthless...nor was there pity nor any softness of woman in their faces...warriors they were...Good! Then not as women but as warriors would I treat them.

And now I saw that archers were posted on the borders of the amphitheatre, bows in readiness, arrows at rest but poised, and the bow-strings lined toward me.

Tibur's doings? Or the priest's--watchful lest I should attempt escape? I had no liking for that, but there was no help for it. Luka, Lovely Goddess--turn your wheel so no arrow flies before I begin the ritual!

I turned and looked for the mystic screen which was Khalk'ru's doorway from the Void. It was a full hundred paces away from me, so broad and deep was the platform of rock. Here the cavern had been shaped into a funnel. The mystic screen was a gigantic disk, a score of times the height of a tall man. Not the square of lucent yellow through which, in the temples of the Mother-land, Khalk'ru had become corporeal. For the first time I felt a doubt--was this Being the same? Was there other reason for the High-priest's malignant confidence than his disbelief in me?

But there in the yellow field floated the symbol of the Greater-than-Gods; his vast black body lay as though suspended in a bubble-ocean of yellow space; his tentacles spread like monstrous rays of black stars and his dreadful eyes brooded on the temple as though, as always, they saw all and saw nothing. The symbol was unchanged. The tide of conscious, dark power in my mind, checked for that instant, resumed its upward flow.

And now I saw between me and the screen a semi-circle of women. Young they were, scarce blossomed out of girlhood--but already in fruit. Twelve of them I counted, each standing in the shallow hollowed cup of sacrifice, the golden girdles of the sacrifice around their waists. Over white shoulders, over young breasts, fell the veils of their ruddy hair, and through those veils they looked at me with blue eyes in which horror lurked. Yet though they could not hide that horror in their eyes from me who was so close, they hid it from those who watched us from beyond. They stood within the cups, erect, proudly, defiant. Ai! but they were brave--those women of Karak! I felt the olden pity for them; stirring of the olden revolt.

In the centre of the semi-circle of women swung a thirteenth ring, held by strong golden chains dropping from the temple's roof. It was empty, the clasps of the heavy girdle open--

The thirteenth ring! The ring of the Warrior's Sacrifice! Open for--me!

I looked at the High-priest. He stood beside his priests squatting at their drums. His gaze was upon me. Tibur stood at the edge of the platform beside the anvil of Tubalka, in his hands the great sledge, on his face reflection of the gloating on that of the High-priest. The Witch-woman I could not see.

The High-priest stepped forward. He spoke into the dark vastness of the temple where was the congregation of the nobles.

"Here stands one who comes to us calling himself--Dwayanu. If he be Dwayanu, then will the Greater-than-Gods, mighty Khalk'ru, hear his prayer and accept the Sacrifices. But if Khalk'ru be deaf to him--he is proven cheat and liar. And Khalk'ru will not be deaf to me who have served him faithfully. Then this cheat and liar swings within the Warrior's Ring for Khalk'ru to punish as he wills. Hear me! Is it just? Answer!"

From the depths of the temple came the voices of the witnesses.

"We hear! It is just!"

The High-priest turned to me as if to speak. But if that had been his mind, he changed it. Thrice he raised his staff of golden bells and shook them. Thrice Tibur raised the hammer and smote the anvil of Tubalka.

Out of the depths of the temple came the ancient chant, the ancient supplication which Khalk'ru had taught our forefathers when he chose us from all the peoples of earth, forgotten age upon forgotten age ago. I listened to it as to a nursery song. And Tibur's eyes never left me, his hand on hammer in readiness to hurl and cripple if I tried to flee; nor did Yodin's gaze leave me.

The chant ended.

Swiftly I raised my hands in the ancient sign, and I did with the ring what the ancient ritual ordered--and through the temple swept that first breath of cold that was presage of the coming of Khalk'ru!

Hai! The faces of Yodin and Tibur when they felt that breath! Would that I could look on them! Laugh now, Tibur! Hai! but they could not stop me now! Not even the Smith would dare hurl hammer nor raise hand to loose arrow storm upon me! Not even Yodin would dare halt me--I forgot all that. I forgot Yodin and Tibur. I forgot, as ever I forgot, the Sacrifices in the dark exultation of the ritual.

The yellow stone wavered, was shot through with tremblings. It became thin as air. It vanished.

Where it had been, black tentacles quivering, black body hovering, vanishing into immeasurable space, was Khalk'ru!

Faster, louder, beat the drums.

The black tentacles writhed forward. The women did not see them. Their eyes clung to me...as though...as though I held for them some hope that flamed through their despair! I...who had summoned their destroyer...

The tentacles touched them. I saw the hope fade and die. The tentacles coiled round their shoulders. They slid across their breasts. Embraced them. Slipped down their thighs and touched their feet. The drums began their swift upward flight into the crescendo of the Sacrifice's culmination.

The wailing of the women was shrill above the drums. Their white bodies became grey mist. They became shadows. They were gone--gone before the sound of their wailing had died. The golden girdles fell clashing to the rock--

What was wrong? The ritual was ended. The Sacrifice accepted. Yet Khalk'ru still hovered!

And the lifeless cold was creeping round me, was rising round me...

A tentacle swayed and writhed forward. Slowly, slowly, it passed the Warrior's Ring--came closer--closer--

It was reaching for me!

I heard a voice intoning. Intoning words more ancient than I had ever known. Words? They were not words! They were sounds whose roots struck back and back into a time before ever man drew breath.

It was Yodin--Yodin speaking in a tongue that might have been Khalk'ru's own before ever life was!

Drawing Khalk'ru upon me by it! Sending me along the road the Sacrifices had travelled!

I leaped upon Yodin. I caught him in my arms and thrust him between me and the questing tentacle. I raised Yodin in my arms as though he had been a doll and flung him to Khalk'ru. He went through the tentacle as though it had been cloud. He struck the chains that held the Warrior's Ring. He swung in them, entangled. He slithered down upon the golden girdle.

Hands upraised, I heard myself crying to Khalk'ru those same unhuman syllables. I did not know their meaning then, and do not know them now--nor from whence knowledge of them came to me...

I know they were sounds the throats and lips of men were never meant to utter!

But Khalk'ru heard--and heeded! He hesitated. His eyes stared at me, unfathomably--stared at and through me.

And then the tentacle curled back. It encircled Yodin. A thin screeching--and Yodin was gone!

The living Khalk'ru was gone. Lucent yellow, the bubble-ocean gleamed where he had been--the black shape floated inert within it.

I heard a tinkle upon the rock, the ring of Yodin rolling down the side of the cup. I leaped forward and picked it up.

Tibur, hammer half raised, stood glaring at me beside the anvil. I snatched the sledge from his hand, gave him a blow that sent him reeling.

I raised the hammer and crushed the ring of Yodin on the anvil!

From the temple came a thunderous shout--

"Dwayanu!"

XVIII. WOLVES OF LUR

I rode through the forest with the Witch-woman. The white falcon perched on her gauntleted wrist and cursed me with unwinking golden eyes. It did not like me--Lur's falcon. A score of her women rode behind us. A picked dozen of my own were shield for my back. They rode close. So it was of old. I liked my back covered. It was my sensitive part, whether with friends or foes.

The armourers had fashioned me a jacket of the light chain-mail. I wore it; Lur and our little troop wore them; and each was as fully armed as I with the two swords, the long dagger and the thonged hammer. We were on our way to reconnoitre Sirk.

For five days I had sat on the throne of the High-priest, ruling Karak with the Witch-woman and Tibur. Lur had come to me--penitent in her own fierce fashion. Tibur, all arrogance and insolence evaporated, had bent the knee, proffering me allegiance, protesting, reasonably enough, that his doubts had been but natural. I accepted his allegiance, with reservations. Sooner or later I would have to kill Tibur--even if I had not promised Lur his death. But why kill him before he ceased to be useful? He was a sharp-edged tool? Well, if he cut me in my handling of him, it would be only my fault. Better a crooked sharp knife than a straight dull one.

As for Lur--she was sweet woman flesh, and subtle. But did she greatly matter? Not greatly--just then. There was a lethargy upon me, a lassitude, as I rode beside her through the fragrant forest.

Yet I had received from Karak homage and acclaim more than enough to soothe any wounded pride. I was the idol of the soldiers. I rode through the streets to the shouts of the people, and mothers held their babes up to look on me. But there were many who were silent when I passed, averting their heads, or glancing at me askance with eyes shadowed by furtive hatred and fear.

Dara, the bold-eyed captain who had warned me of Tibur, and Naral, the swaggering girl who had given me her locket, I had taken for my own and had made them officers of my personal guard. They were devoted and amusing. I had spoken to Dara only that morning of those who looked askance at me, asking why.

"You want straight answer, Lord?"

"Always that, Dara."

She said bluntly:

"They are the ones who looked for a Deliverer. One who would break chains. Open doors. Bring freedom. They say Dwayanu is only another feeder of Khalk'ru. His butcher. Like Yodin. No worse, maybe. No better certainly."

I thought of that strange hope I had seen strangled in the eyes of the sacrifices. They too had hoped me Deliverer, instead of...

"What do you think, Dara?"

"I think as you think, Lord," she answered. "Only--it would not break my heart to see the golden girdles broken."

And I was thinking of that as I rode along with Lur, her falcon hating me with its unwinking glare. What was--Khalk'ru? Often and often, long and long and long ago, I had wondered that. Could the illimitable cast itself into such a shape as that which came to the call of the wearer of the ring? Or rather--would it? My empire had been widespread--under sun and moon and stars. Yet it was a mote in the sun-ray compared to the empire of the Spirit of the Void. Would one so great be content to shrink himself within the mote?

Ai! but there was no doubt that the Enemy of Life was! But was that which came to the summons of the ring--the Enemy of Life? And if not--then was this dark worship worth its cost?

A wolf howled. The Witch-woman threw back her head and answered it. The falcon stretched its wings, screaming. We rode from the forest into an open glade, moss-carpeted. She halted, sent again from her throat the wolf cry.

Suddenly around us was a ring of wolves. White wolves whose glowing green eyes were fixed on Lur. They ringed us, red tongues lolling, fangs glistening. A patter of pads, and as suddenly the circle of wolves was doubled. And others slipped through the trees until the circle was three-fold, four-fold...until it was a wide belt of living white flecked by scarlet flames of wolf-tongues, studded with glinting emeralds of wolf-eyes...

My horse trembled; I smelled its sweat.

Lur drove her knees into the sides of her mount and rode forward. Slowly she paced it round the inner circle of the white wolves. She raised her hand; something she said. A great dog-wolf arose from its haunches and came toward her. Like a dog, it put its paws upon her saddle. She reached down, caught its jowls in her hands. She whispered to it. The wolf seemed to listen. It slipped back to the circle and squatted, watching her. I laughed.

"Are you woman--or wolf, Lur?"

She said:

"I, too, have my followers, Dwayanu. You could not easily win these from me."

Something in her tone made me look at her sharply. It was the first time that she had shown resentment, or at least chagrin, at my popularity. She did not meet my gaze.

The big dog-wolf lifted its throat and howled. The circles broke. They spread out, padding swiftly ahead of us like scouts. They melted into the green shadows.

The forest thinned. Giant ferns took the place of the trees. I began to hear a curious hissing. Also it grew steadily warmer, and the air filled with moisture, and mist wreaths floated over the ferns. I could see no tracks, yet Lur rode steadily as though upon a well-marked road.

We came to a huge clump of ferns. Lur dropped from her horse.

"We go on foot here, Dwayanu. It is but a little way."

I joined her. The troop drew up but did not alight. The Witch-woman and I slipped through the ferns for a score of paces. The dog-wolf stalked just ahead of her. She parted the fronds. Sirk lay before me.

At right arose a bastion of perpendicular cliff, dripping with moisture, little of green upon it except small ferns clinging to precarious root-holds. At left, perhaps four arrow flights away, was a similar bastion, soaring into the haze. Between these bastions was a level platform of black rock. Its smooth and glistening foundations dropped into a moat as wide as two strong throws of a javelin. The platform curved outward, and from cliff to cliff it was lipped with one unbroken line of fortress.

Hai! But that was a moat! Out from under the right-hand cliff gushed a torrent. It hissed and bubbled as it shot forth, and the steam from it wavered over the cliff face like a great veil and fell upon us in a fine warm spray. It raced boiling along the rock base of the fortress, and jets of steam broke through it and immense bubbles rose and burst, scattering showers of scalding spray.

The fortress itself was not high. It was squat and solidly built, its front unbroken except for arrow slits close to the top. There was a parapet across the top. Upon it I could see the glint of spears and the heads of the guards. In only one part was there anything like towers. These were close to the centre where the boiling moat narrowed. Opposite them, on the farther bank, was a pier for a drawbridge. I could see the bridge, a narrow one, raised and protruding from between the two towers like a tongue.

Behind the fortress, the cliffs swept inward. They did not touch. Between them was a gap about a third as wide as the platform of the fortress. In front of us, on our side of the boiling stream, the sloping ground had been cleared both of trees and ferns. It gave no cover.

They had picked their spot well, these outlaws of Sirk. No besiegers could swim that moat with its hissing jets of live steam and bursting bubbles rising continually from the geysers at its bottom. No stones nor trees could dam it, making a causeway over which to march to batter at the fortress's walls. There was no taking of Sirk from this side. That was clear. Yet there must be more of Sirk than this.

Lur had been following my eyes, reading my thoughts.

"Sirk itself lies beyond those gates," she pointed to the gap between the cliffs. "It is a valley wherein is the city, the fields, the herds. And there is no way into it except through those gates."

I nodded, absently. I was studying the cliffs behind the fortress. I saw that these, unlike the bastions in whose embrace the platform lay, were not smooth. There had been falls of rock, and these rocks had formed rough terraces. If one could get to those terraces--unseen...

"Can we get closer to the cliff from which the torrent comes, Lur?"

She caught my wrist, her eyes bright.

"What do you see, Dwayanu?"

"I do not know as yet, Witch-woman. Perhaps nothing. Can we get closer to the torrent?"

"Come."

We slipped out of the ferns, skirted them, the dog-wolf walking stiff-legged in the lead, eyes and ears alert. The air grew hotter, vapour-filled, hard to breathe. The hissing became louder. We crept through the ferns, wet to the skins. Another step and I looked straight down upon the boiling torrent. I saw now that it did not come directly from the cliff. It shot up from beneath it, and its heat and its exhalations made me giddy. I tore a strip from my tunic and wrapped it around mouth and nose. I studied the cliff above it, foot by foot. Long I studied it and long--and then I turned.

"We can go back, Lur."

"What have you seen, Dwayanu?"

What I had seen might be the end of Sirk--but I did not tell her so. The thought was not yet fully born. It had never been my way to admit others into half-formed plans. It is too dangerous. The bud is more delicate than the flower and should be left to develop free from prying hands or treacherous or even well-meant meddling. Mature your plan and test it; then you can weigh with clear judgment any changes. Nor was I ever strong for counsel; too many pebbles thrown into the spring muddy it. That was one reason I was--Dwayanu. I said to Lur:

"I do not know. I have a thought. But I must weigh it."

She said, angrily:

"I am not stupid. I know war--as I know love. I could help you."--

I said, impatiently:

"Not yet. When I have made my plan I will tell it to you."

She did not speak again until we were within sight of the waiting women; then she turned to me. Her voice was low, and very sweet:

"Will you not tell me? Are we not equal, Dwayanu?"

"No," I answered, and left her to decide whether that was answer to the first question or both.

She mounted her horse, and we rode back through the forest.

I was thinking, thinking over what I had seen, and what it might mean, when I heard again the howling of the wolves. It was a steady, insistent howling. Summoning. The Witch-woman raised her head, listened, then spurred her horse forward. I shot my own after her. The white falcon fluttered, and beat up into the air, screeching.

We raced out of the forest and upon a flower-covered meadow. In the meadow stood a little man. The wolves surrounded him, weaving around and around one another in a witch-ring. The instant they caught sight of Lur, they ceased their cry--squatted on their haunches. Lur checked her horse and rode slowly toward them. I caught a glimpse of her face, and it was hard and fierce.

I looked at the little man. Little enough he was, hardly above one of my knees, yet perfectly formed. A little golden man with hair streaming down almost to his feet. One of the Rrrllya--I had studied the woven pictures of them on the tapestries, but this was the first living one I had seen--or was it? I had a vague idea that once I had been in closer contact with them than the tapestries.

The white falcon was circling round his head, darting down upon him, striking at him with claws and beak. The little man held an arm before his eyes, while the other was trying to beat the bird away.

The Witch-woman sent a shrill call to the falcon. It flew to her, and the little man dropped his arms. His eyes fell upon me.

He cried out to me, held his arms out to me, like a child.

There was appeal in cry and gesture. Hope, too, and confidence. It was like a frightened child calling to one whom it knew and trusted. In his eyes I saw again the hope that I had watched die in the eyes of the Sacrifices. Well, I would not watch it die in the eyes of the little man!

I thrust my horse past Lur's, and lifted it over the barrier of the wolves. Leaning from the saddle, I caught the little man up in my arms. He clung to me, whispering in strange trilling sounds.

I looked back at Lur. She had halted her horse beyond the wolves.

She cried:

"Bring him to me!"

The little man clutched me tight, and broke into a rapid babble of the strange sounds. Quite evidently he had understood, and quite as evidently he was imploring me to do anything other than turn him over to the Witch-woman.

I laughed, and shook my head at her. I saw her eyes blaze with quick, uncontrollable fury. Let her rage! The little man should go safe! I put my heels to the horse and leaped the far ring of wolves. I saw not far away the gleam of the river, and turned my horse toward it.

The Witch-woman gave one wild, fierce cry. And then there was the whirr of wings around my head, and the buffeting of wings about my ears. I threw up a hand. I felt it strike the falcon, and I heard it shriek with rage and pain. The little man shrank closer to me.

A white body shot up and clung for a moment to the pommel of my saddle, green eyes glaring into mine, red mouth slavering. I took a quick glance back. The wolf pack was rushing down upon me, Lur at their heels. Again the wolf leaped. But by this time I had drawn my sword. I thrust it through the white wolf's throat. Another leaped, tearing a strip from my tunic. I held the little man high up in one arm and thrust again.

Now the river was close. And now I was on its bank. I lifted the little man in both hands and hurled him far out into the water.

I turned, both swords in hand, to meet the charge of the wolves.

I heard another cry from Lur. The wolves stopped in their rush, so suddenly that the foremost of them slid and rolled. I looked over the river. Far out on it was the head of the little man, long hair floating behind him, streaking for the opposite shore.

Lur rode up to me. Her face was white, and her eyes were hard as blue jewels. She said in a strangled voice:

"Why did you save him?"

I considered that, gravely. I said:

"Because not twice would I see hope die in the eyes of one who trusts me."

She watched me, steadily; and the white-hot anger did not abate.

"You have broken the wings of my falcon, Dwayanu."

"Which do you love best. Witch-woman--its wing or my eyes?"

"You have killed two of my wolves."

"Two wolves--or my throat, Lur?"

She did not answer. She rode slowly back to her women. But I had seen tears in her eyes before she turned. They might have been of rage--or they might not. But it was the first time I had ever seen Lur weep.

With never a word to each other we rode back to Karak--she nursing the wounded falcon, I thinking over what I had seen on the cliffs of Sirk.

We did not stop at Karak. I had a longing for the quiet and beauty of the Lake of the Ghosts. I told Lur that. She assented indifferently, so we went straight on and came to it just as the twilight was thickening. With the women, we dined together in the great hall. Lur had shaken off her moodiness. If she still felt wrath toward me, she hid it well. We were merry and I drank much wine. The more I drank the clearer became my plan for the taking of Sirk. It was a good plan. After awhile, I went up with Lur to her tower and watched the waterfall and the beckoning mist wraiths, and the plan became clearer still.

Then my mind turned back to that matter of Khalk'ru. And I thought over that a long while. I looked up and found Lur's gaze intent upon me.

"What are you thinking, Dwayanu?"

"I am thinking that never again will I summon Khalk'ru."

She said, slowly, incredulously:

"You cannot mean that, Dwayanu!"

"I do mean it."

Her face whitened. She said:

"If Khalk'ru is not offered his Sacrifice, he will withdraw life from this land. It will become desert, as did the Mother-land when the Sacrifices were ended."

I said:

146

"Will it? That is what I have ceased to believe. Nor do I think you believe it, Lur. In the olden days there was land upon land which did not acknowledge Khalk'ru, whose people did not sacrifice to Khalk'ru--yet they were not desert. And I know, even though I do not know how I know, that there is land upon land to-day where Khalk'ru is not worshipped--yet life teems in them. Even here--the Rrrllya, the Little People, do not worship him. They hate him--or so you have told me--yet the land over Nanbu is no less fertile than here."

She said:

"That was the whisper that went through the Mother-land, long and long and long ago. It became louder--and the Mother-land became desert."

"There might have been other reasons than Khalk'ru's wrath for that, Lur."

"What were they?"

"I do not know," I said. "But you have never seen the sun and moon and stars. I have seen them. And a wise old man once told me that beyond sun and moon were other suns with other earths circling them, and upon them--life. The Spirit of the Void in which burn these suns should be too vast to shrink itself to such littleness as that which, in a little temple in this little corner of all earth, makes itself manifest to us."

She answered:

"Khalk'ru is! Khalk'ru is everywhere. He is in the tree that withers, the spring that dries. Every heart is open to him. He touches it-- and there comes weariness of life, hatred of life, desire for eternal death. He touches earth and there is sterile sand where meadows grew; the flocks grow barren. Khalk'ru is."

I thought over that, and I thought it was true enough. But there was a flaw in her argument.

"Nor do I deny that, Lur," I answered. "The Enemy of Life is. But is what comes to the ritual of the ring--Khalk'ru?"

"What else? So it has been taught from ancient days."

"I do not know what else. And many things have been taught from ancient days which would not stand the test. But I do not believe that which comes is Khalk'ru, Soul of the Void, He-to-Whom-All-Life-Must-Return and all the rest of his titles. Nor do I believe that if we end the Sacrifices life will end here with them."

She said, very quietly:

"Hear me, Dwayanu. Whether that which comes to the Sacrifices be Khalk'ru or another matters not at all to me. All that matters is

147

this: I do not want to leave this land, and I would keep it unchanged. I have been happy here. I have seen the sun and moon and stars. I have seen the outer earth in my waterfall yonder. I would not go into it. Where would I find a place so lovely as this my Lake of the Ghosts? If the Sacrifices end, they whom only fear keeps here will go. They will be followed by more and more. The old life I love ends with the Sacrifices--surely. For if desolation comes, we shall be forced to go. And if it does not come, the people will know that they have been taught lies, and will go to see whether what is beyond be not fairer, happier, than here. So it has always been. I say to you, Dwayanu--it shall not be here!"

She waited for me to answer. I did not answer.

"If you do not wish to summon Khalk'ru, then why not choose another in your place?"

I looked at her sharply. I was not ready to go quite that far as yet. Give up the ring, with all its power!

"There is another reason, Dwayanu, than those you have given me. What is it?"

I said, bluntly:

"There are many who call me feeder of Khalk'ru. Butcher for him. I do not like that. Nor do I like to see--what I see--in the eyes of the women I feed him."

"So that is it," she said, contemptuously. "Sleep has made you soft, Dwayanu! Better tell me your plan to take Sirk and let me carry it out! You have grown too tender-hearted for war, I think!"

That stung me, swept all my compunctions away. I jumped up, knocking away the chair, half-raised my hand to strike her. She faced me, boldly, no trace of fear in her eyes. I dropped my hand.

"But not so soft that you can mould me to your will, Witch," I said. "Nor do I go back on my bargains. I have given you Yodin. I shall give you Sirk, and all else I have promised. Till then--let this matter of the Sacrifices rest. When shall I give you Tibur?"

She put her hands on my shoulders and smiled into my angry eyes. She clasped her hands around my neck and brought my lips down to her warm red ones.

"Now," she whispered, "you are Dwayanu! Now the one I love--ah, Dwayanu, if you but loved me as I love you!"

Well, as for that, I loved her as much as I could any woman... After all, there was none like her. I swung her up and held her tight, and the old recklessness, the old love of life poured through me.

"You shall have Sirk! And Tibur when you will."

She seemed to consider.

"Not yet," she said. "He is strong, and he has his followers. He will be useful at Sirk, Dwayanu. Not before then--surely."

"It was precisely what I was thinking," I said. "On one thing at least we agree."

"Let us have wine upon our peace," she said, and called to her serving-women.

"But there is another thing also upon which we agree." She looked at me strangely.

"What is it?" I asked.

"You yourself have said it," she answered--and more than that I could not get her to say. It was long before I knew what she had meant, and then it was too late...

It was good wine. I drank more than I should have. But clearer and clearer grew my plan for the taking of Sirk.

It was late next morning when I awoke. Lur was gone. I had slept as though drugged. I had the vaguest memory of what had occurred the night before, except that Lur and I had violently disagreed about something. I thought of Khalk'ru not at all. I asked Ouarda where Lur had gone. She said that word had been brought early that two women set apart for the next Sacrifice had managed to escape. Lur thought they were making their way to Sirk. She was hunting them with the wolves. I felt irritated that she had not roused me and taken me with her. I thought that I would like to see those white brutes of hers in action. They were like the great dogs we had used in Ayjirland to track similar fugitives.

I did not go into Karak. I spent the day at sword-play and wrestling, and swimming in the Lake of the Ghosts--after my headache had worn off.

Close toward nightfall Lur returned.

"Did you catch them?" I asked.

"No," she said. "They got to Sirk safely. We were just in time to see them half-across the drawbridge."

I thought she was rather indifferent about it, but gave the matter no further thought. And that night she was gay--and most tender toward me. Sometimes so tender that I seemed to detect another emotion in her kisses. It seemed to me that they were--regretful. And I gave that no thought then either.

XIX. THE TAKING OF SIRK

Again I rode through the forest toward Sirk, with Lur at my left hand and Tibur beside her. At my back were my two captains, Dara and Naral. Close at our heels came Ouarda, with twelve slim, strong girls, fair skins stained strangely green and black, and naked except for a narrow belt around their waists. Behind these rode four score of the nobles with Tibur's friend Rascha at their head. And behind them marched silently a full thousand of Karak's finest fighting women.

It was night. It was essential to reach the edge of the forest before the last third of the stretch between midnight and dawn. The hoofs of the horses were muffled so that no sharp ears might hear their distant tread, and the soldiers marched in open formation, noiselessly. Five days had passed since I had first looked on the fortress.

They had been five days of secret, careful preparation. Only the Witch-woman and the Smith knew what I had in mind. Secret as we had been, the rumour had spread that we were preparing for a sortie against the Rrrllya. I was well content with that. Not until we had gathered to start did even Rascha, or so I believed, know that we were headed toward Sirk. This so no word might be carried there to put them on guard, for I knew well that those we menaced had many friends in Karak--might have them among the ranks that slipped along behind us. Surprise was the essence of my plan. Therefore the muffling of the horses' hoofs. Therefore the march by night. Therefore the silence as we passed through the forest. And therefore it was that when we heard the first howling of Lur's wolves the Witch-woman slipped from her horse and disappeared in the luminous green darkness.

We halted, awaiting her return. None spoke; the howls were stilled; she came from the trees and remounted. Like well-trained dogs the white wolves spread ahead of us, nosing over the ground we still must travel, ruthless scouts which no spy nor chance wanderer, whether from or to Sirk, could escape.

I had desired to strike sooner than this, had chafed at the delay, had been reluctant to lay bare my plan to Tibur. But Lur had pointed out that if the Smith were to be useful at Sirk's taking he would have to be trusted, and that he would be less dangerous if informed and eager than if uninformed and suspicious. Well, that was true. And Tibur was a first-class fighting man with strong friends.

So I had taken him into my confidence and told him what I had observed when first I had stood with Lur beside Sirk's boiling moat-- the vigorously growing clumps of ferns which extended in an almost unbroken, irregular line high up and across the black cliff, from the forest on the hither side and over the geyser-spring, and over the para-pets. It betrayed, I believed, a slipping or cracking of the rock which had formed a ledge. Along that ledge, steady-nerved, sure-footed climbers might creep, and make their way unseen into the fortress--and there do for us what I had in mind.

Tibur's eyes had sparkled, and he had laughed as I had not heard him laugh since my ordeal by Khalk'ru. He had made only one com-ment.

"The first link of your chain is the weakest, Dwayanu."

"True enough. But it is forged where Sirk's chain of defence is weakest."

"Nevertheless--I would not care to be the first to test that link."

For all my lack of trust, I had warmed to him for that touch of frankness.

"Thank the gods for your weight then, Anvil-smiter," I had said. "I cannot see those feet of yours competing for toe-holds with ferns. Otherwise I might have picked you."

I had looked down at the sketch I had drawn to make the matter clearer.

"We must strike quickly. How long before we can be in readi-ness, Lur?"

I had raised my eyes in time to see a swift glance pass between the two. Whatever suspicion I may have felt had been fleeting. Lur had answered, quickly.

"So far as the soldiers are concerned, we could start to-night. How long it will take to pick the climbers, I cannot tell. Then I must test them. All that will take time."

"How long, Lur? We must be swift."

"Three days--five days--I will be swift as may be. Beyond that I will not promise."

With that I had been forced to be content. And now, five nights later, we marched on Sirk. It was neither dark nor light in the forest; a strange dimness floated over us; the glimmer of the flowers was our torch. All the fragrances were of life. But it was death whose errand we were on.

The weapons of the soldiers were covered so that there could be no betraying glints; spear-heads darkened--no shining of metal upon any of us. On the tunics of the soldiers was the Wheel of Luka, so that friend would not be mistaken for foe once we were behind the walls of Sirk. Lur had wanted the Black Symbol of Khalk'ru.

I would not have it. We reached the spot where we had decided to leave the horses. And here in silence our force separated. Under leadership of Tibur and Rascha, the others crept through wood and fern-brake to the edge of the clearing opposite the drawbridge.

With the Witch-woman and myself went a scant dozen of the nobles, Ouarda with the naked girls, a hundred of the soldiers. Each of these had bow and quiver in well-protected cases on their backs. They carried the short battleaxe, long sword and dagger. They bore the long, wide rope ladder I had caused to be made, like those I had used long and long ago to meet problems similar to this of Sirk--but none with its peculiarly forbidding aspects. They carried another ladder, long and flexible and of wood. I was armed only with battleaxe and long sword, Lur and the nobles with the throwing hammers and swords.

We stole toward the torrent whose hissing became louder with each step.

Suddenly I halted, drew Lur to me.

"Witch-woman, can you truly talk to your wolves?"

"Truly, Dwayanu."

"I am thinking it would be no bad plan to draw eyes and ears from this end of the parapet. If some of your wolves would fight and howl and dance a bit there at the far bastion for the amusement of the guards, it might help us here."

She sent a low call, like the whimper of a she-wolf. Almost instantly the head of the great dog-wolf which had greeted her on our first ride lifted beside her. Its hackles bristled as it glared at me. But it made no sound. The Witch-woman dropped to her knees beside it, took its head in her arms, whispering. They seemed to whisper together. And then as suddenly as it had appeared, it was gone. Lur arose, in her eyes something of the green fire of the wolf's.

"The guards shall have their amusement."

I felt a little shiver along my back, for this was true witchcraft. But I said nothing and we went on. We came to that place from which I had scanned the cliff. We parted the ferns and peered out upon the fortress.

Thus it was. At our right, a score of paces away, soared the sheer wall of the cliff which, continuing over the boiling torrent, formed this nearer bastion. The cover in which we lurked ran up to it, was thrown back like a green wave from its base. Between our cover and the moat was a space not more than a dozen paces across, made barren by the hot spray that fell on it. Here, the walls of the fortress were not more than a javelin cast distant. The wall and the parapet touched the cliff, but hardly could they be seen through the thick veils of steam. And this was what I had meant when I had said that our weakest link would be forged where Sirk's defences were weakest. For no sentinels stood at this corner. With the heat and steam and exhalations from the geyser, there was no need--or so they thought. How, here at its hottest source, could the torrent be crossed? Who could scale that smooth and dripping cliff? Of all the defences, this spot was the impregnable one, unnecessary to guard--or so they thought. Therefore it was the exact point to attack--if it could be done.

I studied it. Not for full two hundred paces was there a single sentinel. From somewhere behind the fortress came the glare of a fire. It cast flickering shadows on the terraces of fallen rock beyond the bastioning cliffs; and that was good, since if we gained their shelter, we, too, would seem but flickering shadows. I beckoned Ouarda, and pointed to the rocks which were to be the goal of the naked girls. They were close to the cliff where it curved inward beyond the parapet, and they were about the height of twenty tall men above where we hid. She drew the girls to her and instructed them. They nodded, their eyes dropping swiftly to the cauldron of the moat, then turning to the glistening precipice. I saw some of them shudder. Well, I could not hold that against them, no!

We crept back and found the base of the cliff. Here were enough and to spare of rock holds for the grapnels of the ladder. We unwound the rope ladder. We set the wooden ladder against the cliff. I pointed out the ledge that might be the key to Sirk, counselled the climbers as best I could. I knew that the ledge could not be much wider than the span of a hand. Yet above it and below it were small crevices, pockets, where fingers and toes could grip, for clumps of ferns sprouted there.

Hai! But they had courage, those slim girls. We fastened to their belts long strong cords which would slip through our hands as they crept along. And they looked at one another's stained faces and bodies and laughed. The first went up the ladder like a squirrel, got foothold and handhold and began to edge across. In an instant she had vanished, the green and black with which her body was stained merging into the dim green and black of the cliff. Slowly, slowly, the first cord slipped through my fingers.

Another followed her, and another, until I held six cords. And now the others climbed up and crept out on the perilous path, their leashes held in the strong hands of the Witch-woman.

Hai! But that was queer fishing! With will strained toward keeping these girl-fish out of water! Slowly--Gods, but how slowly--the cords crept through my fingers! Through the fingers of the Witch-woman... slowly...slowly...but ever on and on.

Now that first slim girl must be over the cauldron...I had swift vision of her clinging to the streaming rock, the steam of the cauldron clothing her...

That line slackened in my hand. It slackened, then ran out so swiftly that it cut the skin...slackened again...a tug upon it as of a great fish racing away...I felt the line snap. The girl had fallen! Was now dissolving flesh in the cauldron!

The second cord slackened and tugged and snapped...and the third...Three of them gone! I whispered to Lur:

"Three are gone!"

"And two!" she said. I saw that her eyes were tightly closed, but the hands that clutched the cords were steady.

Five of those slim girls! Only seven left! Luka--spin your wheel!

On and on, slowly, with many a halt, the remaining cords crept through my fingers. Now the fourth girl must be over the moat...must be over the parapet...must be well on her way to the rocks...my heart beat in my throat, half-strangling me...Gods--the sixth had fallen! "Another!" I groaned to Lur. "And another!" she whispered, and cast the end of a cord from her hand.

Five left...only five now...Luka, a temple to you in Karak--all your own, sweet goddess!

What was that? A pull upon a cord, and twice repeated! The signal! One had crossed! Honour and wealth to you, slim girl...

"All gone but one, Dwayanu!" whispered the Witch-woman.

I groaned again, and glared at her...Again the twitches--upon my fifth cord! Another safe! "My last is over!" whispered Lur. Three safe! Three hidden among the rocks. The fishing was done. Sirk had stolen three-fourths of my bait.

But Sirk was hooked!

Weakness like none I had known melted bones and muscles. Lur's face was white as chalk, black shadows under staring eyes.

Well, now it was our turn. The slim maids who had fallen might soon have company!

I took the cord from Lur. Sent the signal. Felt it answered.

We cut the cords, and knotted their ends to heavier strands. And when they had run out we knotted to their ends a stronger, slender rope.

It crept away--and away--and away--

And now for the ladder--the bridge over which we must go.

It was light but strong, that ladder. Woven cunningly in a way thought out long and long ago. It had claws at each end which, once they had gripped, were not easily opened.

We fastened that ladder's end to the slender rope. It slipped away from us...over the ferns...out into the hot breath of the cauldron...through it.

Invisible within that breath...invisible against the green dusk of the cliff...on and on it crept...

The three maids had it! They were making it fast. Under my hands it straightened and stiffened. We drew it taut from our end. We fastened our grapnels.

The road to Sirk was open!

I turned to the Witch-woman. She stood, her gaze far and far away. In her eyes was the green fire of her wolves. And suddenly over the hissing of the torrent, I heard the howling of her wolves--far and far away.

She relaxed; her head dropped; she smiled at me--"Yes--truly can I talk to my wolves, Dwayanu!"

I walked to the ladder, tested it. It was strong, secure.

"I go first, Lur. Let none follow me until I have crossed. Then do you, Dara and Naral, climb to guard my back."

Lur's eyes blazed.

"I follow you. Your captains come after me."

I considered that. Well--let it be.

"As you say, Lur. But do not follow until I have crossed. Then let Ouarda send the soldiers. Ouarda--not more than ten may be on the ladder at a time. Bind cloths over their mouths and nostrils before they start. Count thirty--slowly, like this--before each sets forth behind the other. Fasten axe and sword between my shoulders, Lur. See to it that all bear their weapons so. Watch now, how I use my hands and feet."

I swung upon the ladder, arms and legs opened wide. I began to climb it. Like a spider. Slowly, so they could learn. The ladder swayed but little; its angle was a good one.

And now I was above the fern-brake. And now I was at the edge of the torrent. Above it. The stream swirled round me. It hid me. The hot breath of the geyser shrivelled me. Nor could I see anything of the ladder except the strands beneath me...

Thank Luka for that! If what was before me was hidden--so was I hidden from what was before me!

I was through the steam. I had passed the cliff. I was above the parapet. I dropped from the ladder, among the rocks--unseen. I shook the ladder. There was a quivering response. There was weight upon it... more weight...and more...

I unstrapped axe and sword--

"Dwayanu--"

I turned. There were the three maids. I began to praise them-- holding back laughter. Green and black had run and combined under bath of steam into grotesque pattern.

"Nobles you are, maids! From this moment! Green and black your colours. What you have done this night will long be a tale in Karak."

I looked toward the battlements. Between us and them was a smooth floor of rock and sand, less than half a bow-shot wide. A score of soldiers stood around the fire. There was a larger group on the parapet close to the towers of the bridge. There were more at the farther end of the parapet, looking at the wolves.

The towers of the drawbridge ran straight down to the rocky floor. The tower at the left was blank wall. The tower at the right had a wide gate. The gate was open, unguarded, unless the soldiers about the fire were its guards. Down from between the towers dropped a wide ramp, the approach to the bridge-head.

There was a touch on my arm. Lur was beside me. And close after her came my two captains. After them, one by one, the soldiers. I bade them string bows, set arrows. One by one they melted out of the green darkness, slipped by me. They made ready in the shadow of the rocks.

One score--two score...a shriek cut like an arrow through the hissing of the torrent! The ladder trembled. It shook--and twisted...Again the despairing cry...the ladder fell slack!

"Dwayanu--the ladder is broken? At--Ouarda--"

"Quiet, Lur! They may have heard that shrieking. The ladder could not break..."

"Draw it in, Dwayanu--draw it in!"

156

Together we pulled upon it. It was heavy. We drew it in like a net, and swiftly. And suddenly it was of no weight at all. It rushed into our hands--

Its ends were severed as though by knife slash or axe blow.

"Treachery!" I said.

"But treachery...how...with Ouarda on guard."

I crept, crouching, behind the shadow of the rocks.

"Dara--spread out the soldiers. Tell Naral to slip to the farther end. On the signal, let them loose their arrows. Three flights only. The first at those around the fire. The second and the third at those on the walls closest to the towers. Then follow me. You understand me?"

"It is understood, Lord."

The word went along the line; I heard the bowstrings whisper.

"We are fewer than I like, Lur--yet nothing for us but to go through with it. No way out of Sirk now but the way of the sword."

"I know. It is of Ouarda I am thinking..." Her voice trembled.

"She is safe. If treachery had been wide-spread, we would have heard sounds of fighting. No more talking, Lur. We must move swiftly. After the third arrow flight, we rush the tower gate."

I gave the signal. Up rose the archers. Straight upon those around the fire flew their shafts. They left few alive. Instantly upon those around the towers of the bridge whistled a second arrow storm.

Hai! But that was straight shooting! See them fall! Once more--

Whistle of feathered shaft! Song of the bow-string! Gods--but this is to live again!

I dropped down the rocks, Lur beside me. The soldier women poured after us. Straight to the tower door we sped. We were half-way there before those upon the long parapet awakened.

Shouts rang. Trumpets blared, and the air was filled with the brazen clangour of a great gong bellowing the alarm to Sirk asleep behind the gap. We sped on. Javelins dropped among us, arrows whistled. From other gates along the inner walls guards began to emerge, racing to intercept us.

We were at the door of the bridge towers--and through it!

But not all. A third had fallen under javelin and arrow. We swung the stout door shut. We dropped across it the massive bars that secured it. And not an instant too soon. Upon the door began to beat the sledges of the tricked guards.

The chamber was of stone, huge and bare. Except for the door through which we had come, there was no opening. I saw the reason for that--never had Sirk expected to be attacked from within. There were arrow slits high up, looking over the moat, and platforms for archers. At one side were cogs and levers which raised and lowered the bridge.

All this I took in at one swift glance. I leaped over to the levers, began to manipulate them. The cogs revolved.

The bridge was falling!

The Witch-woman ran up to the platform of the archers; she peered out; set horn to lips; she sent a long call through the arrow slit-- summoning signal for Tibur and his host.

The hammering against the door had ceased. The blows against it were stronger, more regular-timed. The battering of a ram. The stout wood trembled under them; the bars groaned, Lur called to me:

"The bridge is down, Dwayanu! Tibur is rushing upon it. It grows lighter. Dawn is breaking. They have brought their horses!"

I cursed.

"Luka, sent him wit not to pound across that bridge on horse!"

"He is doing it...he and Rascha and a handful of others only... the rest are dismounting..."

"Hai--they are shooting at them from the arrow slits...the jave- lins rain among them...Sirk takes toll..."

There was a thunderous crash against the door. The wood split...

A roaring tumult. Shouts and battle cries. Ring of sword upon sword and the swish of arrows. And over it all the laughter of Tibur.

No longer was the ram battering at the door.

I threw up the bars, raised axe in readiness, opened the great gate a finger's breadth and peered out.

The soldiers of Karak were pouring down the ramp from the bridge-head.

I opened the door wider. The dead of the fortress lay thick around tower base and bridge-head.

I stepped through the door. The soldiers saw me.

"Dwayanu!" rang their shout.

From the fortress still came the clamour of the great gong-- warning Sirk.

Sirk--no longer sleeping!

XX. "TSANTAWU-FAREWELL!"

There was a humming as of a disturbed gigantic hive beyond Sirk's gap. Trumpet blasts and the roll of drums. Clang of brazen gongs answering that lonely one which beat from the secret heart of the raped fortress. And ever Karak's women-warriors poured over the bridge until the space behind the fortress filled with them.

The Smith wheeled his steed--faced me. "Gods--Tibur! But that was well done!"

"Never done but for you, Dwayanu! You saw, you knew--you did. Ours the least part."

Well, that was true. But I was close to liking Tibur then. Life of my blood! It had been no play to lead that charge against the bridge end. The Smith was a soldier! Let him be only half loyal to me--and Khalk'ru take the Witch-woman!

"Sweep the fortress clean, Anvil-smiter. We want no arrows at our backs."

"It is being swept, Dwayanu."

By brooms of sword and spear, by javelin and arrow, the fortress was swept clean.

The clamour of the brazen gong died on a part stroke.

My stallion rested his nose on my shoulder, blew softly against my ear.

"You did not forget my horse! My hand to you, Tibur!"

"You lead the charge, Dwayanu!" I leaped upon the stallion. Battleaxe held high I wheeled and galloped toward the gap. Like the point of a spear I sped, Tibur at my left, the Witch-woman at my right, the nobles behind us, the soldiers sweeping after us.

We hurled ourselves through the cliffed portal of Sirk.

A living wave lifted itself to throw us back. Hammers flew, axes hewed, javelins and spears and feathered shafts sleeted us. My horse tottered and dropped, screaming, his hinder hocks cut through. I felt a hand upon my shoulder, dragging me to my feet. The Witch-woman smiled at me. She sliced with her sword the arm drawing me down among the dead. With axe and sword we cleared a ring around us. I threw myself on the back of a grey from which a noble had fallen, bristling with arrows.

We thrust forward against the living wave. It gave, curling round us.

On and on! Cut sword and hew axe! Cut and slash and batter through!

The curling wave that tore at us was beaten down. We were through the gap. Sirk lay before us.

I reined in my horse. Sirk lay before us--but too invitingly!

The city nestled in a hollow between sheer, unscalable black walls. The lip of the gap was higher than the roof of the houses. They began an arrow flight away. It was a fair city. There was no citadel nor forts; there were no temples nor palaces. Only houses of stone, perhaps a thousand of them, flat roofed, set wide apart, gardens around them, a wide street straying among them, tree-bordered. There were many lanes. Beyond the city fertile field upon field, and flowering orchards.

And no battle ranks arrayed against us. The way open.

Too open!

I caught the glint of arms on the housetops. There was the noise of axes above the blaring of trumpets and the roll of the kettle-drums.

Hai! They were barricading the wide street with their trees, preparing a hundred ambushes for us, expecting us to roll down in force.

Spreading the net in the sight of Dwayanu!

Yet they were good tactics. The best defence I had met with it in many a war against the barbarians. It meant we must fight for every step, with every house a fort, with arrows searching for us from every window and roof. They had a leader here in Sirk, to arrange such reception on such brief notice! I had respect for that leader, whoever he might be. He had picked the only possible way to victory--unless those against whom he fought knew the countermove.

And that, hard earned, I did know.

How long could this leader keep Sirk within its thousand forts? There, always, lay the danger in this defence. The overpowering impulse of a pierced city is to swarm out upon its invaders as ants and bees do from their hills and nests. Not often is there a leader strong enough to hold them back. If each house of Sirk could remain linked to the other, each ever an active part of the whole--then Sirk might be unconquerable. But how, when they began to be cut off, one by one? Isolated? The leader's will severed?

Hai! Then it is that despair creeps through every chink! They are drawn out by fury and despair as though by ropes. They pour out--to kill or to be killed. The cliff crumbles, stone by stone. The cake is eaten by the attackers, crumb by crumb.

I divided our soldiers, and sent the first part against Sirk in small squads, with orders to spread and to take advantage of all cover. They were to take the outer fringe of houses, at all costs, shooting their arrows up in the high curved flight against the defenders while others hammered their way into those houses. Still others were to attack farther on, but never getting too far from their comrades nor from the broad way running through the city.

I was casting a net over Sirk and did not want its meshes broken.

By now it was broad daylight.

The soldiers moved forward. I saw the arrows stream up and down, twisting among each other like serpents...I heard the axe-blows on the doors...By Luka! There floats a banner of Karak from one of the roofs! And another.

The hum of Sirk shot higher, became louder, in it a note of madness. Hai! I knew they could not long stand this nibbling! And I knew that sound! Soon it would rise to frenzy. Drone from that into despair!

Hai! Not long now before they came tumbling out...

Tibur was cursing at my elbow. I looked at Lur, and she was trembling. The soldiers were murmuring, straining at the leash, mad to join battle. I looked at their blue eyes, hard and cold; their faces beneath the helmet-caps were not those of women but of young warriors...those who sought in them for woman's mercy would have rude awakening!

"By Zarda! But the fight will be done before we can dip blade!" I laughed.

"Patience, Tibur! Patience is our strong weapon. Sirk's strongest--if they but knew it. Let them be first to lose that weapon."

The turmoil grew louder. At the head of the street appeared half a hundred of Karak's soldiers, struggling against more than equal number which steadily, swiftly, was swelled by others of Sirk pouring from side lanes and dropping from roofs and windows of the beleaguered houses.

It was the moment for which I had waited!

I gave the command. I raised the battle-cry. We drove down upon them. Our skirmishers opened to let us through, melting into the shouting ranks behind. We ripped into the defenders of Sirk. Down they went, but as they fell they fought, and many a saddle of the nobles was empty, and many were the steeds lost before we won to the first barricade.

Hai! But how they fought us there from behind the hastily felled trees--women and men and children hardly big enough to bend the bow or wield the knife!

Now the soldiers of Karak began to harry them from the sides; the soldiers of Karak shot into them from the tops of the houses they had abandoned; we fought Sirk as it had planned to fight us. And those who fought against us soon broke and fled, and we were over the barricade. Battling, we reached the heart of Sirk, a great and lovely square in which fountains played and flowers blossomed. The spray of the fountains was crimson and there were no flowers when we left that square.

We paid heavy toll there. Full half of the nobles were slain. A spear had struck my helmet and well-nigh dropped me. Bare-headed, blood-flecked I rode, shouting, sword dripping red. Naral and Dara both bore wounds, but still guarded my back. The Witch-woman, and the Smith and his scarred familiar fought on, untouched.

There was a thunder of hoofs. Down upon us swept a wave of horsemen. We raced toward them. We struck like two combers. Surged up. Mingled. Flash swords! Hammers smite! Axes cleave! Hai! But now it was hand-to-hand in the way I knew best and best loved!

We swirled in a mad whirlpool. I glanced at right and saw the Witch-woman had been separated from me. Tibur, too, was gone. Well, they were giving good account of themselves no doubt--wherever they were.

I swung to right and to left with my sword. In the front of those who fought us, over the caps of Karak which had swirled between us, was a dark face...a dark face whose black eyes looked steadily into mine--steadily...steadily. At the shoulder of that man was a slighter figure whose clear, brown eyes stared at me...steadily...steadily. In the black eyes was understanding and sorrow. The brown eyes were filled with hate.

Black eyes and brown eyes touched something deep and deep within me...They were rousing that something...calling to it...something that had been sleeping.

I heard my own voice shouting command to cease fighting, and at that shout abruptly all sound of battle close by was stilled. Sirk and Karak alike stood silent, amazed, staring at me. I thrust my horse through the press of bodies, looked deep into the black eyes.

And wondered why I had dropped my sword...why I stood thus...and why the sorrow in those eyes racked my heart...The dark-faced man spoke--two words--

"Leif!...Degataga!"

That something which had been asleep was wide awake, rushing up through me...rocking my brain...tearing at it...shaking every nerve...

I heard a cry--the voice of the Witch-woman.

A horse burst through the ring of the soldiers. Upon it was Rascha, lips drawn back over his teeth, cold eyes glaring into mine. His arm came up. His dagger gleamed, and was hidden in the back of the man who had called me--Degataga!

Had called me--

God--but I knew him!

Tsantawu! Jim!

The sleeping thing that had awakened was all awake...it had my brain...it was myself...Dwayanu forgotten!

I threw my horse forward.

Rascha's arm was up for second stroke--the brown-eyed rider was swinging at him with sword, and Jim was falling, settling over his horse's mane.

I caught Rascha's arm before the dagger could descend again. I caught his arm, bent it back, and heard the bone snap. He howled--like a wolf.

A hammer hummed by my head, missing it by a hair. I saw Tibur drawing it back by its thong.

I leaned and lifted Rascha from his saddle. His sound arm swept up, hand clutching at my throat. I caught the wrist and twisted that arm back I snapped it as I had the other.

My horse swerved. With one hand at Rascha's throat, the other arm holding him, I toppled from the saddle bearing him down with me. I fell upon him. I twisted, and threw him over the bar of my knee. My hand slipped from his throat to his chest. My right leg locked over his.

A swift downward thrust--a sound like the breaking of a faggot. The Back-breaker would break no more backs. His own was broken.

I leaped to my feet. Looked up into the face of the brown-eyed rider...Evalie!...

I cried out to her--"Evalie!"

Abruptly, all about me the battle broke out afresh. Evalie turned to meet the charge. I saw Tibur's great shoulders rise behind her... saw him snatch her from her horse...saw from his left hand a flash of light...It sped toward me...I was hurled aside. None too soon--not soon enough--

Something caught me a glancing blow upon the side of my head. I went down upon my knees and hands, blind and dizzy. I heard Tibur laughing; I strove to conquer blind dizziness and nausea, felt blood streaming down my face.

And crouching, swaying on knees and hands, heard the tide of battle sweep around and over and past me.

My head steadied. The blindness was passing. I was still on my hands and knees. Under me was the body of a man--a man whose black eyes were fixed on mine with understanding--with love!

I felt a touch on my shoulder; with difficulty I looked up. It was Dara.

"A hair between life and death. Lord. Drink this."

She put a phial to my lips. The bitter, fiery liquid coursed through me, brought steadiness, brought strength. I could see there was a ring of soldier-women around me, guarding me--beyond them a ring of others, on horses.

"Can you hear me, Leif?...I haven't much time..."

I lurched aside and knelt.

"Jim! Jim! Oh, God--why did you come here? Take this sword and kill me!"

He reached for my hand, held it tight.

"Don't be a damned fool, Leif! You couldn't help it...but you've got to save Evalie!"

"I've got to save you, Tsantawu--get you out of here--"

"Shut up and listen. I've got mine, Leif, and I know it. That blade went through the mail right into the lungs...I'm trickling out--inside...hell, Leif--don't take it so hard...It might have been in the war...It might have been any time...It's not your fault..."

A sob shook me, tears mingled with the blood upon my face.

"But I killed him, Jim--I killed him!"

"I know, Leif...a neat job...I saw you...but there's something I've got to tell you..." his voice faltered.

I put the phial to his lips--it brought him back.

"Just now...Evalie...hates you! You have to save her...Leif ... whether she does or not. Listen. Word came to us from Sirk through the Little People that you wanted us to meet you there. You were pretending to be Dwayanu...pretending to remember nothing but Dwayanu...to allay suspicion and to gain power. You were going to slip away...come to Sirk, and lead it against Karak. You needed me to stand beside you...needed Evalie to persuade the pygmies..."

"I sent you no message, Jim!" I groaned.

"I know you didn't--now...But we believed it...You saved Sri from the wolves and defied the Witch-woman--"

"Jim--how long was it after Sri's escape that the lying message came?"

"Two days...What does it matter? I'd told Evalie what was-- wrong--with you...gone over your story again and again. She didn't understand...but she took me on faith...Some more of that stuff, Leif...I'm going..."

Again the fiery draught revived him.

"We reached Sirk...two days ago...across the river with Sri and twenty pygmies...it was easy...too easy...not a wolf howled, although I knew the beasts were watching us...stalking us...and the others did, too. We waited...then came the attack...and then I knew we had been trapped...How did you get over those geysers...Big Fellow...never mind...but...Evalie believes you sent the message...you...black treach- ery..."

His eyes closed. Cold, cold were his hands.

"Tsantawu--brother--you do not believe! Tsantawu--come back...speak to me..."

His eyes opened, but hardly could I hear him speak--

"You're not Dwayanu--Leif? Not now--or ever again?"

"No, Tsantawu...don't leave me!"

"Bend...your head...closer, Leif...keep fighting...save Evalie."

Fainter grew his voice:

"Good-bye...Degataga...not your fault..."

A ghost of the old sardonic smile passed over the white face.

"You didn't pick your...damned...ancestors!...Worse luck...We've had...hell of good times...together... Save...Evalie..."

There was a gush of blood from his mouth.

Jim was dead...was dead.

Tsantawu--no more!

BOOK OF LEIF

XXI. RETURN TO KARAK

I leaned over Jim and kissed his forehead. I arose. I was numb with sorrow. But under that numbness seethed a tortured rage, a tortured horror. Deadly rage against the Witch-woman and the Smith--horror of myself, of what I had been...horror of--Dwayanu!

I must find Tibur and the Witch-woman--but first there was something else to be done. They and Evalie could wait.

"Dara--have them lift him. Carry him into one of the houses."

I followed on foot as they bore Jim away. There was fighting still going on, but far from us. Here were only the dead. I guessed that Sirk was making its last stand at the end of the valley.

Dara, Naral and I and half-dozen more passed through the broken doors of what yesterday had been a pleasant home. In its centre was a little columned hall. The other soldiers clustered round the broken doors, guarding entrance. I ordered chairs and beds and whatever else would burn brought into the little hall and heaped into a pyre. Dara said:

"Lord, let me bathe your wound."

I dropped upon a stool, sat thinking while she washed the gash upon my head with stinging wine. Beyond the strange numbness, my mind was very clear. I was Leif Langdon. Dwayanu was no longer master of my mind--nor ever again would be. Yet he lived. He lived within as part of--myself. It was as though the shock of recognition of Jim had dissolved Dwayanu within Leif Langdon.

As though two opposing currents had merged into one; as though two drops had melted into each other; as though two antagonistic metals had fused.

Crystal clear was every memory of what I had heard and seen, said and done and thought from the time I had been hurled from Nansur Bridge. And crystal clear, agonizingly clear, was all that had gone before. Dwayanu was not dead, no! But part of me, and I was by far the stronger. I could use him, his strength, his wisdom--but he could not use mine. I was in control. I was the master.

And I thought, sitting there, that if I were to save Evalie--if I were to do another thing that now I knew, I would do or die in the doing, I must still outwardly be all Dwayanu. There lay my power. Not easily could such transmutation as I had undergone be explained to my soldiers. They believed in me and followed me as Dwayanu. If Evalie, who had known me as Leif, who had loved me as Leif, who had listened to Jim, could not understand--how much less could these? No, they must see no change.

I touched my head. The cut was deep and long; apparently only the toughness of my skull had saved it from being split.

"Dara--you saw who made this wound?"

"It was Tibur, Lord."

"He tried to kill me...Why did he not finish?"

"Never yet has Tibur's left hand failed to deal death. He thinks it cannot fail. He saw you fall--he thought you dead."

"And death missed me by a hair's-breadth. And would not, had not someone hurled me aside. Was that you, Dara?"

"It was I, Dwayanu. I saw his hand dip into his girdle, knew what was coming. I threw myself at your knees--so he could not see me."

"Why, because you fear Tibur?"

"No--because I wanted him to believe he did not miss."

"Why?"

"So that you would have better chance to kill Tibur, Lord. Your strength was ebbing with your friend's life."

I looked sharply at this bold-eyed captain of mine. How much did she know? Well, time later to find that out. I looked at the pyre. It was nearly complete.

"What was it he threw, Dara?"

She drew from her girdle a curious weapon, one whose like I had never seen. Its end was top-shaped, pointed like a dagger and with four razor-edged ribs on its sides. It had an eight-inch metal haft, round, like the haft of a diminutive javelin. It weighed about five pounds. It was of some metal I did not recognize--denser, harder than the finest of tempered steel. It was, in effect, a casting knife. But no mail could turn aside that adamantine point when hurled with the strength of one like the Smith. Dara took it from me, and pulled the short shaft. Instantly the edged ribs flew open, like flanges. The end of each was shaped like an inverted barb. A devilish tool, if I ever saw one. Once embedded, there was no way to get it out except cutting, and any pull would release the flanges, hooking them at the same time into the flesh. I took it back from Dara, and placed it in my own girdle. If I had had any doubts about what I was going to do to Tibur--I had none now.

The pyre was finished. I walked over to Jim, and laid him on it. I kissed him on the eyes, and put a sword in his dead hand. I stripped the room of its rich tapestries and draped them over him. I struck flint and set flame to the pyre. The wood was dry and resinous, and burned swiftly. I watched the flames creep up and up until smoke and fire made a canopy over him.

Then dry-eyed, but with death in my heart. I walked out of that house and among my soldiers.

Sirk had fallen and its sack was on. Smoke was rising every-where from the looted homes. A detachment of soldiers marched by, herding along some two-score prisoners--women, all of them, and little children; some bore the marks of wounds. And then I saw that among those whom I had taken for children were a handful of the golden pygmies. At sight of me the soldiers halted, stood rigid, staring at me unbelievingly.

Suddenly one cried out..."Dwayanu! Dwayanu lives!"...They raised their swords in salute, and from them came a shout..."Dwayanu!"

I beckoned their captain.

"Did you think Dwayanu dead then?"

"So ran the tale among us, Lord."

"And did this tale also tell how I was slain?"

She hesitated.

"There were some who said it was by the Lord Tibur...by acci-dent... that he had made cast at Sirk's leader who was menacing you...and that you were struck instead...and that your body had been borne away by those of Sirk...I do not know..."

"Enough, soldier. Go on to Karak with the captives. Do not loi-ter, and do not speak of seeing me. It is a command. For a while I let the tale stand."

They glanced at each other, oddly, saluted, and went on. The yellow eyes of the pygmies, filled with a venomous hatred, never left me until they had passed out of range. I waited, thinking. So that was to be the story! Hai! But they had fear at their elbows or they would not have troubled to spread that tale of accident! Suddenly I made de-cision. No use to wander over Sirk searching for Tibur. Folly to be seen, and have the counter-tale that Dwayanu lived be borne to the ears of Tibur and Lur! They should come to me--unknowing.

There was only one way out of Sirk, and that by the bridge. It was there I would await them. I turned to Dara.

"We go to the bridge, but not by this road. We take the lanes until we reach the cliffs."

They wheeled their horses, and for the first time I realized that all this little troop of mine were mounted. And for the first time I realized that all were of my own guard, and that many of them had been foot-soldiers, yet these, too, were riding, and that upon a score of saddles were the colours of nobles who had followed me and the Witch-woman and Tibur through the gap of Sirk. It was Naral who, reading my perplexity, spoke, half-impudently as always:

"These are your most faithful, Dwayanu! The horses were idle--or a few we made so. For your better shield should Tibur--make mistake again."

I said nothing to that until we had gone around the burning house and were under cover of one of the lanes. Then I spoke to them:

"Naral--Dara--let us talk apart for a moment."

And when we had drawn a little away from the others, I said:

"To you two I owe my life--most of all to you, Dara. All that I can give you is yours for the asking. All I ask of you is--truth."

"Dwayanu--you shall have it."

"Why did Tibur want to kill me?"

Naral said, dryly:

"The Smith was not the only one who wanted you killed, Dwayanu."

I knew that, but I wanted to hear it from them.

"Who else, Naral?"

"Lur--and most of the nobles."

"But why? Had I not opened Sirk for them?"

"You were becoming too strong, Dwayanu. It is not in Lur or Tibur to take second place--or third...or maybe no place."

"But they had opportunity before--"

"But you had not taken Sirk for them," said Dara.

Naral said, resentfully:

"Dwayanu, you play with us. You know as well as we--better--what the reason was. You came here with that friend we have just left on his fire couch. All knew it. If you were to die--so must he die. He must not live, perhaps to escape and bring others into this place--for I know, as some others do, that there is life beyond here and that Khalk'ru does not reign supreme, as the nobles tell us. Well--here together are you and this friend of yours. And not only you two, but also the dark girl of the Rrrllya, whose death or capture might break the spirit of the little folk and put them under Karak's yoke. The three of you--together! Why, Dwayanu--it was the one place and the one time to strike! And Lur and Tibur did--and killed your friend, and think they have killed you, and have taken the dark girl."

"And if I kill Tibur, Naral?"

"Then there will be fighting. And you must guard yourself well, for the nobles hate you, Dwayanu. They have been told you are against the old customs--mean to debase them, and raise the people. Intend even to end the Sacrifices..."

She glanced at me, slyly.

"And if that were true?"

"You have most of the soldiers with you now, Dwayanu. If it were true you would also have most of the people. But Tibur has his friends--even among the soldiers. And Lur is no weakling."

She twitched up her horse's head, viciously.

"Better kill Lur, too, while you're in the mood, Dwayanu!"

I made no answer to that. We trotted through the lanes, not speaking again. Everywhere were dead, and gutted houses. We came out of the city, and rode over the narrow plain to the gap between the cliffs. There happened to be none on the open road just then; so we entered the gap unnoticed. We passed through it out into the square behind the fortress. There were soldiers here, in plenty, and groups of captives. I rode in the centre of my troop, bent over the neck of my horse. Dara had roughly bandaged my head. The bandages and cap-helmet I had picked up hid my yellow hair. There was much confusion, and I passed through unnoticed. I rode straight to the door of the tower behind which we had lurked when Karak stormed the bridge. I slipped in with my horse, half-closed the door. My women grouped themselves outside. They were not likely to be challenged. I settled down to wait for Tibur.

It was hard waiting, that! Jim's face over the camp-fire. Jim's face grinning at me in the trenches. Jim's face above mine when I lay on the moss bank of the threshold of the mirage--Jim's face under mine on the street of Sirk...

Tsantawu! Aie--Tsantawu! And you thought that only beauty could come from the forest I

Evalie? I cared nothing for Evalie then, caught in that limbo which at once was ice and candent core of rage.

"Save...Evalie!" Jim had bade. Well, I would save Evalie! Beyond that she mattered no more than did the Witch-woman...yes, a little more...I had a score to satisfy with the Witch-woman...I had none with Evalie...

The face of Jim...always the face of Jim...floating before me. ...

I heard a whisper--

"Dwayanu--Tibur comes!"

"Is Lur with him, Dara?"

"No--a group of the nobles. He is laughing. He carries the dark girl on his saddle-bow."

"How far away is he, Dara?"

"Perhaps a bow-shot. He rides slowly."

"When I ride out, close in behind me. The fight will be between me and Tibur. I do not think those with him will dare attack me. If they do..."

Naral laughed.

"If they do, we shall be at their throats, Dwayanu. There are one or two of Tibur's friends I would like to settle accounts with. We ask you only this: waste neither words nor time on Tibur. Kill him quickly. For by the gods, if he kills you, it will be the boiling pot and the knives of the flayers for all of us he captures."

"I will kill him, Naral."

Slowly I opened the great door. Now I could see Tibur, his horse pacing toward the bridge-end. Upon the pommel of his saddle was Evalie. Her body drooped; the hair of blue-black was loosened and covered her face like a veil. Her hands were tied behind her back, and gripped in one of Tibur's. There were a score of his followers around and behind him, nobles--and the majority of them men. I had noticed that although the Witch-woman had few men among her guards and garrisons, the Smith showed a preference for them among his friends and personal escort. His head was turned toward them, his voice, roaring with triumph, and his laughter came plainly to me. By now the enclosure was almost empty of soldiers and captives. There was none between us. I wondered where the Witch-woman was.

Closer came Tibur, and closer.

"Ready Dara--Naral?"

"Ready, Lord!"

I flung open the gate. I raced toward Tibur, head bent low, my little troop behind me. I swung against him with head uplifted, thrust my face close to his.

Tibur's whole body grew rigid, his eyes glared into mine, his jaw dropped. I knew that those who followed him were held in that same incredulous stupefaction. Before the Smith could recover from his paralysis, I had snatched Evalie up from his saddle, had passed her to Dara.

I lifted my sword to slash at Tibur's throat. I gave him no warning. It was no time for chivalry. Twice he had tried treacherously to kill me. I would make quick end.

Swift as had been my stroke, the Smith was swifter. He threw himself back, slipped off his horse, and landed like a cat at its heels. I was down from mine before his great sledge was half-raised to hurl. I thrust my blade forward to pierce his throat. He parried it with the sledge. Then berserk rage claimed him. The hammer fell clanging on the rock. He threw himself on me, howling. His arms circled me, fettering mine to my sides, like living bands of steel. His legs felt for mine, striving to throw me. His lips were drawn back like a mad wolf's, and he bored his head into the pit of my neck, trying to tear my throat with his teeth.

My ribs cracked under the tightening vice of Tibur's arms. My lungs were labouring, sight dimming. I writhed and twisted in the effort to escape the muzzling of that hot mouth and the searching fangs.

I heard shouting around me, heard and dimly saw milling of the horses. The clutching fingers of my left hand touched my girdle--closed on something there--something like the shaft of a javelin--

Tibur's hell-forged dart!

Suddenly I went limp in Tibur's grip. His laughter bellowed, hoarse with triumph. And for a split-second his grip relaxed.

That split-second was enough. I summoned all my strength and broke his grip. Before he could clench me again, my hand had swept down into the girdle and clutched the dart.

I brought it up and drove it into Tibur's throat just beneath his jaw. I jerked the haft. The opened, razor-edged flanges sliced through arteries and muscles. The bellowing laughter of Tibur changed to a hideous gurgling. His hands sought the haft, dragged at it--tore it out-- And the blood spurted from Tibur's mangled throat; Tibur's knees buckled beneath him, and he lurched and fell at my feet...choking...his hands still feebly groping to clutch me...

I stood there, dazed, gasping for breath, the pulse roaring in my ears.

"Drink this, Lord!"

I looked up at Dara. She was holding a wine-skin to me. I took it with trembling hands, and drank deep. The good wine whipped through me. Suddenly I took it from my lips.

"The dark girl of the Rrrllya--Evalie. She is not with you."

"There she is. I set her on another horse. There was fighting, Lord."

I stared into Evalie's face. She looked back at me, brown eyes cold, implacable.

"Better use the rest of the wine to wash your face, Lord. You are no sight for any tender maid."

I passed my hand over my face, drew it away wet with blood.

"Tibur's blood, Dwayanu, thank the gods!"

She brought my horse forward. I felt better when I was in its saddle. I glanced down at Tibur. His fingers were still faintly twitching. I looked about me. There was a shattered company of Karak's archers at the bridge-end. They raised their bows in salute.

"Dwayanu! Live Dwayanu!"

My troop seemed strangely shrunken. I called--"Naral!"

"Dead, Dwayanu. I told you there had been fighting."

"Who killed her?"

"Never mind. I slew him. And those left of Tibur's escort have fled. And now what. Lord?"

"We wait for Lur."

"Not long shall we have to linger then, for here she comes."

There was the blast of a horn. I turned to see the Witch-woman come galloping over the square. Her red braids were loose, her sword was red, and she was nigh as battle-stained as I. With her rode a scant dozen of her women, half as many of her nobles.

I awaited her. She reined up before me, searching me with wild bright eyes.

I should have killed her as I had Tibur. I should have been hating her. But I found I was not hating her at all. All of hate I had held seemed to have poured out upon Tibur. No, I was not hating her.

She smiled faintly:

"You are hard to kill, Yellow-hair!"

"Dwayanu--Witch."

She glanced at me, half-contemptuously.

"You are no longer Dwayanu!"

"Try to convince these soldiers of that, Lur."

"Oh, I know," she said, and stared down at Tibur. "So you killed the Smith. Well, at least you are still a man."

"Killed him for you, Lur!" I jeered. "Did I not promise you?"

She did not answer, only asked, as Dara had before her:

"And now what?"

175

"We wait here until Sirk is emptied. Then we ride to Karak, you beside me. I do not like you at my back, Witch-woman."

She spoke quietly to her women, then sat, head bent, thinking, with never another word for me.

I whispered to Dara:

"Can we trust the archers?"

She nodded.

"Bid them wait and march with us. Let them drag the body of Tibur into some corner."

For half an hour the soldiers came by, with prisoners, with horses, with cattle and other booty. Small troops of the nobles and their supporters galloped up, halted, and spoke, but, at my word and Lur's nod, passed on over the bridge. Most of the nobles showed dismayed astonishment at my resurrection; the soldiers gave me glad salute.

The last skeleton company came through the gap. I had been watching for Sri, but he was not with them, and I concluded that he had been taken to Karak with the earliest prisoners or had been killed.

"Come," I said to the Witch-woman. "Let your women go before us."

I rode over to Evalie, lifted her from her saddle and set her on my pommel. She made no resistance, but I felt her shrink from me. I knew she was thinking that she had but exchanged Tibur for another master, that to me she was only spoil of war. If my mind had not been so weary I suppose that would have hurt. But my mind was too weary to care.

We passed over the bridge, through the curling mists of steam. We were halfway to the forest when the Witch-woman threw back her head and sent forth a long, wailing call. The white wolves burst from the ferns. I gave command to the archers to set arrows. Lur shook her head.

"No need to harm them. They go to Sirk. They have earned their pay."

The white wolves coursed over the barren to the bridge-end, streamed over it, vanished. I heard them howling among the dead.

"I, too, keep my promises," said the Witch-woman.

We rode on, into the forest, back to Karak.

XXII. GATE OF KHALK'RU

We were close to Karak when the drums of the Little People began beating.

The leaden weariness pressed down upon me increasingly. I struggled to keep awake. Tibur's stroke on my head had something to do with that, but I had taken other blows and eaten nothing since long before dawn. I could not think, much less plan what I was going to do after I had got back to Karak.

The drums of the Little People drove away my lethargy, brought me up wide-awake. They crashed out at first like a thunderburst across the white river. After that they settled down into a slow, measured rhythm filled with implacable menace. It was like Death standing on hollow graves and stamping on them before he marched.

At the first crash Evalie straightened, then sat listening with every nerve. I reined up my horse, and saw that the Witch-woman had also halted and was listening with all of Evalie's intentness. There was something inexplicably disturbing in that monotonous drumming. Something that reached beyond and outside of human experience--or reached before it. It was like thousands of bared hearts beating in unison, in one unalterable rhythm, not to be still till the hearts themselves stopped...inexorable...and increasing in steadily widening area...spreading, spreading...until they beat from all the land across white Nanbu.

I spoke to Lur.

"I am thinking that here is the last of my promises, Witch-woman. I killed Yodin, gave you Sirk, I slew Tibur--and here is your war with the Rrrllya."

I had not thought of how that might sound to Evalie! She turned and gave me one long level look of scorn; she said to the Witch-woman, coldly, in halting Uighur:

"It is war. Was that not what you expected when you dared to take me? It will be war until my people have me again. Best be careful how you use me."

The Witch-woman's control broke at that, all the long pent-up fires of her wrath bursting forth.

"Good! Now we shall wipe out your yellow dogs for once and all. And you shall be flayed, or bathed in the cauldron--or given to Khalk'ru. Win or lose--there will be little of you for your dogs to fight over. You shall be used as I choose."

"No," I said, "as I choose, Lur."

The blue eyes flamed on me at that. And the brown eyes met mine as scornfully as before.

"Give me a horse to ride. I do not like the touch of you--Dwayanu."

"Nevertheless, you ride with me, Evalie."

We passed into Karak. The drums beat now loud, now low. But always with that unchanging, inexorable rhythm. They swelled and fell, swelled and fell. Like Death still stamping on the hollow graves--now fiercely--and now lightly.

There were many people in the streets. They stared at Evalie, and whispered. There were no shouts of welcome, no cheering. They seemed sullen, frightened. Then I knew they were listening so closely to the drums that they hardly knew we were passing. The drums were closer. I could hear them talking from point to point along the far bank of the river. The tongues of the talking drums rose plain above the others. And through their talking, repeated and repeated:

"Ev-ah-lee! Ev-ah-lee!"

We rode over the open square to the gate of the black citadel. There I

stopped.

"A truce, Lur."

She sent a mocking glance at Evalie.

"A truce! What need of a truce between you and me--Dwayanu?"

I said, quietly:

"I am tired of bloodshed. Among the captives are some of the Rrrllya. Let us bring them where they can talk with Evalie and with us two. We will then release a part of them, and send them across Nanbu with the message that no harm is intended Evalie. That we ask the Rrrllya to send us on the morrow an embassy empowered to arrange a lasting peace. And that when that peace is arranged they shall take Evalie back with them unharmed."

She said, smiling:

"So--Dwayanu--fears the dwarfs!"

178

I repeated:

"I am tired of bloodshed."

"Ah, me," she sighed. "And did I not once hear Dwayanu boast that he kept his promises--and was thereby persuaded to give him payment for them in advance! Ah, me--but Dwayanu is changed!"

She stung me there, but I managed to master my anger; I said:

"If you will not agree to this, Lur, then I myself will give the orders. But then we shall be a beleaguered city which is at its own throat. And easy prey for the enemy."

She considered this.

"So you want no war with the little yellow dogs? And it is your thought that if the girl is returned to them, there will be none? Then why wait? Why not send her back at once with the captives? Take them up to Nansur, parley with the dwarfs there. Drum talk would settle the matter in a little while--if you are right. Then we can sleep this night without the drums disturbing you."

That was true enough, but I read the malice in it. The truth was that I did not want Evalie sent back just then. If she were, then never, I knew, might I have a chance to justify myself with her, break down her distrust--have her again accept me as the Leif whom she had loved. But given a little time--I might. And the Witch-woman knew this.

"Not so quickly should it be done, Lur," I said, suavely. "That would be to make them think we fear them--as the proposal made you think I feared them. We need more than hasty drum talk to seal such treaty. No, we hold the girl as hostage until we make our terms."

She bent her head, thinking, then looked at me with clear eyes, and smiled.

"You are right, Dwayanu. I will send for the captives after I have rid myself of these stains of Sirk. They will be brought to your chamber. And in the meantime I will do more. I will order that word be sent the Rrrllya on Nansur that soon their captured fellows will be among them with a message. At the least it will give us time. And we need time, Dwayanu--both of us."

I looked at her sharply. She laughed, and gave her horse the spurs. I rode behind her through the gate and into the great enclosed square. It was crowded with soldiers and captives. Here the drumming was magnified. The drums seemed to be within the place itself, invisible and beaten by invisible drummers. The soldiers were plainly uneasy, the prisoners excited, and curiously defiant.

Passing into the citadel I called various officers who had not taken part in the attack on Sirk and gave orders that the garrison on the walls facing Nansur Bridge be increased. Also that an alarm should be sounded which would bring in the soldiers and people from the outer-lying posts and farms. I ordered the guard upon the river walls to be strengthened, and the people of the city be told that those who wished to seek shelter in the citadel could come, but must be in by dusk. It was a scant hour before nightfall. There would be little trouble in car-ing for them in that immense place. And all this I did in event of the message failing. If it failed, I had no desire to be part of a massacre in Karak, which would stand a siege until I could convince the Little People of my good faith. Or convince Evalie of it, and have her bring about a peace.

This done, I took Evalie to my own chambers, not those of the High-priest where the Black Octopus hovered over the three thrones, but a chain of comfortable rooms in another part of the citadel. The little troop, which had stood by me through the sack of Sirk and after, followed us. There I turned Evalie over to Dara. I was bathed, my wound dressed and bandaged, and clothed. Here the windows looked out over the river, and the drums beat through them maddeningly. I ordered food brought, and wine, and summoned Evalie. Dara brought her. She had been well cared for, but she would not eat with me. She said to me:

"I fear my people will have but scant faith in any messages you send, Dwayanu."

"Later we will talk of that other message, Evalie. I did not send it. And Tsantawu, dying in my arms, believed me when I told him I had not."

"I heard you say to Lur that you had promised her Sirk. You did not lie to her, Dwayanu--for Sirk is eaten. How can I believe you?"

I said: "You shall have proof that I speak truth, Evalie, Now, since you will not eat with me, go with Dara."

She had no fault to find with Dara. Dara was no lying traitor, but a soldier, and fighting in Sirk or elsewhere was part of her trade. She went with her.

I ate sparingly and drank heavily. The wine put new life in me, drove away what was left of weariness. I put sorrow for Jim resolutely aside for the moment, thinking of what I intended to do, and how best to do it. And then there was a challenge at the door, and the Witch-woman entered.

Her red braids crowned her and in them shone the sapphires. She bore not the slightest mark of the struggles of the day, nor sign of fa-tigue. Her eyes were bright and clear, her red lips smiling. Her low, sweet voice, her touch upon my arm, brought back memories I had thought gone with Dwayanu.

She called, and through the door came a file of soldiers, and with them a score of the Little People, unbound, hatred in their yellow eyes as they saw me, curiosity too. I spoke to them, gently. I sent for Evalie. She came, and the golden pygmies ran to her, threw themselves upon her like a crowd of children, twittering and trilling, stroking her hair, touching her feet and hands.

She laughed, called them one by one by name, then spoke rapidly. I could get little of what she said; by the shadow on Lur's face I knew she had understood nothing at all. I repeated to Evalie precisely what I had told Lur--and which, at least in part, she knew, for she had betrayed that she understood the Uighur, or the Ayjir, better than she had admitted. I translated from the tongue of the dwarfs for Lur.

The pact was speedily made. Half of the pygmies were to make their way at once over Nanbu to the garrison on the far side of the bridge. By the talking drums they would send our message to the stronghold of the Little People. If they accepted it, the beating of the war drums would cease. I said to Evalie:

"When they talk on their drums, let them say that nothing will be asked of them that was not contained in the old truce--and that death will no longer lie in wait for them when they cross the river."

The Witch-woman said:

"Just what does that mean, Dwayanu?"

"Now Sirk is done, there is no longer much need for that penalty, Lur. Let them gather their herbs and metals as they will; that is all."

"There is more in your mind than that--" Her eyes narrowed.

"They understood me, Evalie--but do you also tell them."

The Little People trilled among themselves; then ten of them stepped forward, those chosen to take the message. As they were moving away, I stopped them.

"If Sri escaped, let him come with the embassy. Better still--let him come before them. Send word through the drums that he may come as soon as he can. He has my safe-conduct, and shall stay with Evalie until all is settled."

They chattered over that, assented. The Witch-woman made no comment. For the first time I saw Evalie's eyes soften as she looked at me.

When the pygmies were gone, Lur walked to the door, and beckoned. Ouarda entered.

181

"Ouarda!"

I liked Ouarda. It was good to know she was alive. I went to her with outstretched hands. She took them.

"It was two of the soldiers, Lord. They had sisters in Sirk. They cut the ladder before we could stop them. They were slain," she said.

Would to God they had cut it before any could, have followed me!

Before I could speak, one of my captains knocked and entered.

"It is long after dusk and the gates are closed, Lord. All those who would come are behind them."

"Were there many, soldier?"

"No, Lord--not more than a hundred or so. The others refused."

"And did they say why they refused?"

"Is the question an order, Lord?"

"It is an order."

"They said they were safer where they were. That the Rrrllya had no quarrel with them, who were but meat for Khalk'ru."

"Enough, soldier!" The Witch-woman's voice was harsh. "Go! Take the Rrrllya with you."

The captain saluted, turned smartly and was gone with the dwarfs. I laughed.

"Soldiers cut our ladder for sympathy of those who fled Khalk'ru. The people fear the enemies of Khalk'ru less than they do their own kind who are his butchers! We do well to make peace with the Rrrllya, Lur."

I watched her face pale, then redden and saw the knuckles of her hands whiten as she clenched them. She smiled, poured herself wine, lifted it with a steady hand.

"I drink to your wisdom--Dwayanu!"

A strong soul--the Witch-woman's! A warrior's heart. Somewhat lacking in feminine softness, it was true. But it was no wonder that Dwayanu had loved her--in his way and as much as he could love a woman.

A silence dropped upon the chamber, intensified in some odd fashion by the steady beating of the drums. How long we sat in that silence I do not know. But suddenly the beat of the drums became fainter.

And then all at once the drums ceased entirely. The quiet brought a sense of unreality. I could feel the tense nerves loosening like springs long held taut. The abrupt silence made ears ache, slowed heart-beat.

"They have the message. They have accepted it," Evalie spoke. The Witch-woman arose.

"You keep the girl beside you to-night, Dwayanu?"

"She sleeps in one of these rooms, Lur. She will be under guard. No one can reach her without passing through my room here," I looked at her, significantly. "And I sleep lightly. You need have no fear of her escape."

"I am glad the drums will not disturb your sleep--Dwayanu."

She gave me a mocking salute, and, with Ouarda, left me.

And suddenly the weariness dropped upon me again. I turned to Evalie, watching me with eyes in which I thought doubt of her own deep doubt had crept. Certainly there was no scorn, nor loathing in them. Well, now I had her where all this manoeuvring had been meant to bring her. Alone with me. And looking at her I felt that in the face of all she had seen of me, all she had undergone because of me--words were useless things. Nor could I muster them as I wanted. No, there would be plenty of time...in the morning, perhaps, when I had slept...or after I had done what I had to do...then she must believe...

"Sleep, Evalie. Sleep without fear...and believe that all that has been wrong is now becoming right. Go with Dara. You shall be well guarded. None can come to you except through this room, and here I will be. Sleep and fear nothing."

I called Dara, gave her instructions, and Evalie went with her. At the curtains masking the entrance to the next room she hesitated, half turned as though to speak, but did not. And not long after Dara returned. She said:

"She is already asleep, Dwayanu."

"As you should be, friend," I told her. "And all those others who stood by me this day. I think there is nothing to fear to-night. Select those whom you can trust and have them guard the corridor and my door. Where have you put her?"

"In the chamber next this, Lord."

"It would be better if you and the others slept here, Dara. There are half a dozen rooms for you. Have wine and food brought for you--plenty of it."

She laughed.

"Do you expect a siege, Dwayanu?"

"One never knows."

"You do not greatly trust Lur, Lord?"

"I trust her not at all, Dara."

She nodded, turned to go. Upon the impulse I said:

"Dara, would it make you sleep better to-night and those with you, and would it help you in picking your guard if I told you this: there will be no more sacrifices to Khalk'ru while I live?"

She started; her face lightened, softened. She thrust out her hand to me:

"Dwayanu--I had a sister who was given to Khalk'ru. Do you mean this?"

"By the life of my blood! By all the living gods! I mean it!"

"Sleep well, Lord!" Her voice was choked. She walked away, through the curtain, but not before I had seen the tears on her cheeks.

Well, a woman had a right to weep--even if she was a soldier. I myself had wept to-day.

I poured myself wine, sat thinking as I drank. Mainly my thoughts revolved around the enigma of Khalk'ru. And there was a good reason for that.

What was Khalk'ru?

I slipped the chain from round my neck, opened the locket and studied the ring. I closed it, and threw it on the table. Somehow I felt that it was better there than over my heart while I was doing this thinking.

Dwayanu had had his doubts about that dread Thing being any Spirit of the Void, and I, who now was Leif Langdon and a passive Dwayanu, had no doubts whatever that it was not. Yet I could not accept Barr's theory of mass hypnotism--and trickery was out of the question.

Whatever Khalk'ru might be, Khalk'ru--as the Witch-woman had said--was. Or at least that Shape which became material through ritual, ring and screen--was.

I thought that I might have put the experience in the temple of the oasis down as hallucination if it had not been repeated here in the Shadowed-land. But there could be no possible doubt about the reality of the sacrifice I had conducted; no possible doubt as to the destruction--absorption--dissolvement--of the twelve girls. And none of Yodin's complete belief in the power of the tentacle to remove me, and none of his complete effacement. And I thought that if the sacrifices and Yodin were standing in the wings laughing at me, as Barr had put it--then it was in the wings of a theatre in some other world than this. And there was the deep horror of the Little People, the horror of so many of the Ayjir--and there was the revolt in ancient Ayjirland born of this same horror, which had destroyed Ayjirland by civil war.

184

No, whatever the Thing was, no matter how repugnant to science its recognition as a reality might be--still it was Atavism, superstition--call it what Barr would--I knew the Thing was real! Not of this earth--no, most certainly not of this earth. Not even supernatural. Or rather, supernatural only insofar as it might come from another dimension or even another world which our five senses could not encompass.

And I reflected, now, that science and religion are really blood brothers, which is largely why they hate each other so, that scientists and religionists are quite alike in their dogmatism, their intolerance, and that every bitter battle of religion over some interpretation of creed or cult has its parallel in battles of science over a bone or rock.

Yet just as there are men in the churches whose minds have not become religiously fossilized, so there are men in the laboratories whose minds have not become scientifically fossilized...Einstein, who dared challenge all conceptions of space and time with his four dimensional space in which time itself was a dimension, and who followed that with proof of five dimensional space instead of the four which are all our senses can apprehend, and which apprehends one of them wrongly...the possibility of a dozen worlds spinning interlocked with this one...in the same space...the energy which we call matter of each of them keyed to the different vibration, and each utterly unaware of the other...and utterly overturning the old axiom that two bodies cannot occupy the same place at the same time.

And I thought--what if far and far back in time, a scientist of that day, one of the Ayjir people, had discovered all that! Had discovered the fifth dimension beyond length, breadth, thickness and time. Or had discovered one of those interlocking worlds whose matter streams through the interstices of the matter of ours. And discovering dimension or world, had found the way to make dwellers in that dimension or that other world both aware of and manifest to those of this. By sound and gesture, by ring and screen, had made a gateway through which such dwellers could come--or at least, appear! And then what a weapon this discoverer had--what a weapon the inevitable priests of that Thing would have! And did have ages gone, just as they had here in Karak.

If so, was it one dweller or many who lurked in those gateways for its drink of life? The memories bequeathed me by Dwayanu told me there had been other temples in Ayjirland besides that one of the oasis. Was it the same Being that appeared in each? Was the Shape that came from the shattered stone of the oasis the same that had fed in the temple of the mirage? Or were there many of them--dwellers in other dimension or other world--avidly answering the summons? Nor was it necessarily true that in their own place these Things had the form of the Kraken. That might be the shape, through purely natural laws, which entrance into this world forced upon them.

I thought over that for quite awhile. It seemed to me the best explanation of Khalk'ru. And if it was, then the way to be rid of Khalk'ru was to destroy his means of entrance. And that, I reflected, was precisely how the ancient Ayjirs had argued.

But it did not explain why only those of the old blood could summon--

I heard a low voice at the door. I walked softly over to it, listened. I opened the door and there was Lur, talking to the guards.

"What is it you are seeking, Lur?"

"To speak with you. I will keep you only a little time, Dwayanu."

I studied the Witch-woman. She stood, very quietly, in her eyes nothing of defiance nor resentment nor subtle calculation--only appeal. Her red braids fell over her white shoulders; she was without weapon or ornament. She looked younger than ever I had seen her, and somewhat forlorn. I felt no desire to mock her nor to deny her. I felt instead the stirrings of a deep pity.

"Enter, Lur--and say all that is in your mind."

I closed the door behind her. She walked over to the window, looked out into the dim greenly glimmering night. I went to her.

"Speak softly, Lur. The girl is asleep there in the next chamber. Let her rest."

She said, tonelessly:

"I wish you had never come here, Yellow-hair." I thought of Jim, and I answered:

"I wish that too, Witch-woman. But here I am." She leaned towards me, put her hand over my heart. "Why do you hate me so greatly?"

"I do not hate you, Lur. I have no hate left in me--except for one thing."

"And that--?"

Involuntarily I looked at the table. One candle shone there and its light fell on the locket that held the ring. Her glance followed mine. She said:

"What do you mean to do? Throw Karak open to the dwarfs? Mend Nansur? Rule here over Karak and the Rrrllya with their dark girl at your side? Is it that...and if it is that--what is to become of Lur? Answer me. I have the right to know. There is a bond between us...I loved you when you were Dwayanu...you know how well..."

"And would have killed me while I was still Dwayanu," I said, sombrely.

"Because I saw Dwayanu dying as you looked into the eyes of the stranger," she answered. "You whom Dwayanu had mastered was killing Dwayanu. I loved Dwayanu. Why should I not avenge him?"

"If you believe I am no longer Dwayanu, then I am the man whose friend you trapped and murdered--the man whose love you trapped and would have destroyed. And if that be so--what claim have you upon me, Lur?"

She did not answer for moments; then she said:

"I have some justice on my side. I tell you I loved Dwayanu. Something I knew of your case from the first, Yellow-hair. But I saw Dwayanu awaken within you. And I knew it was truly he! I knew, too, that as long as that friend of yours and the dark girl lived there was danger for Dwayanu. That was why I plotted to bring them into Sirk. I threw the dice upon the chance of killing them before you had seen them. Then, I thought, all would be well. There would be none left to rouse that in you which Dwayanu had mastered. I lost. I knew I had lost when by whim of Luka she threw you three together. And rage and sorrow caught me--and I did...what I did."

"Lur," I said, "answer me truly. That day you returned to the Lake of the Ghosts after pursuit of the two women--were they not your spies who bore that lying message into Sirk? And did you not wait until you learned my friend and Evalie were in the trap before you gave me word to march? And was it not in your thought that you would then--if I opened the way into Sirk--rid yourself not only of those two but of Dwayanu? For remember--you may have loved Dwayanu, but as he told you, you loved power better than he. And Dwayanu threatened your power. Answer me truly."

For the second time I saw tears in the eyes of the Witch-woman. She said, brokenly:

"I sent the spies, yes. I waited until the two were in the trap. But I never meant harm to Dwayanu!"

I did not believe her. But still I felt no anger, no hate. The pity grew.

"Lur, now I will tell you truth. It is not in my mind to rule with Evalie over Karak and the Rrrllya. I have no more desire for power. That went with Dwayanu. In the peace I make with the dwarfs, you shall rule over Karak--if that be your desire. The dark girl shall go back with them. She will not desire to remain in Karak. Nor do I..."

"You cannot go with her," she interrupted me. "Never would the yellow dogs trust you. Their arrows would be ever pointed at you."

I nodded--that thought had occurred to me long before.

"All that must adjust itself," I said. "But there shall be no more sacrifices. The gate of Khalk'ru shall be closed against him for ever. And I will close it."

Her eyes dilated.

"You mean--"

"I mean that I will shut Khalk'ru for ever from Karak--unless Khalk'ru proves stronger than I."

She wrung her hands, helplessly.

"What use rule over Karak to me then...how could I hold the people?"

"Nevertheless--I will destroy the gate of Khalk'ru."

She whispered:

"Gods--if I had Yodin's ring..."

I smiled at that.

"Witch-woman, you know as well as I that Khalk'ru comes to no woman's call."

The witch-lights flickered in her eyes; a flash of green shone through them.

"There is an ancient prophecy, Yellow-hair, that Dwayanu did not know--or had forgotten. It says that when Khalk'ru comes to a woman's call, he--stays! That was the reason no woman in ancient Ay-jilrand might be priestess at the sacrifice."

I laughed at that.

"A fine pet, Lur--to add to your wolves."

She walked toward the door, paused.

"What if I could love you--as I loved Dwayanu? Could make you love me as Dwayanu loved me? And more! Send the dark girl to join her people and take the ban of death from them on this side of Nanbu. Would you let things be as they are--rule with me over Karak?"

I opened the door for her.

"I told you I no longer care for power, Lur."

She walked away.

I went back to the window, drew a chair to it, and sat thinking. Suddenly from somewhere close to the citadel I heard a wolf cry. Thrice it howled, then thrice again.

"Leif!"

I jumped to my feet. Evalie was beside me. She peered at me through the veils of her hair; her clear eyes shone upon me--no longer doubting, hating, fearing. They were as they were of old.

"Evalie!"

My arms went round her; my lips found hers.

"I listened, Leif!"

"You believe, Evalie!"

She kissed me, held me tight.

"But she was right--Leif. You could not go with me again into the land of the Little People. Never, never would they understand. And I would not dwell in Karak."

"Will you go with me, Evalie--to my own land? After I have done what I must do...and if I am not destroyed in its doing?"

"I will go with you, Leif!"

And she wept awhile, and after another while she fell asleep in my arms. And I lifted her, and carried her into her chamber and covered her with the sleep silks. Nor did she awaken.

I returned to my own room. As I passed the table I picked up the locket, started to put it round my neck. I threw it back. Never would I wear that chain again, I dropped upon the bed, sword at hand. I slept.

XXIII. IN KHALK'RU'S TEMPLE

Twice I awakened. The first time it was the howling of the wolves that aroused me. It was as though they were beneath my window. I listened drowsily, and sank back to sleep.

The second time I came wide awake from a troubled dream. Some sound in the chamber had roused me, of that I was sure. My hand dropped to my sword lying on the floor beside my bed. I had the feeling that there was someone in the room. I could see nothing in the green darkness that filled the chamber. I called, softly:

"Evalie! Is that you?"

There was no answer, no sound.

I sat up in the bed, even thrust a leg out to rise. And then I remembered the guards at my door, and Dara and her soldiers beyond, and I told myself that it had been only my troubled dream that had awakened me. Yet for a time I lay awake listening, sword in hand. And then the silence lulled me back to sleep.

There was a knocking upon my door, and I struggled out of that sleep. I saw that it was well after dawn. I went to the door softly so that I might not awaken Evalie. I opened it, and there with the guards was Sri. The little man had come well armed, with spear and sickle-sword and between his shoulders one of the small, surprisingly resonant talking drums. He looked at me in the friendliest fashion. I patted his hand and pointed to the curtains.

"Evalie is there, Sri. Go waken her."

He trotted past me. I gave greeting to the guards, and turned to follow Sri. He stood at the curtains, looking at me with eyes in which was now no friendliness at all. He said:

"Evalie is not there."

I stared at him, incredulously, brushed by him and into that chamber. It was empty. I crossed to the pile of silks and cushions on which Evalie had slept, touched them. There was no warmth. I went, Sri at my heels, into the next room. Dara and a half dozen of the women lay there, asleep. Evalie was not among them. I touched Dara on the shoulder. She sat up, yawning.

"Dara--the girl is gone!"

"Gone!" she stared at me as incredulously as I had at the golden pygmy. She leaped to her feet, ran to the empty room, then with me through the other chambers. There lay the soldier women, asleep, but not Evalie.

I ran back to my own room, and to its door. A bitter rage began to possess me. Swiftly, harshly, I questioned the guards. They had seen no one. None had entered; none had gone forth. The golden pygmy listened, his eyes never leaving me.

I turned toward Evalie's room. I passed the table on which I had thrown the locket. My hand fell on it, lifted it; it was curiously light...I opened it...The ring of Khalk'ru was not there! I glared at the empty locket--and like a torturing flame realization of what its emptiness and the vanishment of Evalie might signify came to me. I groaned, leaned against the table to keep from falling.

"Drum, Sri! Call your people! Bid them come quickly! There may yet be time!"

The golden pygmy hissed; his eyes became little pools of yellow fire. He could not have known all the horror of my thoughts--but he read enough. He leaped to the window, swung his drum and sent forth call upon call--peremptory, raging, vicious. At once he was answered--answered from Nansur, and then from all the river and beyond it the drums of the Little People roared out.

Would Lur hear them? She could not help but hear them...but would she heed...would their threat stop her...it would tell her that I was awake and that the Little People knew of their betrayal...and Eva-lie's.

God! If she did hear--was it in time to save Evalie?

"Quick, Lord!" Dara called from the curtains. The dwarf and I ran through. She pointed to the side of the wall. There, where one of the carved stones jointed another, hung a strip of silk.

"A door there, Dwayanu! That is how they took her. They went hurriedly. The cloth caught when the stone closed."

I looked for something to batter at the stone. But Dara was pressing here and there. The stone swung open. Sri darted past and into the black passage it had masked. I stumbled after him, Dara at my heels, the others following. It was a narrow passage, and not long. Its end was a solid wall of stone. And here Dara pressed again until that wall opened.

191

We burst into the chamber of the High-priest. The eyes of the Kraken stared at me and through me with their inscrutable malignancy. Yet it seemed to me that in them now was challenge.

All my senseless fury, all blind threshing of my rage, fell from me. A cold deliberation, an ordered purpose that had in it nothing of haste took its place...Is it too late to save Evalie?...It is not too late to destroy you, my enemy...

"Dara--get horses for us. Gather quickly as many as you can trust. Take only the strongest. Have them ready at the gate of the road to the temple...We go to end Khalk'ru. Tell them that."

I spoke to the golden pygmy.

"I do not know if I can help Evalie. But I go to put an end to Khalk'ru. Do you wait for your people--or do you go with me?"

"I go with you."

I knew where the Witch-woman dwelt in the black citadel, and it was not far away. I knew I would not find her there, but I must be sure. And she might have taken Evalie to the Lake of the Ghosts, I was thinking as I went on, past groups of silent, uneasy, perplexed and sa- luting soldiers. But deep in me I knew she had not. Deep within me I knew that it had been Lur who had awakened me in the night. Lur, who had stolen through the curtains to take the ring of Khalk'ru. And there was only one reason why she should have done that. No, she would not be at the Lake of the Ghosts.

Yet, if she had come into my room--why had she not slain me? Or had she meant to do this, and had my awakening and calling out to Evalie stayed her? Had she feared to go further? Or had she deliber- ately spared me?

I reached her rooms. She was not there. None of her women was there. The place was empty, not even soldiers on guard.

I broke into a run. The golden pygmy followed me, shrilling, javelins in left hand, sickle-sword in right. We came to the gate to the temple road.

There were three or four hundred soldiers awaiting me. Mounted--and every one a woman. I threw myself on a horse Dara held for me, swung Sri up on the saddle. We raced toward the temple.

We were half-way there when out from the trees that bordered the temple road poured the white wolves. They sprang from the sides like a white torrent, threw themselves upon the riders. They checked our rush, our horses stumbled, falling over those the fangs of the wolves had dropped in that swift, unexpected ambuscade; soldiers fal- ling with them, ripped and torn by the wolves before they could struggle to their feet. We milled among them--horses and men and wolves in a whirling, crimson-flecked ring.

Straight at my throat leaped the great dog-wolf, leader of Lur's pack, green eyes naming. I had no time for sword thrust. I caught its throat in my left hand, lifted it and flung it over my back. Even so, its fangs had struck and gashed me.

We were through the wolves. What was left of them came coursing behind us. But they had taken toll of my troop.

I heard the clang of an anvil...thrice stricken...the anvil of Tubalka!

God! It was true...Lur in the temple...and Evalie...and Khalk'ru!

We swept up to the door of the temple. I heard voices raised in the ancient chant. The entrance swarmed...It bristled with swords of the nobles, women and men.

"Ride through them, Dara! Ride them down!"

We swept through them like a ram. Sword against sword, hammers and battleaxes beating at them, horses trampling them.

The shrill song of Sri never ceased. His javelin thrust, his sickle-sword slashed.

We burst into Khalk'ru's temple. The chanting stopped. The chanters arose against us; they struck with sword and axe and hammer at us; they stabbed and hacked our horses; pulled us down. The amphitheatre was a raging cauldron of death...

The lip of the platform was before me. I spurred my horse to it, stood upon its back and leaped upon the platform. Close to my right was the anvil of Tubalka; beside it, hammer raised to smite, was Ouarda. I heard the roll of drums, the drums of Khalk'ru's evocation. The backs of the priests were bent over them.

In front of the priests, the ring of Khalk'ru raised high, stood Lur.

And between her and the bubble ocean of yellow stone that was the gate of Khalk'ru, fettered dwarfs swung two by two in the golden girdles...

Within the warrior's ring--Evalie!

The Witch-woman never looked at me; she never looked behind her at the roaring cauldron of the amphitheatre where the soldiers and nobles battled.

She launched into the ritual!

Shouting, I rushed on Ouarda. I wrested the great sledge from her hands. I hurled it straight at the yellow screen...straight at the head of Khalk'ru. With every ounce of my strength I hurled that great hammer.

The screen cracked! The hammer was thrown back from it...fell.

The Witch-woman's voice went on...and on...never faltering.

There was a wavering in the cracked screen. The Kraken floating in the bubble ocean seemed to draw back...to thrust forward...

I ran toward it...to the hammer.

An instant I halted beside Evalie. I thrust my hands through the golden girdle, broke it as though it had been wood. I dropped my sword at her feet.

"Guard yourself, Evalie!"

I picked up the hammer. I raised it. The eyes of Khalk'ru moved... they glared at me, were aware of me...the tentacles stirred! And the paralysing cold began to creep round me...I threw all my will against it.

I smashed the sledge of Tubalka against the yellow stone...again... and again--

The tentacles of Khalk'ru stretched toward me!

There was a crystalline crashing, like a lightning bolt striking close. The yellow stone of the screen shattered. It rained round me like sleet driven by an icy hurricane. There was an earthquake trembling. The temple rocked. My arms fell, paralysed. The hammer of Tubalka dropped from hands that could no longer feel it. The icy cold swirled about me ... higher...higher...there was a shrill and dreadful shrieking...

For an instant the shape of the Kraken hovered where the screen had been. Then it shrank. It seemed to be sucked away into immeasurable distances. It vanished.

And life rushed back into me!

There were jagged streamers of the yellow stone upon the rocky floor...black of the Kraken within them...I beat them into dust...

"Leif!"

Evalie's voice, shrill, agonized. I swung round. Lur was rushing upon me, sword raised. Before I could move Evalie had darted between us, flung herself in front of the Witch-woman, struck at her with my own sword.

The blade of Lur parried the stroke, swept in...bit deep...and Evalie fell...Lur leaped toward me...I watched her come, not moving, not caring...there was blood upon her sword...Evalie's blood...

Something like a flash of light touched her breast. She halted as though a hand had thrust her back. Slowly, she dropped to her knees. She sank to the rock.

Over the rim of the platform leaped the dog-wolf, howling as it ran. It hurled itself straight at me. There was another flash of light. The dog-wolf somersaulted and fell--in mid-leap.

I saw Sri, crouching. One of his javelins was in Lur's breast, the mate to it in the dog-wolf's throat...I saw the golden pygmy running to Evalie...saw her rise, holding a hand to a shoulder from which streamed blood...

I walked toward Lur, stiffly, like an automaton. The white wolf tried to stagger to its feet, then crawled to the Witch-woman, dragging itself on its belly. It reached her before I did. It dropped its head upon her breast. It turned its head, and lay glaring at me, dying.

The Witch-woman looked up at me. Her eyes were soft and her mouth had lost all cruelty. It was tender. She smiled at me.

"I wish you had never come here, Yellow-hair!"

And then--

"Ai--and--Ai! My Lake of the Ghosts!"

Her hand crept up, and dropped on the head of the dying wolf, caressingly. She sighed--

The Witch-woman was dead.

I looked into the awed faces of Evalie and Dara. "Evalie--your wound--"

"Not deep, Leif...Soon it will heal...it does not matter..."

Dara said:

"Hail--Dwayanu! It is a great thing you have done this day!"

She dropped on her knees, kissed my hand. And now I saw that those of mine who had survived the battle in the temple had come up on the platform, and were kneeling--to me. And that Ouarda lay beside Tubalka's anvil, and that Sri too was on his knees, staring at me, eyes filled with worship.

I heard the tumult of the drums of the Little People...no longer on Nanbu's far side...in Karak...and closer.

Dara spoke again:

"Let us be going back to Karak, Lord. It is now all yours to rule."

I said to Sri:

"Sound your drum, Sri. Tell them that Evalie lives. That Lur is dead. That the gate of Khalk'ru is closed forever. Let there be no more killing."

Sri answered:

"What you have done has wiped out all war between my people and Karak. Evalie and you we will obey. I will tell them what you have done."

He swung the little drum, raised his hands to beat it I stopped him.

"Wait, Sri, I shall not be here to obey."

Dara cried: "Dwayanu--you will not leave us!"

"Yes, Dara...I go now to that place whence I came...I do not return to Karak. I am done with the Little People, Sri."

Evalie spoke, breathlessly:

"What of me--Leif?"

I put my hands on her shoulders, looked into her eyes:

"Last night you whispered that you would go with me, Evalie. I release you from that promise...I am thinking you would be happier here with your small folk..."

She said, steadily:

"I know where happiness lies for me. I hold to my promise...unless you do not want me..."

"I do want you--dark girl!"

She turned to Sri: "Carry my love to my people, Sri. I shall not see them again."

The little man clung to her, cast himself down before her, wailed and wept while she talked to him. At last he squatted on his haunches, and stared long at the shattered gate of the Kraken. I saw the secret knowledge touch him. He came to me, held up his arms for me to lift him. He raised my lids and looked deep into my eyes. He thrust his hand in my breast, and placed his head on my breast, and listened to the beating of my heart. He dropped, bent Evalie's head to his, whispering.

Dara said: "Dwayanu's will is our will. Yet it is hard to understand why he will not stay with us."

"Sri knows...more than I do. I cannot, Dara."

Evalie came to me. Her eyes were bright with unshed tears.

"Sri says we must go now, Leif...quickly. My people must--not see me. He will tell them a tale upon his drum...there will be no fighting...and henceforth there will be peace."

The golden pygmy began to beat the talking drum. At the first strokes the hosts of other drums were silent. When he had ended they began again...jubilant, triumphant...until in them crept a note of questioning. Once more he beat a message...the answer came--angry, peremptory--in some queer fashion, incredulous.

196

Sri said to me: "Haste! Haste!"

Dara said: "We stay with you, Dwayanu, until the last."

I nodded, and looked at Lur. Upon her hand the ring of Khalk'ru sent out a sudden gleam. I went to her, lifted the dead hand and took from it the ring. I smashed it on the anvil of Tubalka as I had the ring of Yodin.

Evalie said: "Sri knows a way that will lead us out into your world, Leif. It lies at the head of Nanbu. He will take us."

"Is the way past the Lake of Ghosts, Evalie?"

"I will ask him...yes, it passes there."

"That is good. We go into a country where the clothing I wear would be hardly fitting. And some provision must be made for you."

We rode from the temple with Sri on my saddle, and Evalie and Dara on either side. The drums were very close. They were muted when we emerged from the forest upon the road. We went swiftly. It was mid-afternoon when we reached the Lake of the Ghosts. The drawbridge was down. There was no one in the garrison. The Witch-woman's castle was empty. I searched, and found my roll of clothes; I stripped the finery of Dwayanu from me. I took a battle-ax, thrust a short sword in my belt, picked javelins for Evalie and myself. They would help us win through, would be all we had to depend upon to get us food later on. We took food with us from Lur's castle, and skins to clothe Evalie when she passed from the Mirage.

I did not go up into the chamber of the Witch-woman. I heard the whispering of the waterfall--and did not dare to look upon it.

All the rest of that afternoon we galloped along the white river's banks. The drums of the Little People followed us...searching... questioning...calling..."Ev-ah-lee...Ev-ah-lee... Ev-ah-lee..."

By nightfall we had come to the cliffs at the far end of the valley. Here Nanbu poured forth in a mighty torrent from some subterranean source. We picked our way across. Sri led us far into a ravine running steeply upward, and here we camped.

And that night I sat thinking long of what Evalie must meet in that new world awaiting her beyond the Mirage--the world of sun and stars and wind and cold. I thought long of what must be done to shield her until she could adjust herself to that world. And I listened to the drums of the Little People calling her, and I watched her while she slept, and wept and smiled in dream.

She must be taught to breathe. I knew that when she emerged from this atmosphere in which she had lived since babyhood, she would cease instantly to breathe--deprivation of the accustomed stimulus of the carbon-dioxide would bring that about at once. She must will herself to breathe until the reflexes again became automatic and she need give them no conscious thought. And at night, when she slept, this would be trebly difficult. I would have to remain awake, watch beside her.

And she must enter this new world with eyes bandaged, blind, until the nerves accustomed to the green luminosity of the Mirage could endure the stronger light. Warm clothing we could contrive from the skins and furs. But the food--what was it Jim had said in the long and long ago--that those who had eaten the food of the Little People would die if they ate other. Well, that was true in part. Yet, only in part--it could be managed.

With dawn came a sudden memory--the pack I had hidden on Nanbu's bank when we had plunged into the white river with the wolves at our heels. If that could be found, it would help solve the problem of Evalie's clothing at least. I told Dara about it. And she and Sri set out to find it. And while they were gone the soldier-women foraged for food and I instructed Evalie upon what she must do to cross in safety that bridge which lay, perilous, between her world and mine.

Two days they were gone--but they had found the pack. They brought word of peace between the Ayjir and the Little People. As for me--

Dwayanu the Deliverer had come even as the prophecy had promised... had come and freed them from the ancient doom...and had gone back as was his right to that place from which, answering the prophecy, he had come...and had taken with him Evalie as was also his right. Sri had spread the tale.

And next morning when the light showed that the sun had risen over the peaks that girdled the Valley of the Mirage, we set forth-- Evalie like a slim boy beside me.

We climbed until we were within the green mists. And here we bade farewell, Sri clinging to Evalie, kissing her hands and feet, weeping. And Dara clasped my shoulders:

"You will come back to us, Dwayanu? We will be waiting!"

It was like the echo of the Uighur captain's voice--long and long ago...

I turned and began to climb, Evalie following. I thought that so might Euridice have followed her lover up from the Land of Shades in another long and long ago.

The figures of Sri and the watching women became dim. They were hidden under the green mists...

I felt the bitter cold touch my face. I caught Evalie up in my arms--and climbed up and on--and staggered at last out into the sun-lit warmth of the slopes beyond the pit of the precipices.

The day dawned when we had won the long, hard fight for Evalie's life. Not easily was the grip of the Mirage loosed. We turned our faces to the South and set our feet upon the Southward trail.

And yet...

Ai! Lur--Witch-woman! I see you lying there, smiling with lips grown tender--the--white wolf's head upon your breast! And Dwayanu still lives within me!

Also from Benediction Books ...
Wandering Between Two Worlds: Essays on Faith and Art
Anita Mathias
Benediction Books, 2007
152 pages
ISBN: 0955373700

Available from www.amazon.com, www.amazon.co.uk

In these wide-ranging lyrical essays, Anita Mathias writes, in lush, lovely prose, of her naughty Catholic childhood in Jamshedpur, India; her large, eccentric family in Mangalore, a sea-coast town converted by the Portuguese in the sixteenth century; her rebellion and atheism as a teenager in her Himalayan boarding school, run by German missionary nuns, St. Mary's Convent, Nainital; and her abrupt religious conversion after which she entered Mother Teresa's convent in Calcutta as a novice. Later rich, elegant essays explore the dualities of her life as a writer, mother, and Christian in the United States-- Domesticity and Art, Writing and Prayer, and the experience of being "an alien and stranger" as an immigrant in America, sensing the need for roots.

About the Author

Anita Mathias is the author of *Wandering Between Two Worlds: Essays on Faith and Art.* She has a B.A. and M.A. in English from Somerville College, Oxford University, and an M.A. in Creative Writing from the Ohio State University, USA. Anita won a National Endowment of the Arts fellowship in Creative Nonfiction in 1997. She lives in Oxford, England with her husband, Roy, and her daughters, Zoe and Irene.

Visit Anita at http://www.anitamathias.com, and on
http://theoxfordchristian.blogspot.com, her Christian blog;
http://wanderingbetweentwoworlds.blogspot.com/, her personal blog, and
http://thegoodbooksblog.blogspot.com, her literary and writing blog.

The Church That Had Too Much
Anita Mathias
Benediction Books, 2010
52 pages
ISBN: 9781849026567

Available from www.amazon.com, www.amazon.co.uk

The Church That Had Too Much was very well-intentioned. She wanted to love God, she wanted to love people, but she was both hampered by her muchness and the abundance of her posses-sions, and beset by ambition, power struggles and snobbery. Read about the surprising way The Church That Had Too Much began to resolve her problems in this deceptively simple and en-chanting fable.

About the Author

Anita Mathias is the author of *Wandering Between Two Worlds: Essays on Faith and Art.* She has a B.A. and M.A. in English from Somerville College, Oxford University, and an M.A. in Creative Writing from the Ohio State University, USA. Anita won a National Endowment of the Arts fellowship in Creative Nonfiction in 1997. She lives in Oxford, England with her hus-band, Roy, and her daughters, Zoe and Irene.

Visit Anita at http://www.anitamathias.com, and on
http://theoxfordchristian.blogspot.com, her Christian blog;
http://wanderingbetweentwoworlds.blogspot.com/, her personal blog, and
http://thegoodbooksblog.blogspot.com, her literary and writing blog.

CPSIA information can be obtained
at www.ICGtesting.com
Printed in the USA
LVOW12s1433271216

518847LV00001B/35/P